THE TRUTH BETWEEN

THE WESTWICK UNIVERSITY SERIES

BRI BLACKWOOD

BRETAGEY PRESS

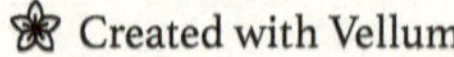 Created with Vellum

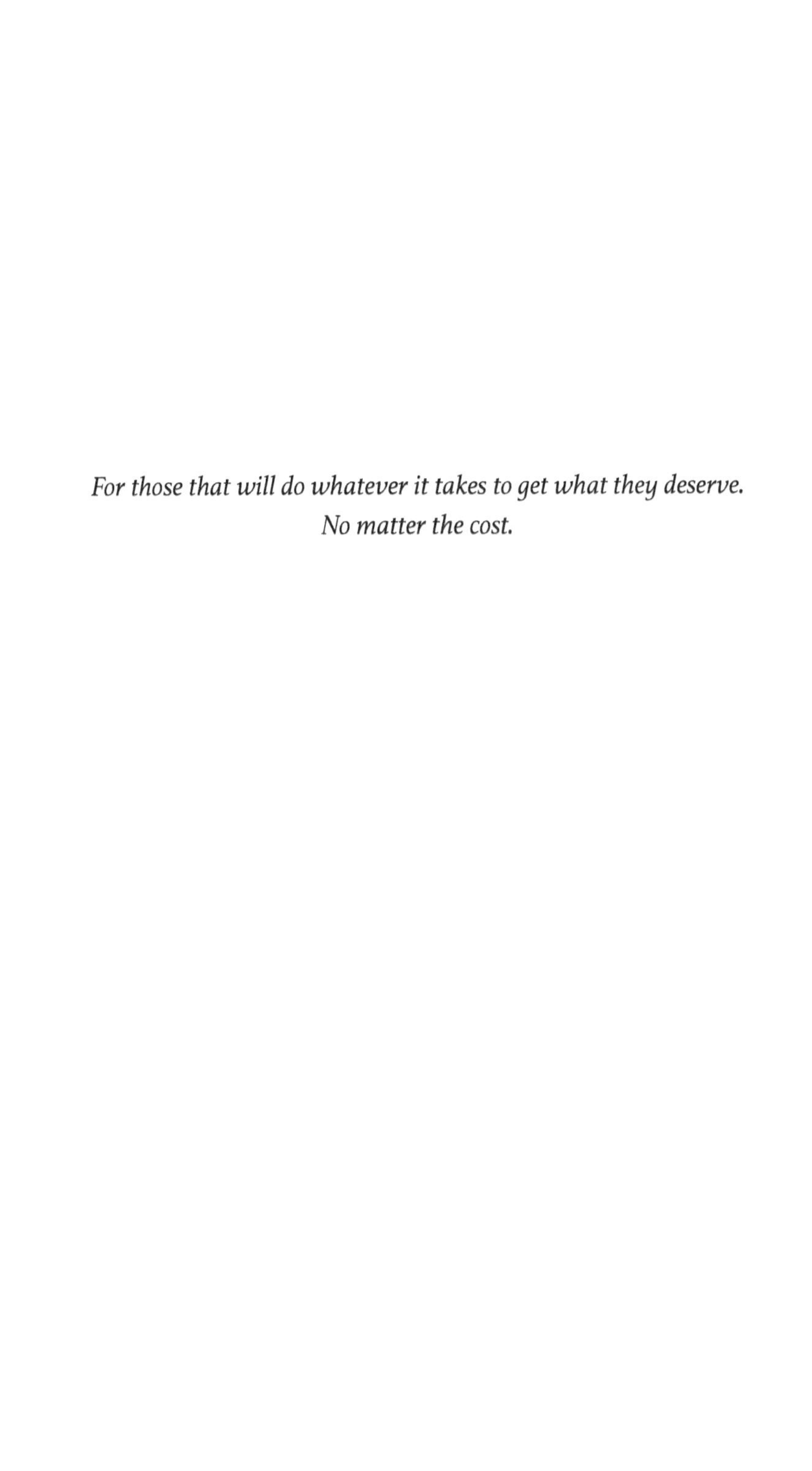

For those that will do whatever it takes to get what they deserve.
No matter the cost.

NOTE FROM THE AUTHOR

Hello!

Thank you for taking the time to read this book. The Truth Between is a dark college billionaire enemies-to-lovers forbidden romance. It is not recommended for minors and contains situations involve kidnapping and dubious/noncon-sent (related to birth control) and could be triggering.

For a more detailed trigger and content warning list, you can find it on my website.

It isn't a standalone and but Iris and Soren's story is complete. Aria and Landon's story will be in The Whispers Below.

BLURB

Curiosity has its consequences...

Westwick University conceals the truth in its ancient walls.

Some will do whatever it takes to keep it buried.

That includes Soren Grant.

My stalker.

My professor.

I never expected things to end up this way,

But I should have done my research.

After all, no one knows what really happened to his wife.

Now I'm trapped in nothing more than a gilded cage,

Forced to do his bidding.

Because whatever Professor Grant wants,

Professor Grant gets...

PLAYLIST

Writing's On The Wall - Sam Smith
Disturbia - Rihanna
Superhero - Alan Wake, Mougleta
False God - Taylor Swift
Fine Line - Harry Styles
Habits (Stay High) - Tovo Lo
The One That Got Away - Katy Perry
Stay - Rihanna, Mikky Ekko
The Heart Wants What It Wants - Selena Gomez
Mirrors - Justin Timberlake

The playlist can be found on Spotify.

1

IRIS

A sob fell from my lips. I hated that I couldn't control my emotions.

My hand trembled as I reached out to rub my face. My skin felt damp. I wasn't sure why. Had I started to sweat at some point last night? But that didn't make sense. The thin blanket, flimsy pillow, and shitty mattress I'd slept on didn't seem to hold much warmth, not to mention this room was cool and mostly dark.

Except for now.

I looked up toward the source of light breaking through the darkness. It was shining in from the small windows near the ceiling and told me that day had broken. I wished they were an option as an escape plan. They were too tiny for me to fit through, but even if I could have gotten through, there were some iron bars strategically placed across them. This only further confirmed that it wasn't a way out. I was a prisoner here.

The light allowed me to see the set of stairs that I was convinced would lead me to salvation. From what I saw, it was the only way out of this room, and somehow, some way, I needed to figure out a way to get there. But with me chained to this wall, the chance of getting to that door was basically zero.

What the hell was all of this?

It had to all be a bad dream. There was no other way I could describe it. Any second now, I would wake up from all this and be in my bed in my dorm room at Westwick University. Maybe Gran would surprise me with some of her home-made treats and spend the day with me on campus.

But I knew that was a lie. This whole situation was well suited for a nightmare that had flipped and become my new reality. Remaining positive was pointless. There was nothing happy or go-lucky about this.

I was in hell.

I shifted my foot and felt the gentle resistance due to the chain wrapped around my ankle, another reminder about where I was. I was being held captive by a man who had gone so far as to become my professor in order to stalk me. A man who had no issue with breaking into my dorm to stare at me when I was supposed to be asleep. Someone who I'd let fuck me until it felt like I couldn't breathe.

And the moments we shared, where he was telling me all those filthy things? They were the only times I liked him. The only times that I wished that the circumstances that we met under were different.

I shifted my body until I was leaning up against the cool wall and took a deep breath. But all I could smell was the musty air that surrounded me. A slight headache was beginning to form, but there was nothing I could do about it. Finding a way to alert Soren that I wasn't feeling well was out of the question. It would be showing weakness, something I couldn't afford to disclose.

There were so many things and factors that I didn't know about this situation, making it hard to wrap my head around it. Then again, I was pretty fucking traumatized about what had happened. I wanted to ask why he had chosen me of all people, but prior to him stalking me, I'd only seen him once that I could remember. Being alone with my own thoughts has helped me piece together why this might be.

It was obvious to me that he was somehow connected to the Chevaliers because he was at the party. He'd also known who Eddison Payne was. He mentioned how I would never stop digging to find what I perceived to be the truth.

And he was damn right.

However, what didn't make sense was why wait for the party? He could have easily taken me from my dorm room or from my class.

The only thing I could think of was that he was trying to keep me from finding anything related to Payne in Chevalier Manor. For that, I couldn't fault him because it had been my mission all along.

As I shifted my legs, once again becoming physically aware of the cuff around my ankle, my stomach growled. I placed my hands on my belly and cringed. I didn't know the last time I'd eaten a full meal. Someone had left food for me yesterday, but I'd barely touched it. That was feeling more and more like a mistake and could be feeding into the headache that was slowly becoming stronger. I swallowed hard to try to ignore the hunger pains I was feeling. I knew that I needed to eat something, but—

My thoughts were cut off when I heard footsteps overhead. I could hear them going back and forth, back and forth. Every time the steps grew closer overhead, the panic within me grew. Maintaining a sense of calm wasn't an option; however, the only thing I could focus on in order to not completely spiral was to wonder if that was him pacing, wondering what the hell he was going to do with me. Because, at some point, he had to do something.

Right? Of course he had to make his move. He couldn't keep me down here forever.

But it felt as if I was just trying to convince myself more than anything else.

Even though there was plenty of space in this room, the suffocating feeling that weighed heavy on my chest was strong. Part of me yearned to try to reach the door or the windows, but even if I wasn't chained to the wall, I would draw attention to myself before I could snap my fingers. And based on my experience, Soren Grant would have no issue killing me where I was.

But I couldn't just sit here and not try to do something. But what?

My mind raced, trying to think of different ways I could get out of this situation. Maybe if I screamed for help, then someone would come and find me? But I didn't know exactly where I was. And did I want to alert him if it actually was him walking around upstairs? Also, who knew how well sound could travel within these walls?

I turned slightly and used my fist to knock on the wall behind me. It sounded solid, making me lose even more hope. There was no way I would be able to break through it.

But I refused to give up.

I started brainstorming other ideas and remembered,

once more, the chain around my ankle. I moved my leg to see how much resistance was there. Were there any weak points in the chain? Was there some type of object nearby that I could slam into it?

I knew there was no way for me to slip this cuff over my foot. Its grip was snug, likely on purpose. Maybe if I found some sharp objects in the room, like a nail or screwdriver, I could use them to try to loosen it enough until it snapped?

I carefully scanned the area, but I didn't see much and definitely nothing within arm's distance.

Fuck.

With a deep breath, I slowly stood, bracing my weight on the wall so that I wouldn't fall. I was still wobbly from the lack of food, but I didn't crash to the floor once I was fully upright so that was a win. I heard the chain clank, reminding me of my imprisonment and what was at stake every second that I remained here. There was one room that I hadn't explored yet that might be my last opportunity to escape.

Soren ensured that I couldn't slip the cuff off my ankle, but he'd also made sure that he gave me enough chain to use the bathroom unassisted. I'd been in the bathroom a few times, but I hadn't taken the time to fully explore.

Chances were, there wasn't anything in there that would help me. I could only assume that he or someone on his team had done a thorough job of clearing out anything that might be used as a tool or a weapon.

Before I could move, I adjusted my clothes—the same gown I'd worn to the Chevalier Masquerade Ball. I could only imagine the state it was in, as well as how I must look. As I began to walk, my chain dragged behind me, sounding louder than necessary in the empty space I was in. Each step

I took felt precious because I didn't know what was waiting on the other side.

I stepped inside the small, separate room and flipped the light switch. The light didn't do much to illuminate the space and it was obvious the area had been neglected, much like the room I was trapped in. I closed the door behind me just in case Soren had some sort of camera system and was watching my every move. There was the potential that he'd also put cameras in here, which disgusted me, but this was a risk I needed to take.

I scanned the cracked tiles and the rusted faucet and sink with new eyes. When I'd come in here to use it, I did my best to get in and get out because this room gave me the creeps more than the rest of the basement. He'd been nice enough to put soap and hand towels in here for me to wash my hands, but that was as far as his generosity went. Now, I was looking for something, anything, that could be the light at the end of the tunnel for me. However, on its surface, this room was bare, probably as bare as Soren's soul.

My eyes stared at my reflection, the age and state of the mirror reflecting everything I felt about being trapped here. I glanced down at the sink and found nothing but a cool ceramic surface. I bent down and opened the drawers below the sink, but I was only met with disappointment. There was nothing in them.

Reality slammed into me, almost taking my breath away even though this was what I had expected would happen. Soren had done exactly what I thought he would do, and I shouldn't have been shocked. However, having that last bit of hope snatched from my grasp wasn't something I had prepared for.

I placed my hands on both sides of the sink and leaned against it, trying to come to terms with the situation at hand. I hadn't expected any of this to be easy, but having the door slammed in my face still stung.

What else could I do?

I refused to believe there was nothing. I was missing something. Maybe there was a mistake he'd made, a detail he'd overlooked that would give me the opportunity I needed to strike. After all, he was human, and we all made mistakes. My eyes flew shut and I let my head fall forward as I gritted my teeth in frustration. There was a war going on inside of me and I didn't know which side would be victorious.

What I did know was that my chances of getting out of here seemed to be growing smaller with every breath I took. Seconds ticked by as I tried to think of a solution, finding none. The only thing that was flashing through my mind was when he appeared at my side at the Chevalier Masquerade Ball. The shadow he cast over me when I was talking to Raven and Nash. The way his touch felt against my skin while we danced. How the tension in the air only increased when we left the dance floor and ended up in the library of the manor.

Where we...

A tear dropped from my face, and I angrily wiped it away. Soren didn't deserve my tears, and I refused to give them to him.

My eyes snapped open, and I jumped slightly when I heard more footsteps overhead. I turned to flush the toilet and turned on the faucet to wash my hands, pretending that was what I'd been doing the entire time.

The last thing I wanted to do was alert anyone in the house to what I was doing.

I quickly dried off my hands and looked around the room once more in hopes of finding something. When I came up empty-handed once more, I put the towel back, opened the door, and turned out the lights.

As I walked back into the main area of the basement, something caught my eye. In the corner of the room, closest to the bathroom door, there was something resting on the floor. I bent down to pick it up and stared at the folded-up piece of paper in my hand.

Before I could open it, I heard something loud hit the floor above me.

My heart began to race as I wrapped my fist around the piece of paper. I walked as quickly as I could back to the mattress and blanket I'd been using to sleep. With my hands still shaking, I sat there, my body trembling with fear. Part of me wanted to know what was going on up there, but the other part of me wanted whatever was happening to stay on that floor.

I clenched the piece of paper in my hand as I waited to see if another sound followed the loud bang. I was convinced that the air in the basement was growing thicker and an almost suffocating feeling was taking over. The sound of my breathing filled the room until one sound stopped it all: footsteps growing closer to the door that would lead whoever it was down to me.

2

IRIS

I was willing to swear that every step I heard was forcing my heart to jump into my throat. There was no doubt in my mind that whoever was standing on the other side of that door was about to come down here. At the last moment, I opened my hand discreetly, glanced down at the folded piece of paper and as smoothly as possible, shifted my body so that I was now sitting on the note. The last thing I wanted was for it to be taken away from me before I had a chance to read it.

Once I was settled, I sat as still as possible. The only sound that cut through the silence was the footsteps that were approaching the door. Thoughts slammed through my mind at a million miles an hour as I tried to prepare for the unexpected. But there was no way I could mentally pull myself together for something I didn't know was coming. If it was Soren on the other side of that door, I was screwed. The sight of him would send me into a frenzy, and I knew that would lead to me not being able to think straight.

The sound of distant footsteps grew closer until they

slowed just outside the door, but my heart rate didn't. I bit my lip so hard I swore I could taste blood. After swiping my tongue along my lips, I swallowed hard as I waited for the door to open. When I heard what sounded like a doorknob turning, my heart moved from my throat to my stomach. I grabbed the blanket that lay next to me and placed it over my legs, covering the large split in the gown that I still had on. The door began to move, and I wished I'd thought to pretend I was asleep sooner.

Then again, given my experiences with Soren, what had pretending to be asleep gotten me? Soren had only called me out because he knew I hadn't been.

But it wasn't Soren who entered the room.

I figured that out immediately. While I suspected that Soren was six-three or six-four, this man looked to be slightly shorter and had a thinner frame. When he stepped into the dim light in the room, I noticed that he was older, with hair that had gone mostly gray. He was wearing a dark suit that was tailored to fit him perfectly. Given how professional he looked, he stood out like a sore thumb in this room.

I did know I hadn't seen him before. Did he work here? Where was here? I could only assume that Soren had hired him to be a butler of sorts because that was the only explanation I could think of for what was happening in front of me.

He came closer to me, his eyes focused on what he was carrying instead of on me. In his hands, he balanced a tray with a cloche and a glass of water on it. My first thought was that he must be bringing me food even though I couldn't smell anything indicating that it was so. Maybe that was wishful thinking.

I watched as he put the tray down near me with more

grace than one should have in this situation. An idea appeared in my head, and I couldn't stop myself from seeing where it might lead. It almost felt foolish for me to say anything, but I needed to try because the worse he would say was no. "Help me, please."

Any hope that might have sprouted quickly vanished in the silence that surrounded us. He didn't respond. The man didn't even bother to look at me; it was as if I wasn't there. I did notice that he shifted slightly at my voice, so I suspected he did hear me. What he did instead was pull the cloche off the tray, and underneath it was a sandwich on a white plate and a bowl of fruit. The setup looked more pristine and fancier than I would expect a sandwich to appear on. While I'd been expecting food, the sandwich somehow surprised me. Even if my stomach hadn't chosen that moment to growl, I still would have been tempted to grab the food before this man left the room.

I didn't want to stare at him, but I found my eyes drifting back over to his form, watching his every move. His presence here with me, being my first interaction with someone else in who knew how long, should have been welcomed, but I felt nothing but frostiness between the two of us.

"Please," I begged as I stared at him, hoping that maybe, deep down, my plea would resonate with him. However, it was pretty clear where his loyalty lay.

He again remained silent as if I hadn't said a thing. It seemed to add to the feeling of suffocation I was having, or maybe it was just due to being locked in this room.

"I'll do anything if you let me out of here right now." For some reason, I couldn't give up pleading. After searching and spending who knew how much time down here, I was desperate, and to be honest, I didn't care.

While my thoughts seemed a little shaky, I knew I needed to play this carefully. Threatening and screaming at the top of my lungs at him wasn't going to solve anything. I was already taking a risk by asking him to help as many times as I had, but I suspected that Soren, and by extension, this man in front of me, expected that I would do this.

My words seemed to get to him for only a millisecond because I saw a slight change in the stoic expression that he wore like a badge. However, it was gone in an instant. That change forced me to realize that I was alone. That feeling of isolation had returned, stronger than ever.

The man didn't spare me a glance as he turned away, walking back up the stairs from where he came. When I heard the door click shut, I waited a beat until I was sure I was alone again.

I finally moved my attention away from the mysterious man and down to the sandwich that felt as if it was staring at me, daring me to eat it. I didn't really want to eat the meal for fear that something might have been put into it to poison me. But if there wasn't anything in it, it could provide the strength I needed to get the hell out of here. I was leaning toward it being fine because wouldn't it be easier to just shoot me dead and dispose of my body if Soren's plan had been to kill me?

Poisoning me would potentially take longer and be more torturous, and that son of a bitch would probably get off on me suffering for a long time. A tear fell from my eyes as I debated my decision. I was desperate and needed the nutrients, but the potential of being poisoned—

My thoughts were interrupted by the growling of my

stomach. I needed to eat, and I didn't have a choice on what I could eat at the moment, so this sandwich was it. I sniffed the food before pulling back the bread to see if I could tell if something had been done to tamper with it. Not that I could see much in this room anyway. When my stomach began to hurt from hunger pains, I brought the sandwich up to my lips and took a big bite.

The first chew was euphoric as the flavors took over my entire mouth. I had no idea how long it had been since I'd eaten because I'd lost all meaning of time. It could have been the lack of food, but I was willing to say that this was the best-tasting sandwich I'd ever had. When I didn't feel any numbness or pain, nor did I drop dead immediately, I felt more comfortable with taking another bite.

That initial bite turned into an all-out feast. I was practically inhaling the sandwich by taking large bites and then washing it down with gulps of water. In addition to the sandwich, there was a side dish of freshly cut fruit that I ate as well. I wiped away some of the pineapple juice that dribbled down my chin and took a deep breath. It felt so good to be full again.

Once I was done, I put everything back on the tray and pushed it away. I assumed at some point, Soren's butler would return to pick it up, and if I was awake, we would have a staredown. I would ask him questions, and he would continue to ignore me.

But the time to think of that was later. I needed to focus on getting the hell out of here.

It was then that I remembered what I'd found just outside the bathroom door. In case there were cameras on me, I wanted to be as discreet as possible in order to not alert anyone about what I'd found. I might be taking precautions against being seen for absolutely no reason, but I didn't want to chance it.

I once again moved the blanket so that it was spread out more, hopefully covering myself from what I was about to do. Once I'd accomplished that task, I sat up slightly and swept my hand underneath me, grasping the piece of paper in my hand before I settled back down. I waited a beat before I moved again, staying still to see if I could hear anything that would indicate that someone was coming. When I didn't hear a sound for a few seconds, I felt comfortable enough to move on to the next step.

Underneath the blanket, I used my hands to unfold the note and let it sit on my lap for a moment, allowing myself to calm my racing heart before I attempted to read it. I hoped the light that was shining into the room was enough for me to study whatever was on the paper. When I was once again certain that I hadn't alerted anyone of my actions, I slowly moved the blanket back, giving myself full access to the note on my lap.

The note only had five words on it in a beautiful script, weaving together almost whimsically. It didn't take much for me to appreciate the penmanship, but what was on the note left me more than slightly puzzled.

The scales must be balanced.

The piece of paper itself looked somewhat weathered and worn, and I wondered exactly when the note was written. Who was this note intended for? What did it mean?

I ran a finger across the handwriting, slightly frustrated

by my discovery. What I'd hoped would be an answer to many of the questions I'd had, and the biggest problem I'd hoped to solve did neither. In fact, it only forced more questions into my already turbulent mind.

I quickly folded the piece of paper back up and bent down to stick it under the mattress, not caring any longer if there were cameras on me. The note, as it stood now, was pointless for me anyway.

What I needed to focus on was what was going to come next for me because, at some point, I was going to see Soren again, and I needed to get out of here. And if meeting his butler was any indication, this was my battle to fight by myself. I would be the one to save myself from this nightmare because there was no prince to save me from all of this. And none of this would deter me from finding out the truth about Margaret Turner and her connection to the Chevaliers.

3

SOREN

Nightfall had never felt more fitting than it did right now. After all, what I was about to do should only be committed under the guise of darkness. My car, parked in this quiet neighborhood, was hidden in the shadows, away from the full moon that decided to make its appearance tonight. Thankfully for me, the skies were somewhat cloudy, helping to cover the bright light that the moon was trying to bless me with.

It would be daylight soon, and I needed to get this done as quickly as possible.

My gaze was fixated on the home across the street from where I was parked.

I clenched my fists as my nails bit into my palms. I'd been waiting for the opportunity to make my move. I wanted to get this over and done with so I could move on to my next target.

For what I had planned, most people would feel fear or remorse, but none of those thoughts had entered my mind. This needed to get done, and it would get done, but my impatience was beginning to show its ugly head.

My patience was usually a strength of mine.

For years, I had built my reputation of succeeding in any challenge set before me by always taking the time and making sure everything was properly thought through. I never took shortcuts or cut corners; I did things the way they needed to be done in all avenues of my life.

But then I ran into Iris and my world imploded. All of that changed. Suddenly, waiting felt like an eternity. Waiting until I could hold and touch her had been my kryptonite, and it seemingly bled into other areas of my life. My frustration grew each day as I watched those around me move on while I still waited for something that felt so far away.

The home I was watching seemed to mock me, its darkened windows showcasing that no one was awake yet. All it was doing was reminding me that I couldn't make my move yet because it wasn't the right time.

Not yet at least.

I took a deep breath and exhaled slowly, trying to ignore the tension that was vibrating through my body. It wasn't a nervous energy because there was no need to be. My plan was foolproof and while there was always a chance that something could go wrong, I knew that this wouldn't. I would prevail in the end, one way or another.

To my utter frustration, my thoughts drifted back to Iris, trapped in the basement of my home. Locking her down there had been a blessing and a curse. There was no more of me wondering what she was doing or who she was with because I knew exactly where she was at all times.

But now that she was under lock and key, I could feel an even bigger storm brewing. What she'd been up to, trying to find out more about the Chevaliers, was the biggest mistake she could have ever made. Allowing history to remain buried would have been beneficial to her. Now, it was up to Parker Townsend and whoever else he decided to bring into the fold to decide what her fate would be.

There was nothing I could do to save her. Hell, the better question was if I even wanted to save her.

I shook my head, trying to snap out of it. This wasn't the time for distractions. I had a job to do, and this would need all my focus. I reached for the bag on the passenger seat and checked its contents for the hundredth time. Nothing was missing and I had everything I needed.

I took one last look at the house, and that's when I saw it. A small light in the living room. Someone was awake.

About fucking time, but I waited to make my move.

I checked the time on my dashboard and saw that he was a little later than normal. I swallowed that irritation and focused on what was about to happen. It would be easy to break into his house and kill him now, but I decided to switch things up a bit.

Instead, I waited for Derrick Wilson to step out of his house to go for his very early morning jog. While I waited, I put my gloves on and grabbed some of the tools that I would need to avoid having to bring a bag with me. The last thing I needed was to be weighed down by anything.

After I was done, I watched as the front door of Derrick's house opened. Stepping out was a man in his late forties, fit and trim, wearing a pair of running shorts with leggings underneath and a T-shirt. He had a water bottle in his right hand and a set of keys in his left. Once he locked the front door, he jogged down the driveway, passing within a few feet of my car. I held my breath as I watched him jog past, then waited a few more seconds before getting out of my car.

I followed him away from his house and into a more secluded area, keeping a safe distance between us. All of this looked familiar to me because I'd taken the time to study his routine before making my move. It was obvious that his having a routine that he didn't change up at all was an important part of his life, but it would also lead to his downfall. My heart was slamming in my chest as the adrenaline pumped through my veins. The thrill of a kill was returning even if I hadn't committed the act yet.

Derrick slowed down to a walk and seemed to be in his own little world. It would have been nice for him to make me work for what I was about to do by chasing after him, but beggars couldn't be choosers.

When Derrick slowed to take a sip of his water, I knew this was my chance. Plus, I had the element of surprise on my side.

I ran up behind him, grabbed him by the neck, and pulled him into a choke hold.

"Rumor has it that you're a little fucking spy," I said in his ear as he continued to fight me. "Trying to have a role in taking down the Chevaliers, are we?"

When I said the name of the organization that had changed my life, he froze for a split second before his movements became even more erratic.

"No, please no," Derrick's strained voice made me smile as he continued to struggle.

I tightened my grip, and he stopped fighting me.

"Good," I said. "Now I have a few questions to ask you and I want the truth, no matter how much it fucking hurts," I said as I pushed him to the ground. I made sure to tie his wrists behind his back with a zip tie before I turned him over onto his back.

"Okay, yes, fine. Please don't kill me," he said, taking in deep breaths.

I smirked and took a small step back from him so I could get a better look at the man who wanted to fuck with us.

"Please don't kill me," he said again.

I ignored his desperate pleas and kneeled down beside him, my eyes boring into his as I began my interrogation.

"Who are you working for?" I asked, my voice cold and unforgiving.

Derrick hesitated for a moment before finally answering, "I can't tell you that."

I moved my hand toward my coat, pulling out a knife. Derrick's eyes widened with fear as he stared at the blade.

"Are you sure?" I asked him, pressing the sharp edge of the knife against his cheek. "I think you can easily answer my very simple question."

Derrick winced as the point of the knife dug into his skin, drawing a small bead of blood. He shook his head frantically, trying to buy himself some time. "Okay, okay, I'll talk. Just don't hurt me anymore or hurt my wife."

I pulled the knife away but didn't confirm or deny that I wouldn't hurt him again. I watched as the blood dripped from his body. I had no intention of harming his family. It was him that I had the issue with. I stood over him, staring down at the damage I'd done with a small smirk playing on my lips.

"Who are you working for?" I repeated, this time with more emphasis.

"I don't know," he repeated, his voice shaking. "I swear I don't know."

"How the hell don't you know who you're working for?"

Derrick hesitated before answering, his eyes darting around nervously. "I was just given instructions to gather information on the Chevaliers. They never gave me a name or anything; they just told me what to do."

I raised an eyebrow, trying to decide if he was telling the truth or not. "And you just went along with it?"

"The money was too great not to."

I cursed under my breath before returning my stare to him. "Not all money is good money. Was your next target Iris Bennington? Were you supposed to be digging up information on her?"

His eyes widened enough that I knew I'd been right. Iris was next on his list, and even though I wasn't going to kill him because of her after the orders I'd received, a small part of me was going to be happy to not have him lurking in the background when it came to her.

"Did you really think that whoever hired you would be able to protect you from us? Do you think he or she gives two shits about you, and that's why you took the job?"

Derrick didn't respond, but the look of panic on his face spoke volumes.

I rolled my eyes at his naivety. "Now, here's the thing," I continued, my voice low and ominous. "I can't have anyone else trying to harm the Chevaliers. It's my duty to protect my organization."

Derrick nodded quickly, his eyes wide with terror.

"So, any last words?" I said, my hand reaching for the knife once more.

Derrick's eyes widened even further, and he began to beg for his life, but in reality, all he was doing was pissing me off further.

I let out a sigh and shook my head, disappointed by the display in front of me. "You're pathetic," I said before plunging the knife into his chest, his desperate cries for mercy coming to a stop. I stared as he lay there motionless, taking his last breath. Watching as the life left his eyes caused a sense of satisfaction to wash over me.

There it was, finally. The thrill of taking another life.

I stood up, pulling a handkerchief from my coat and wiping the blood from the knife on it before putting it away. Without a second glance back at the man bleeding out, I walked back to my car and closed the door behind me. I watched as the sun began to rise, on the brink of showing signs of life, just as I was about to drive back to my sanctuary.

Then again, was it much of a sanctuary anymore? The woman in my basement caused more turmoil than anything. Because of her, I needed to hire my staff back to meet her needs. Things were anything but peaceful at the moment.

As I pulled away from the curb, I couldn't help but think that, although I didn't get all the answers I wanted, this was still a job well done.

4

IRIS

The damp air clung to me like a second skin as my heart pounded against my rib cage. Yet the only thing I was doing was standing up, staring into the darkness that covered this barely lit basement.

Panic grew in my chest, tightening around my lungs with each shallow breath that I took. The walls seemed to close in around me, further trapping me in this godforsaken place. I yanked at the chain binding my ankle, the rusted metal cutting into my skin. The panic spread through my veins, becoming an unstoppable force that drowned out all my other feelings and thoughts.

For the millionth time, I tried to search for a way out but found none. The walls began to spin as the floor shifted beneath me. I gasped, tasting bile on my tongue as the world became distorted and turned into a kaleidoscope of shapes and shadows.

I knew exactly what was happening. The panic attack crashed over me in waves, robbing me of control and reason. My legs buckled and I sank to the floor. I gasped for air as my body trembled and I landed on the mattress that had become my bed. Tears streamed down my face because I couldn't stop this. I couldn't prevent any of this.

I was filled with fear. With desperation. With helplessness.

I fought for every breath as my chest burned because of the panic that had its hold on me. I curled into a ball, hugging my arms tight around my knees as my body shook. Darkness crowded my vision, and I could feel the threats it tossed at me, wanting to swallow me whole. My thoughts descended into chaos. I told myself that I was going to die down here, all alone in this fucking basement. No one would save me. It was unlikely my dead body would even be found.

I squeezed my eyes shut, trying to block out the darkness, the dampness, the fear threatening to overwhelm my senses. But it was no use. The panic had me in its hold, tearing at my mind in an attempt to leave nothing left.

No. I couldn't give in. I refused to do so. I had to stay strong.

An eerie calm flowed over me as my body felt like it was going numb. With shaking hands, I wiped the tears from my face as the walls began to slow down. My breaths came slower now and my breathing evened out as the panic eased the grip it had on me. Exhaustion took its place as I lay there, pulling the blanket over me. The panic would pass, as it always did. But it would return, again and again, to remind me of where I was and how I'd gotten here.

Beneath all of it, the only thing I wanted was peace. But when would I get it?

I lay there motionless on the mattress, too drained to

move. I closed my eyes, willing my body to relax. To rest for the first time in days.

I was determined not to break.

Because I would make Soren pay for what had been done to me.

My eyes opened with my heart pounding in my chest as I tried to make sense of my surroundings. The panic that had been deep within my soul stirred but didn't explode. It took me a second to remember that I was in this stone room and not in my warm bed at Westwick University. Would I ever get used to being here?

I hoped not. That more than likely would mean that I'd given up on making it out of here alive.

I stretched, shifting on the shitty mattress, and I closed my eyes again temporarily. This stretch was absolutely necessary and a temporary reprieve from the problems I was trying to solve.

I turned my head and my eyes met those of Soren Grant, his intense gaze piercing through me like a dagger. I screamed, the sound bouncing off the walls of the mostly empty room as I grabbed the blanket to wrap around myself. If I had been panicking before, I was definitely freaking the hell out now.

Soren's lips twitched into a smirk as he watched me scramble for cover. "Good morning, petal," he drawled, his voice deep and rough. Every word he said made my skin crawl. "Did I scare you?"

I scowled at him, my heart still racing. "What the fuck? Why are you watching me sleep?"

His smirk widened into a grin. "I find it entertaining."

"You know what would be entertaining for me? You letting me go home. If you do, I would pretend that none of this happened."

I expected him to say something slick or to laugh at me. Instead, his gaze held mine for what seemed like an eternity, neither of us willing to back down. There was something about the way he looked at me that freaked me the hell out. It was a mixture of curiosity and something darker and more dangerous that I couldn't quite put my finger on. Despite being one-hundred-percent afraid of what he might do, I couldn't tear myself away from the pull he had over me.

Then he finally spoke. "Let you go? You think that you have any negotiating power here?"

I stared at him, wondering who the hell I was dealing with and feeling completely out of my depth. I was still trying to wrap my mind around the fact that Soren had somehow managed to sneak into my prison cell.

"There's something wrong with you," I muttered, pulling the blanket tighter around me. I shifted my leg and was quickly reminded of the chain that was still clamped around it.

Soren raised an eyebrow. "Something wrong with me? That's a bit harsh, don't you think? I prefer to think of myself as... unconventional."

I rolled my eyes. "Yeah, well, unconventional doesn't cover the fact that you're a psychopath. What do you want, Soren? What is the purpose of keeping me here?"

Soren leaned forward in the chair he'd been sitting in. "You already know, Iris."

His saying my first name instead of the nickname he'd given me sent a strong tremble down my spine. "You should have let the past stay buried instead of trying to find out more."

"I couldn't do that."

He shrugged nonchalantly. "Then we have nothing more to discuss about that. Anyway, I just wanted to check in on my favorite captive. Make sure you're comfortable and you feel at home here."

I snorted. "Comfortable? Aren't you the charitable host?"

"I want to make sure that you're relaxed and have your needs catered to in my home."

So I was at his place, but where that was, I had no idea. His words did nothing to dissuade me from what was coming out of my mouth next.

"Are you fucking kidding me? I'm locked up in a basement like a damn prisoner, you asshole!"

Anger radiated from every word that spilled from my lips. When I was alone, I'd tried to prepare myself for when I would see Soren again. I told myself I would try to keep my cool, not allowing him to rattle me because showing emotion would be like showing weakness in this situation. I didn't want to give Soren the satisfaction of seeing my frustration, but something about him saying the word comfortable made me snap.

I was stuck here. No one knew where I was outside of potentially Nash and Raven, the former serving for the organization that Soren is trying to protect. My poor grandmother was probably trying to figure out what had happened to me. She was probably going out of her mind with worry.

I repeated the mantra that I hated Soren. I hated him with every fiber of my being. He was delusional, and I was willing to do whatever it took for him to let me go.

Soren frowned and stood, moving toward me. I shifted my body in an attempt to get as far away from him as I possibly could. I didn't know what would happen with me being so close to him.

"Why are you avoiding the inevitable?"

"Nothing is set in stone here. Just unlock me, and then we can talk about this."

Soren looked at me and then shrugged. "Look, petal, there's no point in trying to fight me. I'll win. Because I always do."

My lips curled up into a snarl before I could gain control of my feelings. I couldn't believe what I was hearing. I took a deep breath to keep from flipping out on him. "I'm not trying to compete with you. This isn't some kind of competition," I said through clenched teeth.

"You and I both know that's a lie. I can see that you're trying to find a way out of this. You're working out a plan that you hope to enact, and that's smart, but you need to stop. Trying to escape while the Chevaliers are still deciding what to do with you will just end up with you getting hurt."

Soren walked toward me and bent down, our eyes meeting because we were now on the same level. He leaned in toward me, his lips brushing against my forehead, and I moved my hands so I could push him away. It all happened so fast, and Soren was left trying to find his footing. He glared at me, but I was way too proud of myself for what I'd done.

The heat in Soren's eyes was downright scary, but I didn't care. I was determined to go down swinging. I wasn't going down without a fight and Soren should have known that.

When he moved toward me again, I was prepared for him. I had my hands curled into fists and ready to go.

When his lips were a whisper away from mine, I was fully prepared to hit him, but instead, he grabbed my hair and yanked it, forcing me to look up into his eyes. "I can do anything I want to you and no one but you and me would be any wiser."

"The hell you will."

"Do you want to test me, petal?"

The challenging look in his eyes made me want to shrivel up into a ball on the floor, but I refused to let him see me like that. Just like I refused to give him the satisfaction of seeing me cry.

Neither of us said a word before he released me, and I immediately brought my hands up to grab the back of my head in an attempt to ease the tension. My scalp stung slightly from where he'd pulled my hair.

I sat there while he stood over me, both of us in silence for a moment because there wasn't anything else to say.

What I did know was that I didn't trust Soren Grant any more than I trusted the devil. He was used to getting what he wanted by any means necessary, no matter the cost.

"I can't wait to fuck you again, especially that pretty little mouth," Soren said, seemingly out of nowhere.

"That's never going to happen."

"Never say never," he said quickly.

"How about over my dead body?"

"That can also be arranged."

My eyes widened slightly at what he was alluding to, but the smirk on his face told me he was bullshitting me.

Soren waited a beat before he snatched the blanket off me. Immediately, I felt embarrassed.

I was still in the formerly pretty black gown that I'd worn to the masquerade ball. It had seen better days, and I definitely looked worse for wear now too. That's what being locked up in a basement would do to you.

His eyes studied me as if I were a piece of art, and I couldn't help but wonder what he was seeing that I wasn't. I was dirty and probably needed to soak in bleach in order to be clean again. This was a far cry from how I looked leaving my dorm room for Chevalier Manor.

A shiver flew through my body as I felt his stare, looking me up and down. He hadn't even touched me again, and my body was having involuntary reactions to him. Most of me wanted to throw up on him and see if that made him understand how I felt about him, but a small part of me wanted him to take me right here, right now, on this mattress. My mind veered to the times we'd spent together fucking each other until I cut myself off rather abruptly.

I couldn't let my mind go there. I had more important things to worry about.

Like how to get out of here.

"You haven't attempted to escape?" Soren's words cut through my thoughts like a knife as I drew my full attention back to him.

"Depends on your definition of attempting escape. I did ask the guy who served me food to help me, but obviously, he didn't."

"Obviously," Soren said smugly, and I wanted to slap the

look off his face. "Franklin knows better than to do such a thing."

"Because he works for you?"

When Soren nodded, I stored that piece of information away in my mind in case it came in handy at some point. "I was wondering if you were going to lie about that or not."

It seemed as if I'd made the right decision by being honest, but when Soren's eyes grew slightly darker, I began to regret my decision. I could see the wheels in his head turning and I didn't like that one bit.

"Maybe you deserve a reward, petal. Would you like to take a shower?"

5

IRIS

Soren's question hung in the air as I traced the edge of the cold metal cuff that wrapped around my ankle with my fingers. His offer to allow me to take a shower hung in the air between us, tempting me with the promise of a tiny bit of normalcy in this whirlwind of chaos that he'd turned my life into. I couldn't trust him as far as I could throw him, so what else did he have up his sleeve when it came to this reward?

"I'm not sure what more there is to think about, Iris. It's a yes or no question."

I was half expecting him to tell me that I stunk, but he didn't, choosing only to stare at me with an unreadable expression.

"What's the catch?"

"Catch? There is no catch," Soren said, but I didn't believe him.

However, a shower sounded wonderful. I just hoped it wasn't in a bathroom that was in a similar state as this room.

"Fine," I muttered, struggling to keep my voice steady. "I'll take a shower."

Soren's lips curved into a sly smile as if he knew how much I struggled to say that. Our eyes remained locked for a moment longer before I watched him produce a key from his pants pocket and bend down toward my feet. His hand held my leg in a firm grip as he undid the cuff and remained there a second longer than necessary before he stood up once more. He turned toward the stairs and moved to the door that had teased me with my freedom. I waited a beat before I followed him.

We began climbing the staircase that had taunted me, and he opened the door that I'd found myself staring at more times than I could count. It opened into what looked to be a hallway with tall walls covered in dark, soft wallpaper. Light fixtures reminiscent of candles hung from the walls, emanating low light that gave the hallway an alluring and creepy quality.

In between the lights, the walls were lined with old portraits. I tried to shake off the feeling that we were being watched by the painted eyes, but I couldn't. Not one of the paintings I passed showed anyone smiling, making me wonder if anyone in this house had ever shown a glimmer of happiness.

The floor was made of polished dark wood, so shiny it reflected some of the light from the lamps on the wall. We walked up another set of stairs as Soren led me to a guest room with a huge four-poster bed and dark furniture. He continued to walk until he opened another door in the room and flicked on the light.

I followed him into the room and found myself standing

in a bathroom. The walls were decorated with these deep-colored tiles that I was convinced were black. There was just a bit of light coming from old-fashioned lamps on the walls, much like the hallway we walked through.

The bathtub was, without a doubt, the focal point of the room. It was huge and black, with gold trimming and a showerhead attached to the tile. Above the sink, there was a big mirror. Its frame was gold but looked old and worn out, but the glass was clear, looking as if it was brand new. There was not a speck of dirt around, telling me how well cared for this room was.

There were already towels and toiletries in the bathroom, along with what looked to be a T-shirt, sweatpants, and underwear for me to put on. Soren had clearly thought all of this through and was expecting me to say yes to the shower. Giving in to this "reward" felt as if I was selling a piece of my soul to him, but even having a second of peace under the pressure of the water flowing down on me might just make all this worth it.

"Undress," Soren said, his voice low and gravelly. I glanced at him, confused by his statement.

"I will once you leave the room."

A harsh chuckle left his lips. "That's not part of the plan, petal."

It was then that the other shoe dropped. This was his catch. He wanted to watch me while I was naked and even more vulnerable than I was in this moment for his own joy and amusement.

My heart hammered in my chest at the realization. "I don't want you here. Leave."

"You're not going to tell me what to do. Ever. Let alone in my own home. Now strip before I do it for you."

I shook my head and swallowed hard. "I won't let you degrade me like this."

Soren took a step closer to me, his eyes darkening with anger. "Degradation doesn't turn you on? Or maybe it's when I praise you?"

I swallowed hard at what he was implying but didn't back down. "This is not the same as what consenting adults do when they are in the bedroom."

"Are you saying that you aren't consenting to this?"

I stared at him silently, wondering how I should respond to that absurd question. I knew if I said no, Soren would take it as a challenge and try to push me until he got what he wanted. On the other hand, if I said yes, then I would be giving in to his demands. But I couldn't fight the response that was hanging at the tip of my tongue.

"I didn't consent to getting kidnapped or any of the events that followed, and you fucking know it. Stop insulting my intelligence."

A few beats passed before Soren spoke, and I took a small amount of glee in the fact that I'd stumped him, even temporarily. "Iris, you consented to this treatment when you kept investigating something that didn't pertain to you. Now, take off your clothes before I do it for you."

I backed away from him as I debated whether I should follow his directive. Part of me wanted to run out of the room, screaming my head off to get attention, but I knew I wouldn't be fast enough to outrun him. I couldn't remember the last time I'd been out on a run at this point, and my lack of food and having been drugged who knows how long ago would work against me. I also didn't know the layout of this home, so the chances of me getting lost before I made it out of the house were high.

He leaned toward the tub to turn on the showerhead before he turned back to me. "This is your final warning," he said as he closed the gap between us.

Soren's eyes told me all I needed to know about the state of mind he was in. He looked slightly unhinged, and if I was being honest with myself, I wasn't sure what he was capable of. Deep down, I knew I had no choice but to comply with his demands. As I began to undress, I felt his gaze on me, burning into my skin as he watched my every move. I turned around to give him my back because I knew that I would need his help unzipping the gown.

With gentleness I didn't expect of him, especially after everything that had transpired between us, he pulled the zipper of my dress as I held the fabric up to my chest. Once it was all the way down, his hands left my body and he said, "Turn around. I want to see you."

I slowly turned around awkwardly because of the looseness of the gown and faced him. His gaze set every nerve in my body off, and I hated him for it. I hated myself for it too, because I couldn't stand the effect he was having on me.

Finally, with a deep breath, I let the fabric fall from my body. I was left in the black strapless bra and panties I'd worn to the masquerade ball.

Soren's eyes roamed over my body as if he was taking inventory of every inch of me. It was somewhat ironic, given that he'd seen me completely bare, but I didn't say a word. His gaze was intense and unsettling. It was as if he was committing everything to memory. His attention did nothing to settle the pounding of my heart.

"Take the rest of it off."

I hesitated for a moment before I stood up straighter and unclasped my bra. I watched his face as the garment fell from my body. I wasn't going to give him the opportunity to see that his attempts to break me were working. If he could hide behind a mask, then I could too.

I grabbed my panties and pushed them down my legs until I was standing in nothing. I glanced down at the mark that had formed on my ankle as a result of being chained to a wall before I stood up straight once more. A shuddering breath passed through my body, but I didn't say a word even though a million different things were floating through my mind.

His fists clenched and then unclenched, showcasing how hard he was trying to restrain himself. He rubbed a hand down his face before shaking his head. "Go ahead. Take your shower."

I shifted my body so I could step into the warm water. I sighed as the water washed over me, washing away the grime and dirt of the past few days. This was what I needed to soothe and calm my soul, even temporarily.

But even as I enjoyed the sensation of the water on my skin, I couldn't help but feel uneasy with Soren still being in the room, watching me. I didn't know what he was thinking or planning to do with me, and until I did, it would leave a huge pit in the middle of my stomach.

After I used my hands to wipe the water from my face, I glanced over my shoulder at him. He'd managed to move, so he was now leaning against the bathroom counter, still watching my every move.

"Are you satisfied?" I spat out, unable to keep the anger from my voice.

"Hardly," he replied. "There are plenty more things I would love to do to you right now. In fact, you've just given me an idea."

It was easy for me to figure out what he was referring to and it only made me despise him even more. My heart dropped to my stomach as I waited for him to continue. What had I just walked into?

"I want you to fuck yourself."

"Absolutely not." I'd suspected that he would allude to something along those lines, but I wasn't expecting that.

Soren stared at my body but refused to look at my face. "The thought of fucking yourself in front of me excites you. Your body betrays what your brain is telling you to feel."

I followed where his gaze had landed and noticed that he was staring at my nipples. They were hard, but that could be attributed to anything. "You do realize that they can also get hard when they are exposed to cool air?"

"It's awfully hot in here..." Soren's voice trailed off as he adjusted his position. "Have you ever fucked yourself, Iris?"

"That's none of your business."

"Show me. Now."

The sternness in his voice sent a shiver down my spine. I could see the challenge in his eyes, and I couldn't back down.

I refused to do so.

I tossed my wet hair to one side before my hands landed on my breasts. I allowed the water to fall all over my face as I massaged them, trying to ignore the thoughts that were going through my head as he watched my every move. With a quick breath, I moved my foot to give Soren a better view of where my hand was about to go.

My fingers moved in a slow, circular motion as I explored my body. The feeling of pleasure was intense, and it grew with every move I made. My breathing became heavier as my other hand started to explore lower, finding its way to my pussy. I could feel the heat radiating from me and I suspected that Soren could too.

Out of the corner of my eye, I saw him shift his body, but I refused to give him my attention. While thoughts of whether he would attempt to join me on this excursion did cross my mind, I refused to let it consume me. The quicker I fell over the edge, the quicker he would leave me alone.

When my fingertips finally touched my clit, I thought my legs were going to give out. I allowed myself to close my eyes and throw my head back as the water pelted my skin, further adding to the sensations I was feeling.

"Oh fuck," I moaned. The words had left my lips without warning, not giving a damn that I didn't want to give him the reaction he was looking for. If I had to guess, he was smirking at me, pleased that he was able to push me to this point.

I wished that this was all pretend and that it hadn't been a result of his words forcing me into this predicament. But the closer I inched toward my climax, the less of a fuck I gave. All that mattered was me getting to the finish line, even if it meant he had to watch me in such a vulnerable state.

I wasn't surprised that he didn't say a word, probably due to the fact that his voice would be like the shower water suddenly turning ice cold, and if he ruined this for me, I would lose all sense of control.

As if he knew this was the case, the only sounds that could be heard in the room were the water spraying from the showerhead and small sighs and moans that fell from my lips.

When I was bracing for the explosion that was about to burst from my body, I tried my hardest to steady myself using the tiles in the shower, but it was futile. I used my other hand to continue playing with myself, making sure to increase the speed.

My breathing became shallower as a cry fell from my lips, marking the point that I'd reached. It would be a wonderful downhill ride from here.

With a groan, my orgasm took over, to the point where I had to quickly move my body so that I could lean against the wall in order to stay upright. All the sensations coursing through me were overwhelming, and they left me completely spent. I hadn't expected to come as hard as I did, but here I was.

I kept my eyes closed as I tried to catch my breath, but the heat that I felt from Soren's stare was still on me. As the last waves of pleasure washed over me, I opened my eyes and met his gaze once more.

"That was an excellent job, petal, and I don't say those words lightly. Now clean up."

Without saying a word, I leaned over to grab the wash-cloth from the towel bar in the bathroom. I opened up the bodywash that had been left for me to use, and the scent of coconut permeated the room. It was one of my favorite aromas, and I didn't even want to begin to question if it was a coincidence or if he'd planned that out too.

I lathered my body quickly as I tried to recover from the

orgasm I'd just experienced. Once I'd managed to clear my mind, I asked, "Why are you doing this?"

"Because I have no other choice," he confessed. "You went digging where you shouldn't have, and there are consequences to those actions."

"So, because I was looking to prove Margaret Turner was heavily involved in the Chevaliers, you kidnapped me and locked me up in your basement? Because that makes a whole lot of fucking sense."

I jumped when I heard Soren slam his hand down on the countertop, and the sound vibrated throughout the whole room. "You're really fucking lucky that's all that has happened and that you're here. You have no idea the shit you've stirred by going on your little detective adventure because things could be a lot worse for you. A whole lot worse."

The silence that passed between us moved way past awkward and was stuck in the fearful territory. How was someone supposed to react to this?

"Are you just going to keep me here forever?" I blurted out without thinking about it.

"Would you rather be dead?"

The question made me freeze because that wasn't the response I was expecting. The only thing that kept me moving was the fact that I refused to let him see just how much what he said affected me. "I'd rather be free, Soren."

"Freedom is an illusion," he said coldly. "You're alive because I chose to keep you alive. You're still able to take your next breath because I'm allowing you to do so. You're here because I brought you here. And you will remain here until I decide otherwise."

6

IRIS

I couldn't believe I'd done what I did, but there was no time to dwell on it. Stepping out of the shower, I shivered as cold air assaulted my wet skin. The contrast between the warmth of the water and the slight chill in the room was enough to jolt me out of the small reprieve I'd had as a result of the best shower I'd had in who knows how long.

As much as it pained me to admit it, it included the orgasm I'd given myself as well. What would have made it better is if I'd been alone. Soren stood there studying my every move, thinking who knew what. Then again, I didn't care what he thought unless it meant he was going to kill me.

Soren didn't bother to grab my towel for me, not that I expected him to. No, he just stood there with his hands crossed over his chest, glaring at me. I turned away from him and snatched the towel off the bar. I quickly wrapped it around myself, happy to have hidden my body from his hungry gaze.

"Get dressed," he barked, his voice sharp, as if I was

inconveniencing him. His tone was different from the praise he'd just given me for doing what he wanted. No one told him to stay in here with me while I washed my body. I picked up the pile of what I hoped would be comfortable sweatpants and a baggy T-shirt.

I quickly threw the garments on and realized that while they were comfortable, they were extremely big. I rolled the waistband of the sweatpants down as far as I could in an effort to get them to fit me better, but it didn't work. I rolled my eyes and looked back up at Soren.

"Are these your clothes? Couldn't snap your fingers and buy something better than this?"

"What? Would you rather I gave you Eden's clothes?"

His question nearly made my eyes pop out of my skull. I didn't even know Soren knew I knew his wife's name, so that was surprising enough, let alone him throwing out the fact that he could have given me clothes that previously belonged to a dead woman.

I quickly pushed the thought out of my mind. Soren didn't make any moves to show that he was going to continue, as if he was truly waiting on an answer from me.

"No, I don't want her clothes," I said finally, my voice barely above a whisper. "These are absolutely perfect. Nothing wrong with them at all."

"Thought so. Now it's time to head down to breakfast."

"Wait. I'm eating... with you?"

"It's either that, or I'll chain you back up and have Franklin deliver your food in the basement."

I fought the eye roll and scream I wanted to let loose. Honestly, the former option was tempting because I didn't want to see Soren's face if I could help it. It caused unnecessary stress and the desire to strangle him with my bare hands. "Lead the fucking way," I muttered.

Soren's glare sent a shiver down my spine, but he didn't say another word. He turned and walked away, and I could only hope that he was leading me to the dining room.

As I followed him, I took the opportunity to look around, this time not for aesthetic purposes but to get a layout of the house to plan my escape. I wouldn't act out now because the last thing I wanted to do was piss him off. Even though I wanted to express every single one of my emotions, I needed to reel myself in and remain cool, calm, and collected.

As we walked through his home, the silence between the two of us was more than welcomed. It gave me more time to concentrate on my surroundings as I created a mental map of the place in my mind. I'd found what I thought was the entrance of his house and made a mental note of it. I eyed the windows as well in case that was my only option for getting out.

Finally, we arrived in the dining room, where a long table had two table settings with a bunch of food in the middle. The food that my eyes danced over was enough for a feast.

"Sit," Soren said as he gestured for me to take a seat at the end of the table. He walked farther into the room and sat at the head of the table, putting a lot of distance between the two of us. With a heavy sigh, I sat where he told me to. My stomach growled at the sight of all the food, but I also couldn't help but wonder why the hell all this food was made in the first place if it was for just him and me.

The table contained a bunch of different foods, including

flaky croissants on a big white plate and a bowl of fresh fruit. I noticed that there were strawberries, blueberries, and slices of mango in it. It was the most inviting thing in the room.

Next, my eyes landed on the bacon. It was cooked perfectly for me, not too crispy but not too soft either. The eggs next to it looked super fluffy. Everything on the table looked as if it had come out of a food magazine.

I glanced at the cup of black coffee and glass of water that had been placed near my table setting before I glanced at Soren. He was in the middle of serving himself some food and started eating without a word or a glance. I followed his lead and started dishing out some food for myself. The first bite was even better than the sandwich I'd had yesterday, and my body was happy that I had even more food to consume.

Seemingly out of nowhere, a woman who had a blend of silver and black hair pinned back into a low bun and an apron over her clothes walked into the room. If I had to guess, she looked to be older than both Soren and me, maybe in her fifties or sixties. She immediately walked over to Soren. "Is everything to your liking, Mr. Grant?"

Soren nodded. "It is, Molly. Thank you."

Molly gave a small nod and walked back from where she came without bothering to glance in my direction. Had Soren given everyone working here strict orders not to talk to me?

"Eat," Soren said, bringing me out of the daydream I'd found myself in.

I stared at him for a moment before I stood up and began to put things on my plate. It took me multiple attempts to remind myself that I needed to maintain my composure. However, once again, Soren's presence made me want to lash out. I shoved the food in my mouth and nearly moaned.

It was delicious, better than anything I had tasted in a long time. I savored each bite, trying to ignore the fact that every so often, Soren would look up at me and watch me eat. Thankfully, he didn't seem to have any interest in making small talk, making the silence even more pleasurable.

As I was eating, Soren cleared his throat. I looked up at him as I placed my fork down, wondering what he was going to say. But it only took a second for me to realize that he wasn't preparing his voice to talk to me.

Franklin entered the room from the door my back was facing and walked over to Soren. The two men talked in hushed whispers, and I could only make out a word every so often. It wasn't enough context for me to put together what the conversation might be about and that slightly frustrated me. What could they be talking about right now that couldn't wait until after breakfast was done?

"Is this something you would like me to have done?" Franklin asked, his words barely audible.

Soren nodded. "Yes, make sure that it is done properly." His gaze returned to me, and I hated it. Did their conversation have anything to do with me? Was I just being paranoid?

"Will do, sir," Franklin turned on his heel and walked out of the door that I saw Molly enter and leave from just a few minutes ago.

The conversation had stopped everything in my mind. My appetite was long gone, having walked out of the room right behind Franklin. I used my fork to move the food on my plate from left to right as I felt Soren's stare on me once more.

"How is the food?" he asked.

"It's great."

"Then why aren't you eating it?"

"I've lost my appetite." At least that wasn't a lie.

Soren leaned forward, resting his elbows on the table and his chin on his hands. "That's unfortunate. I figured you would be hungry after the early dinner you had the night before."

That was a reasonable assumption because dinner, for whatever reason, had been early. I just shrugged and tucked a piece of my hair behind my ear.

Soren clearly wasn't letting it go because next, he said, "Is it because of what Franklin and I were discussing?"

I tensed at the question, knowing it was foolish to think their conversation had nothing to do with me. "What were you talking about?"

Soren's lips curved into a smirk. "That's not important."

"It is if it concerns me," I shot back, feeling the anger I'd been trying to suppress boiling to the surface.

"You'll find out soon enough."

I pushed my plate away, standing up from my seat. I was over his games and being in his vicinity. "I'm done eating."

Soren raised an eyebrow. "You're sure?"

"Yes. I told you I lost my appetite," I repeated. "And I've had enough of your mind games for one day."

"Who said I'm done playing with you, petal?"

I could hear the double meaning in his words. This was just one of the things I'd been afraid of. Him tossing back barbs, trying to get under my skin, to upset me and to get a reaction that he could feed off of.

"Then it's time for us to head back to the basement."

I nodded, knowing that my opportunity to be a little freer than I'd been in what felt like days was coming to an end.

However, this time, I was slightly happy about being alone down there again. It would give me some distance from the man who was determined to make my life a living hell.

And for now, that was all that I could ask for.

7

SOREN

As evening arrived, showcasing a pretty warm glow throughout my bedroom, I adjusted my black tie before fixing the collar of my shirt. Once my reflection told me it was perfect, I took a step back, gave myself one final look, and left the room.

Within seconds, I'd walked down the stairs leading to the front door, where Franklin was standing with my coat. I grabbed it from him and asked, "Anything more from downstairs?"

Franklin's eyes darted to the floor as if he could see through it before he looked back at me. "Nothing. She's been nothing but the perfect guest."

"Very well. Let me know if anything changes, and I'll keep a lookout when I can."

Once he gave me a short nod, I walked to my door and stepped out of the house.

As I got into the black sedan that was idling in front of my home, I tried to push away any other thoughts aside from the ones related to the Chevaliers. We were holding a meeting at a location that was an equal distance from my home and New York City, a change from where we usually held meetings.

It made sense for me to travel to New York City because many of the higher-ranking officials within the Chevaliers had homes or apartments there. But with me holding the one person who has gotten closest to shaking our organization's very foundation, we'd decided as a group that we didn't want me too far away in case something happened.

It was more precautionary than anything because I knew there was no way that Iris was getting out of where I stashed her.

As the car drove down the winding road toward the home where we would be meeting, I couldn't stop the image of Iris that kept flashing in my mind. All I could see was her skin glistening with water droplets as she washed her body. Had I needed to stay in the bathroom while she took a shower? No, but the desire to torture myself by only being able to watch her was more appealing than standing on the other side of the door.

It had done little to satisfy my craving for her. Things were even more complicated than they had been before, and the only thing I could focus on now was the organization that I'd dedicated my life to. I shook my head, trying to push those thoughts away, but they kept creeping back.

I adjusted my cock to relieve the pressure my slacks were now inflicting on it. I needed to fucking cool it because the last thing I needed to do was walk in there with a hard-on.

Finally, we arrived at the location, a large mansion about an hour from my home. The mansion was surrounded by high walls and guarded by two heavily armed men. As I stepped out of the car, I moved my gaze around the home of

Parker Townsend, chairman of the Chevaliers. In all my years as a part of this organization, I think I'd only been here one other time.

Not that I'd expected to be here every weekend. Parker and I mostly kept our relationship about the Chevaliers and nothing else. It was an unspoken agreement between the two of us and how we both preferred it.

As I approached the door, it opened without me having to knock. I was greeted by Parker's butler.

"Welcome, Mr. Grant," he said.

"Thank you," I replied as I handed him my coat.

"The meeting will be taking place in here." He led me to a closed double door. He knocked once and then twisted the doorknob before moving out of the way so I could walk through.

It seemed as if I was the last one to arrive.

Parker, Beck Chamberlain, Hudson Thorne, Ioan Cavanaugh, and another guy that I didn't recognize were all settling down at the large table.

One of these men didn't belong. Parker must have noticed the look on my face because he said, "Landon here will be on a special assignment for me. He won't be staying too long."

I looked at the man in question and couldn't help but be curious about what sort of assignment Parker had planned for him. He looked younger than everyone else in the room, college-aged or maybe a couple of years removed.

I stuck my hand out to shake his. While he returned the gesture, Parker spoke once more.

"Please, everyone, have a seat."

We all took our seats and our focus shifted to the man of the hour. Parker, as chairman of the Chevaliers, commanded respect and authority. He cleared his throat before beginning the meeting.

"Let's address the assignment that Soren successfully completed," he said, locking eyes with me for a moment. It was his way of acknowledging my murder of Derrick Wilson just days prior. He explained the version of events I'd given him before he looked over at Landon and said, "You might have to do something similar when the time comes. Are you okay with that?"

Landon nodded once. "Yes, sir. I am."

That answer was good enough for Parker because he turned his attention back to the rest of us. The meeting unfolded basically the way I expected it to. Landon left after a few minutes, and we were able to discuss things more freely.

"Soren, how's the girl doing at your place?" Parker's voice sliced through any thoughts I was having. Everyone's attention snapped toward me as they waited for my response.

"She's fine," I replied, making sure to choose my words carefully. "She hasn't tried to escape or anything."

This time, Beck spoke up. "Do we know how much she's found out?"

I couldn't deny that I was a bit annoyed that this had become the topic of conversation, but I understood why it had. "I don't think she was able to find much," I said, locking eyes with Beck. "She was on the right path though. Who knows what she might have been able to find if I hadn't grabbed her at the masquerade ball."

Parker lifted a hand, signaling everyone to be quiet. "We'll keep an eye on things and the people who seem to think that she is the key to our puzzle."

I had a question of my own. "Are we going to continue to keep her at my home?"

Parker nodded. "Nothing changes for now."

The meeting continued as we talked about different measures that we were taking to ensure that we protected the Chevalier organization at all costs. My mind drifted back to Iris occasionally, and I attributed that to her being a topic of conversation. I was annoyed that just the thought of her was providing a distraction to me, but there wasn't anything I could do about it.

As the meeting ended, I hung back and waited to get an opportunity to talk to Parker alone. He spoke to everyone else, and as they exited the room, Parker walked back over to me.

When Parker stepped up next to me, he said, "Your work with Derrick was... excellent."

"Thank you. I didn't hear anything about the body being found by the police. I assume that means the person he was working for got the message then?"

Parker nodded. "I assume so, which is what we want. This was their warning."

"And are you sure that you don't have plans for Iris? Was what you said during the meeting just lip service?"

Parker stared at me for longer than necessary and I wondered what he was thinking. "She is a potential loose end."

I adjusted my stance. "I agree, but does that mean you've made a decision on what you want to do with her?"

"No, I haven't. As long as everything is fine where she is, then I'm truly fine with not making any moves yet. While it would be easy to take her out, I know she's friends with

Bianca Henson, and that could lead to more unrest with the younger generation of leaders, including her brother."

"I have everything under control."

"Good, because I would hate for that loose end to truly end up becoming a problem."

"That I can agree with. If that is it, I'll see myself out now."

Parker looked as if he was deciding what he wanted to do next. "There is something I wanted to share with you that I didn't want to say in front of everyone else."

My eyebrow rose involuntarily. "What's that?"

"Iris isn't wrong."

It took a lot to surprise me, but I was willing to admit that Parker's words had stunned me. "What do you mean Iris isn't wrong?"

"Margaret Turner was involved in the founding of the Chevaliers."

The news shocked me to my core. "How has this been kept under wraps for so long?"

"You mean, how will this continue to be kept under wraps? If this gets out, I would have failed as chairman of the Chevaliers. And I refuse to fail."

"You're going to have to give me more information than that, Parker."

"That's all I can say for now. So when I ask if you've gotten that situation at your home handled, this is what I'm talking about. You must do whatever it takes to keep all of this under wraps, or I'll be forced to make the call on her life."

Parker didn't wait for me to respond. He turned and walked away from me, ending our conversation on that note. I walked out of the room and stood in the hallway as I waited for Parker's butler to get my coat. I waited until I stepped out into the cool evening air and got back into the car I'd hired for the evening before I tried to digest the information that Parker had just told me.

The car glided along the interstate, and the ride back to my home went as smoothly as anticipated. However, my mind was nothing but chaos. I'd tried to focus on some things I needed to complete for work, but I couldn't. Nothing could stop the replaying of Parker's words in my brain.

The meeting at Parker's had left me feeling somewhat angry, but my talk with him after had sent me over the edge. I needed to protect the Chevaliers at all costs, but knowing that there might be some truth to what Iris was searching for sent me down another path of thinking. But I shoved it to the side. I needed to keep a clear head in order to not fuck something up.

"Whatever it takes," I whispered to myself as I mindlessly tapped the leather seat I was sitting on. I went back to trying to focus on the emails I needed to answer, deciding that, at the moment, they were worth more of my brainpower than focusing on what Parker did and didn't say.

"Welcome home," I muttered to myself as the driver I'd hired for the evening pulled up to the front of my home. He put the car into park, and I opened my own door without waiting for him to get out of his seat. Without a backward glance, I quickly walked to the entrance, and the front door opened almost silently before me, revealing Franklin standing in the doorway.

We exchanged a brief nod, acknowledging each other's presence. "Did anything happen while I was gone?"

Franklin shook his head. "Everything has been quiet here.

Molly has just finished preparing dinner. Do you want me to bring Ms. Bennington upstairs to sit at the table with you?"

I thought about it for a second before I shook my head. "I'll be having dinner alone tonight."

"Very well. I'll make sure she gets served."

"Thank you and I'll also take my dinner in my office."

"Excellent, sir."

With that, I left Franklin in the hallway and headed to my office to lock myself away from my thoughts of Parker's revelation, which changed everything I thought I knew.

8

IRIS

My hand flew to my chest as my eyes popped open. It took me a second to realize that I was awake, still trapped in this dreary basement. The grogginess started to fade as my brain tried to piece together exactly what it was that caused me to wake up with such a start.

The creaking of the basement door brought my attention to the staircase. The sound signaled that someone was about to make their presence known, giving me little time to mentally prepare. Then again, could I ever be mentally prepared for this shit? Having spent days down here now, my loneliness only broken when Franklin brought me food, was starting to take its toll. But I refused to let them see what being down here was doing to me.

Soren Grant was determined to break me. And I wouldn't let him.

This didn't mean that every time I heard footsteps over my head or the basement door opening, my heart didn't freeze before beating rapidly. There was a mixture of fear and anger bubbling beneath the surface, which I was forced to contain.

When the door opened and I heard the first couple of footsteps coming down the stairs, I knew it was Franklin bringing me breakfast. I'd gotten better at being able to tell the difference in their strides and the sounds of the steps that they took. When Franklin appeared at the foot of the stairs without a tray in his hands, I was confused.

Where was my food? Was Soren planning on starving me now?

Then Franklin looked up, his piercing eyes boring into me, making me wish that he would find some other place to look. "Mr. Grant wants you to eat breakfast with him this morning."

"Do I need to—"

Franklin took a step closer to me and looked at me with a blank expression. "Mr. Grant did not give me any further instructions. He only said that he wants you to join him for breakfast."

I had to take Franklin at his word, but I didn't know what to make of this. Much like the shower incident, what was the catch here?

I wouldn't find out unless I went along with this farce.

"Okay," I said finally. "I'll go."

Franklin nodded and bent down at my feet to unchain my ankle. Then he turned around, signaling for me to follow him. I removed the blanket from my body and got up from the mattress to follow him up the stairs.

As I climbed the steps, I knew this was just another one of Soren's games. I didn't know what to expect, but I needed to keep cool no matter what happened.

Once we reached the top of the stairs, Franklin led me to the dining room, although I would have had no issue getting there on my own now if I were alone. I stepped into the room and noticed a similar setup as the day before. Soren was already seated at the head of the table, his eyes trained on me as I entered.

"Ah, Iris," he greeted me. "How did you sleep last night?"

So, the games had already begun. It didn't take a rocket scientist to know how well I slept on a shitty mattress on the floor while being chained to a wall. "No complaints," I said as I started to pull the chair out for me to sit in.

"No, I want you to sit right here. Next to me."

Of course that's what he wanted me to do. I bit back a sigh, instead choosing to take a deep breath to calm my emotions. I sat down in the chair to Soren's left. We filled our plates and ate in silence until Soren spoke up.

Without looking up from his plate, he asked, "How is the food?"

The way he asked the question triggered me. His tone was condescending, and I couldn't believe his audacity. Then again, I should have expected it, but apparently, controlling my temper wasn't in the cards.

The words flew out of my mouth before I could stop them. "It's great, but you make it seem like I should be grateful. Like, should I be begging you on my knees for not letting me starve?"

"There are reasons why I could see you being on your knees. Begging me for food isn't one of them."

I froze. The double entendre was not lost on me, and I could feel the heat rising in my cheeks even though I wished I wasn't having that reaction. Soren smirked, his eyes darkening even more than they normally were. If this was the game he wanted to play, then by all means, I was going to play it.

I matched Soren's smirk with a sly smile of my own. I did my best to match his confidence, even though I was definitely lacking there, given what had happened. "Was I supposed to come crawling to you, begging you to let me go? That still hasn't happened, has it?"

I watched as Soren's jaw clenched before he leaned forward, his eyes locked onto mine. "Oh, I think you'll beg eventually. We all have our breaking point, petal. And I intend to find yours."

I refused to let him get the upper hand. "You seem awfully confident in that, Soren. But I'm not so easily broken, as you can see."

Soren chuckled and I hated how it made me feel. "We'll see, Iris. We'll see." He raised his glass to me and said, "You know, this really all could have been avoided."

"Avoided? You are the one that brought me here and then locked me in the fucking basement! Hell, all of this is because of you. A little bit hard to forget that detail," I spat back.

"You chose to dive into things you had no business getting into. I merely reacted." The coldness in his voice sent shivers down my spine.

"I'm looking for the truth, Soren. That's it."

He leaned toward me, and I instinctively moved back. "Some truths, Iris, are better left buried."

The weight of his stare shook me, and I tried to maintain my composure. I failed. He'd pissed me off to the point of no return. "Or perhaps the truth will come out anyway. Like revealing what happened to Eden, right?"

I regretted the words as soon as I said them. Bringing up his dead wife was the cruelest thing I could think of, and I just said it.

I had crossed a line.

Soren's face shifted into something I'd never seen before. It morphed from cold anger to something far more terrifying. He looked like I had slapped him, and to be honest, it felt like I'd slapped him too.

Everything changed in an instant. There was a storm brewing in Soren's eyes. The tension in the room snapped, crossing over into a place of no return. His gaze was pinned on me, but he was silent. It felt as though he was trying to decipher my every thought. There was nothing to be said.

But then he wasn't.

Before I could respond, he reacted, choosing to knock all the china in his vicinity off the table with one swipe of his arm. I gasped as dishware flew off the table and shattered onto the wood floor. The sound was deafening, each plate turning into shiny shards that reflected in the light. The action was so unexpected that I flinched hard, and it made me stumble out of my chair.

My heart hammered in my chest as adrenaline pumped through my veins. I almost wished for the silence that we had shared before versus the chaos that had now erupted. I glanced at the door before looking back at Soren. The urge to run out of this house was more prevalent than ever, but he was too quick. He stormed toward me. I backed away from him, stumbling over my now fallen chair until my back hit the wall.

There was nowhere to go.

Nowhere to hide.

Cornered, with no means of escape, I looked up at him and put my hands out in front of me in hopes of providing a small barrier between him and me. I was confronted by every ounce of his rage, which had now contorted his usually handsome features. Even if I hated the man, I was willing to admit he was still so fucking attractive.

"Never speak of her again."

The threat hung between us, but there was something else in his eyes. I saw something beneath the surface, a subtle shift in the hardened exterior he liked to portray. I noticed a glimmer of something raw and vulnerable. Pain.

It was as if, for a brief moment, the walls he'd built around himself had crumbled just a little, revealing something he'd made sure to keep hidden. It was surprising, unsettling even. I was too afraid to move because of what I'd seen and what he might be planning to do. Not that it mattered because he sprung first.

Soren's hand was around my throat before I had the chance to react. He squeezed, not enough to cut off my air supply but enough to make me gasp for breath. Adrenaline continued to churn through my veins, but it was now joined by fear. My hands flew to his in an effort to break free from his hold. His grip only tightened, his fingers digging into my skin.

"You have no idea what you're playing with," he growled, his face only inches from mine. My vision blurred as salty tears ran down my cheeks and my breath caught in my throat. Each inhalation was a battle against the growing lump in my chest. Then the unthinkable happened.

Soren's lips crashed onto mine. His hands moved from my throat to my hips and pulled me flush against him. This time, his touch was more firm than punishing. I was so shocked I didn't know what to do other than to let him kiss me. As much as my brain told me to pull away, my body refused because the sensations that I was feeling drowned out rational thought.

He bit down on my lower lip, causing me to gasp just before he deepened the kiss. His tongue pushed its way into my mouth, and I moaned. I was ashamed to admit it, but I was enjoying this. I was enjoying being kissed like this, being wanted like this.

Was it my fear or my excitement filling my brain? I couldn't be sure because both had melded together. I found myself sliding my arms around Soren's neck and leaned into our kiss.

However, that seemed to shift the dynamic. The kiss abruptly ended, leaving me breathless and wanting more. Soren pulled away from me, his eyes still dark with desire.

"Franklin," he called out. "Get her out of my sight."

Franklin appeared out of the corner of my eye, and I quickly turned on my heel and ran out of the room. I was gone before Franklin could follow. I needed to put distance between Soren and me—now.

I needed to be alone to calm my nerves and lick the wounds that Soren had ripped open when he terrified me.

9

SOREN

I stormed into my study and slammed the door shut behind me. I was still pissed as Iris's words played on repeat in my mind. My hand impulsively reached for the crystal decanter and clean glass on my desk, something that I should have put back in its place the last time I used it. I poured myself a glass of whiskey, getting a small thrill as I watched the amber liquid fall into the glass.

"Damn her," I muttered under my breath, my voice filled with anger. The truth was, she had struck a nerve, and I wasn't sure if she completely understood the effect she'd had before I reacted. Her words were a mirror reflecting the darkest parts of myself that I had done my best to ignore. My grip tightened around the glass, and I watched as my knuckles turned white.

She didn't know what the fuck she was talking about.

As I stared into the depths of the liquid in my hand, memories that I wanted to keep buried began to resurface. I'd done my damnedest to hide them, but they erupted within me and now I had to deal with them once more.

I was the reason why Eden was dead. It was all because of me.

The feeling of the slightly chilled glass pressed against my lips was a stark contrast to the fire that was brewing inside of me. I took a sip, feeling the burning sensation spread through my throat and enjoying the feel of it. It all was a temporary escape from the world outside the walls of my study.

"Or perhaps the truth will come out anyway. Like revealing what happened to Eden, right?" Iris's words rang in my ears, and they only made my anger grow. Her piercing blue eyes shined with defiance and fear, and I had to admit, she was brave for saying the words out loud.

My fist clenched as I recalled our argument once more. I began to pace across the floor of my study as I tried to calm myself. The drink didn't help, but it was better than me going to her and taking my fucked-up emotions out on her. Hell, maybe fucking her emotions out of her until the only thing left was her writhing under my body, crying out my name.

I shook my head to remove the idea from my mind. I had no business thinking about fucking her when she was determined to tear the Chevaliers apart seam by seam. What kind of man would that make me?

Then again, I'd made some interesting choices in my life, so that wouldn't be the strangest thing I've ever done. I took another sip from my glass and allowed the bitterness of the drink to mingle with the bitterness that filled my heart. The liquid was slowly scorching away the lingering traces of Iris's words in my brain.

However, no amount of alcohol could erase the memories

of that night. The night when everything went to shit, and I lost the woman I was supposed to protect. Eden's face flashed before my eyes, haunting me like a ghost. Hell, I wouldn't be surprised if that was something she'd decided to do.

I downed the rest of my drink and slammed the glass on the desk, the sound echoing through the room. I needed to think. To figure out what my next move was going to be. I wandered over to the window, my eyes scanning my landscape.

Iris had struck a nerve, and I wasn't sure if I could keep ignoring it any longer. Maybe it was time to face my demons head-on, no matter how painful it might be. But I needed to go back to when things weren't as shitty as they were now.

I stared out the window of my study and let my mind drift back to Eden and our wedding day.

THE WARM SUN cast a golden haze over the garden as the aroma of flowers filled the air, unsurprising given where we were.

I stood next to Eden as her eyes darted all over the scenery before us. She was dressed in a soft, elegant ivory gown made of lace. Her chestnut curls cascaded down her back and were caught in the light breeze that blew around us.

"Eden, you look beautiful," I said without a hint of humor. Normally, we would tease each other about things like this, but this wasn't the time to do so.

She turned to face me, a smile playing on her full lips. "Thank you. Today wasn't exactly how I imagined my wedding day would go, but this is a beautiful day nonetheless."

I agreed with her only because I never imagined getting married, but I was willing to do it for her. All of this was for her.

"Are you ready?" I asked.

"Yes, I'm ready," she whispered. She offered me her trembling hand and I grabbed it, trying to steady her in any way I could.

This hadn't been the first choice of either of us, but we were going through with it anyway.

There wasn't much of a crowd here to witness our big event. We didn't need it. Franklin and Molly served as our witnesses as we walked up to the officiant, who gave us a big smile.

"Eden, Soren," the officiant began, "today is a day of celebration. A day where love comes together to create something even more beautiful."

I glanced over at Eden, noticing the tears welling up in her eyes as she looked at me. The officiant continued to speak, but I barely heard the words. We recited the standard vows, choosing not to waste any time creating our own. We just needed to get this done as quickly as possible.

"Eden, do you take Soren to be your lawfully wedded husband, to have and to hold, to love and to cherish, in sickness and in health, till death do you part?" the officiant said.

"I do," she whispered, and her voice quivered slightly. Her eyes were locked onto mine. I offered a reassuring smile, letting her know that we were making the right choice.

"Soren, do you take Eden to be your lawfully wedded wife, to have and to hold, to love and to cherish, in sickness and in health, till death do you part?" the officiant asked.

"I do," I said with confidence.

"By the power vested in me, I now pronounce you husband and wife. Soren, you may kiss the bride."

And as the officiant pronounced us husband and wife, the

sound of birds chirping announced the end of our ceremony. Franklin, Molly, and our officiant offered a small round of applause as Eden and I leaned in and gave each other a small kiss on the cheek. Before she could completely pull away, I put a kiss on her forehead. It was a tender gesture that spoke volumes about the foundation of our relationship. It was one built on respect and understanding.

Almost everyone here knew the score about why this wedding was happening.

But it didn't matter. What mattered was that Eden was now my wife. And I would do whatever it took to protect her.

As we turned to face our small group of witnesses, Franklin stepped forward with a bottle of champagne in his hand.

"Congratulations, Mr. and Mrs. Grant," he said, popping the cork and pouring us each a glass.

We raised our glasses in a toast. The bubbles tickled our noses as we sipped the sweet liquid, and I turned to Eden as she giggled because of the champagne. It was a small, intimate celebration, but it was perfect in its own way.

As the day progressed, we took a stroll through the gardens, hand in hand, taking in the beautiful scenery and enjoying each other's company. It was a moment of calm away from the chaos that swirled around us.

We clasped our hands together and walked into the small restaurant that I'd rented out for this occasion. Even though we'd gotten married for an unusual reason, I still wanted this to be a day that Eden would remember. She deserved to have a day where she could relax amid everything, and I wanted to give it to her.

Franklin and Molly sat at our table, and together, we had a delicious meal. I was grateful for what they'd done to ensure that this plan went off without a hitch. It had taken quite a few people to pull this together on short notice, but it needed to be done in order to save a life.

"Soren."

I turned my head to look at Eden. "Do you remember the incident at the river when we were eight or nine?"

"Of course," I murmured, not too thrilled to have that memory appear in my mind again.

"You jumped into the water without a second thought when you saw me struggling to get out," she said. "Do you remember what you said when you rescued me?"

"I do."

"You promised to always save me. No matter where in the world we were or what was going on. Including what you've done today."

I nodded. "It's a promise I intend to keep. There was no way I was letting him do that to you." I knew what she was referring to. Her father's plans that we'd now foiled because of us signing our names on that certificate.

"You will never understand how grateful I am for you and our friendship." I could see tears starting to pool in the corner of her eyes.

"I know that you'll be there for me too, if something were to occur. This was a no-brainer. Now stop crying, or else everyone is going to think that I upset you on our wedding day."

That made Eden chuckle. "Fine. That would be the last thing I want."

～

THE MEMORY soon faded to black as I took another sip of the whiskey in my glass. Thinking better of it, I polished off the rest and placed the glass down gently on my desk, feeling much calmer than I'd been when I walked into this room.

Even when I thought of Iris, who always seemed to be present in my mind, I couldn't get rid of the thoughts no matter how hard I tried.

It was then that I finally decided that it was time I did something about it.

10

IRIS

I could still feel the stinging sensation from Soren's kiss on my lips. But I didn't need to feel it because I'd been playing his last interaction with me on repeat in my mind. My thoughts raced as I tried to make sense of what had just happened and how all of this had come to be.

Nothing made sense, and I needed to embrace the fact that I might never figure this out.

I pulled the blanket next to me over my lap in the spirit of keeping myself warm. Although it could be thicker, I was grateful to have anything. I was sitting back down on what had become my makeshift bed in this basement, and I hated that I was trembling from the anger he'd caused.

My fingers ran across my throat, but where I expected to wince due to the hold he'd had on me, I didn't. Even in his rage, he'd known the exact amount of pressure to put on my neck to make it feel more erotic than hurtful. Another thing I could add to the list of things I hated about him.

I took a deep breath and closed my eyes in an attempt to push out all thoughts of Soren. However, it was impossible.

Even with my eyes tightly shut, I could feel his presence. He was everywhere in this house but also nowhere at the same time.

A shiver forced my body to shake as the hair on the back of my neck stood up. I felt as if I was walking a tightrope, flirting with the potential of falling to my death. I was playing with fire.

I brushed a hand through my hair and opened my eyes. Why hadn't I found a way out of here yet? Why did it seem as if he was always ten steps ahead of me?

Until this morning, he hadn't been expecting me to throw the dead wife card out. Hell, I hadn't been expecting it either, if I was being honest. But I'd been pushed to the brink by him, and it fell from my lips. While I did feel bad on some level because I understood how it felt to lose people you loved, it didn't give him the right to treat me as such.

I moved my legs and immediately felt the weight of the chain attached to my left ankle. I drew my leg up to my chest to give myself an opportunity to scrutinize the cuff. I pulled on the chain for the billionth time. The heavy iron links were unforgiving, and I wondered why I even bothered.

He'd done everything he could do to make sure that I was locked down here for as long as he wanted me to be. I lay back down and pulled the blanket over me more, hoping I could get some sleep to make time pass by faster.

But this time, it hadn't worked.

Instead, I found myself staring at the ceiling, reviewing how I'd gotten to this point. Soren was right in a way. Eddison Payne and the desire to prove everyone wrong was what had gotten me here. But also, Soren didn't have to do all of this.

Nothing he'd done had changed my mind. Not even being

locked away like a prisoner had done anything to dim the fire that burned in me to seek out the truth. Though my movements were restricted, and my questions went unanswered, my restless mind never stopped trying to piece together the mystery or a way out of here.

I must have been close to discovering something by the night of the masquerade ball. It didn't make sense for Soren to wait until then to strike if I hadn't been. Unless... he was taking orders from someone who didn't tell him to snatch me until the party.

My eyes darted around the room as I began to think of the possibilities. There were two other men in the room that we'd entered, where I was forced to drink whatever it was they'd given me. Could one of them have been the person who told Soren to kidnap me?

But what was in Chevalier Manor that made them decide that was the right time? Soren could have kidnapped me right before the party or made sure I didn't get an invitation. There was a reason why I'd been invited to the party, and I still didn't know why. It was obvious that he had no issue with me being seen there or there being witnesses to the crime. Not that any of them would come forward against him.

But perhaps Payne's papers or something alluding to the location of them was somewhere in that building, somewhere that I might have had access to. But in order to figure any of this out, I needed to get out of here.

How though?

My gaze landed on the tiny windows up above. No matter how many times I looked up at them, nothing had changed. The windows were still too small for me to fit through, up too high for me to reach, and had bars on them. There was no way I was going to be able to get out that way. My eyes drifted toward the basement door. I needed to get out of here and that seemed like the only way.

With a small glance at the chain I was attached to, I looked around the room. Maybe I was becoming delusional, but there had to be something I was missing.

I threw my blanket off my body, got off the mattress and stretched, trying to soothe the soreness that was a result of sleeping in these conditions. I once again started to search for something that could help me break the chain. I checked in the corners of the room, even behind a few boxes. But I came up empty.

I went to the bathroom once more in hopes that there was something inside that could help me. Maybe, just maybe, I'd missed something before, and it could be my ticket out of this nightmare. With each step I took, the cold floor beneath my feet made me tremble slightly, but I pushed on.

The bathroom door creaked slightly as I opened it. The same scene I saw every time I walked in here greeted me once more. I began searching again, hoping for a different outcome than before. My heart sank a little more with each place I checked. The hope that had forced me to walk into this room began to wane as I realized, once again, there was nothing here to help me get out of this basement. The echoing sound of my own frustrated sigh figuratively slapped me in the face. Once again, I left the bathroom feeling defeated, despite knowing it was silly for me to do the same thing and hope for a different outcome.

I sighed as I walked back to where I'd been sitting before. I slid down the wall and landed on the mattress as the feelings of defeat crowded my brain.

What the hell was I missing?

I sighed as my eyes darted around the empty space again. This place was getting to me. I brought my knees close to my chest and hugged them. I could feel myself slowly losing my mind. We all had our own demons to fight, and I'd seen Soren's up close and personal this morning.

Heck, maybe the reason I was down here was to slowly make me feel like I was losing a handle on it all, to make me feel as if my entire world was crashing down.

And then it hit me. I thought about Gran, the only family I had left. I missed her warm, comforting hugs and the way her eyes would light up when she smiled at me. I could almost smell her homemade apple pie baking in the oven as I walked through the door. I could only imagine what she was thinking about me not being with her right now.

Then there was Bianca. There was no doubt in my mind she'd noticed I was missing by now and she knew her brother and his girlfriend were at the party. They'd seen Soren walk up to me and dance with me, so why hadn't anyone come and questioned him yet? Was anyone even looking for me?

My hot tears grew more prevalent as the sharp pang of missing the people I loved hit me right in the heart. The feelings coursing through me reminded me of when I lost my parents. And now my life was in Soren's hands, and I may never see my loved ones again if I remained trapped in this fucking basement.

I squeezed my eyes shut as I tried to wash away the anger and fear and convince myself that the dominant feeling I needed to have was determination. I had to survive this. I clung to the warm memories of them as I dozed off to sleep on this mattress because that was the only thing I could do at the moment.

I only slightly moved my head when I heard footsteps sounding from above. I assumed it was Franklin moving, but hearing them move back and forth in the same place made me think differently.

Was the person pacing?

It wasn't as if any of that mattered. I leaned back against the cold wall and closed my eyes again. I allowed myself to listen to every sound that the house made.

As I sat still, I found myself hoping that something would change. Something needed to change.

11

SOREN

Late at night, my home was completely silent, just as I preferred. The large windows reflected the soft glow of the moon, casting shadows into my office. The only sound was the gentle ticking of the grandfather clock, indicating how much time had passed since I entered this room. I sat in my office chair, nursing a glass of whiskey, having calmed down from my earlier explosion against Iris.

However, she wasn't the only person I was thinking of.

Eden's face danced in my mind, her laughter playing like a melody. For a brief moment, I lost myself in the illusion that she was still alive. But the bitter truth came crashing down like a sledgehammer.

I thought back to us sitting in here, Eden looking through my books. I could tell that something was on her mind because she hadn't been acting like herself. That day, she seemed to be more reserved and when she turned to look at me, I could see the vulnerability in her eyes. The memory was so vivid it replayed in my mind as if it were happening again now.

"My father is trying to force me to marry someone that I've never met. He thinks this will propel our family's status in New York."

It wasn't the first time I'd heard of a marriage taking place due to an arrangement between families, but I'd never expected it to happen to Eden. "Your father is doing what?" There was no way I'd heard her correctly.

"He's selling off my hand in marriage to the highest bidder in hopes of having more money and status."

She looked away, but I saw the way that her face fell before she moved. And that only made me angrier. "You can't let him control you like this."

Eden sighed. "What choice do I have? If I refuse, we'll have nothing."

I shook my head, not believing what I was hearing, but at the same time, I wasn't shocked at Anthony Marsden's audacity. "No, we can figure something out. There must be another way."

My mind raced with possibilities of how to help Eden escape her father's plans. Confronting her father would only make things worse for her. Offering her financial compensation without the marriage would only fix one of her issues because while I can give her money, there wouldn't be any change in social status for her.

While I did move in many powerful social circles, I preferred to remain in the shadows instead of being the center of attention. Nothing I came up with in my mind as a potential solution seemed to fit the bill until it finally hit me.

"Marry me instead." The words tumbled out before I could stop them.

Eden stared at me. "What?"

"Marry me," I repeated. "Your father wants you to wed for money. I can give you that. Getting married to me would prevent him from forcing you down the aisle with anyone else. You won't have to marry a stranger, and your family will be provided for."

"Soren, we can't. I won't bring you into this and tie you to me because we aren't actually in love." A watery chuckle left her lips.

"This isn't about falling in love. We love each other and our friendship can make this work," I walked over to her and grasped her hands, willing her to understand. "This is about protecting you, Eden. Marry me, and I'll keep you safe. No matter what."

Eden searched my face as the floodgates opened and tears spilled down her cheeks. At last, she nodded. "Thank you."

I pulled her into my arms and hoped to soothe the pain she felt. "Of course. You've saved me more times than I can count."

"Hardly, Soren. You never needed anyone to save you. I still feel terrible bringing you into this. You should find someone to spend the rest of your life with, to treat with love, dignity, and respect."

"I'm choosing to help you. And that's the end of it."

As the memory faded, I found myself standing up and pacing back and forth. I took one last sip of my whiskey and placed the glass back on my desk, knowing that Franklin would retrieve it in the morning.

I paced back and forth in my office, my thoughts consuming me before I finally left to head upstairs and go to bed.

I walked down the hallway and up the stairs but found myself unable to go to my bedroom. Instead, I stopped in front of the locked door that haunted me to this very day. Before I could convince myself otherwise, I found myself opening the door and slipping inside.

This room was filled with Eden's things, and I couldn't help but sigh as I took it all in. Dusty beams of moonlight filtered through the curtains, falling across items of our unconventional marriage: a faded bouquet of wildflowers Eden had used as a bouquet on our wedding day, a book of poetry I'd given her when we were teens, and her wedding dress.

All of this was a memorial to the woman with whom I had shared a wonderful friendship but who I hadn't been able to secure justice for. No matter how long it took me, I was determined to make her father pay for her death. I assumed she wanted the same, and that was why her ghost still haunted the halls of Chevalier Manor to this day. I couldn't help but reflect on the many ways she practiced empathy and kindness to others and yet she was still snatched away from this world before her time.

I knew that Eden wouldn't want me to isolate myself forever. Hell, she'd even debated the option of marrying me because it would tie us together versus giving me the ability to find everlasting love, according to her.

And now I had that opportunity once again with Iris. I couldn't deny that Iris had sparked something inside me. A flicker of warmth in the dark, a breath of hope that I'd never expected even if I didn't show it to her. I might have been masterful at hiding it, but beneath the layers, something was shifting.

Maybe now was the time for a change.

This short walk down memory lane had been enough. I found myself walking to the door, stepping out of it, and locking it behind me once more.

12

IRIS

Two days after my last encounter with Soren, Franklin walked down the stairs of the basement and approached me. This wasn't out of the norm since he was the one who continued to deliver my meals, but he'd just delivered lunch to me about thirty minutes ago. Without saying a word, he crouched down by my side and carefully unlocked the chain around my ankle.

"Ms. Bennington," he said softly, "Mr. Grant has decided to let you stay in one of our guest rooms."

I eyed him warily, unsure of what to make of this sudden change. Why would Soren want to do me a favor after the big fight we had? It didn't make any sense. I brought my ankle closer to my body and rubbed it gently as the thoughts in my mind raced. "Why?"

"He mentioned that you might be more comfortable in a real bed. All your accommodations are set up."

This sounded too good to be true. Trusting anyone in this place was the worst decision I could make. In fact, it made me more anxious than anything because I could already see a million ways that I could get stabbed in the back. However, the idea of staying chained up in this room was unbearable. I wanted to get out and move around more freely even if it still meant being locked in this mansion.

"Okay," I nodded, hesitantly standing up. "Please show me to the room I'll be staying in."

Franklin led me through the home, giving me a short tour of where some of the main rooms were, including the kitchen and the bathrooms. His footsteps were nearly silent on the floor, while I thought I sounded like an elephant stomping through the house. As we walked around the house, we didn't run into the one person I felt was lurking around every corner. Soren was nowhere to be found, but I couldn't help but feel as if I was still under his watchful eye. I couldn't deny that I was happy he hadn't appeared, but I refused to ask Franklin anything about him.

"Here," Franklin gestured to an ornate wooden door. "This will be your room."

"Thank you," I murmured, stepping inside. I immediately recognized it as the room Soren had brought me to when he'd invited me to take a shower.

"The bathroom is right through that door. If there is anything else you need, I'll be downstairs."

Franklin was already across the threshold when I spoke. "Wait, can I ask you one more thing?"

"Sure."

"What is today's date?"

He remained silent, so still and quiet that I began to question if he'd even heard me. The moments stretched on, agonizingly, until he finally spoke, "December nineteenth."

The date echoed in my mind like I was playing it on repeat. *Shit.* By now, festive lights would be twinkling everywhere, and the air would be filled with the scent of pine and gingerbread cookies. The holidays were in full swing. I would usually be spending this time with Gran and celebrating the fact that she and I were together. All the festive cheer out there was a stark contrast to my current reality. The thought made me sick to my stomach.

Franklin walked out of the room without another word, the door clicking shut behind him.

I found myself in a room that felt dark and old yet still retained its beauty. It was as if time had frozen in here and had decided to preserve the charm of the room. Vaulted ceilings rose high above, with beautiful molding and a chandelier that hung almost like a crown.

The four-poster bed in the center of the room was made from what looked to be dark mahogany. The bedding was a deep red and looked as if it would be smooth to the touch. Two nightstands surrounded the bed, each with a lamp on its rich, glossy surface. A dresser that matched the nightstands and the bed stood along one of the walls in the room. The room had your standard bedroom furniture and a small desk in the corner with a notebook on it.

The first place I walked to was the window, which currently had its heavy curtains open, allowing the sunlight to shine in. At least from this window, there was nothing that could be seen for miles. This home was very isolated, making an escape even harder because there was nowhere I could run to for help.

"Freedom is an illusion... and the scales must be balanced," I whispered to myself as unease flowed from every pore in my body. Being out of the basement and having the ability to move around more was great, but I was still confined to this building.

I assumed there were some sort of security measures in place that would prevent me from walking out the front door. After all, since I was a captive, allowing me to just waltz out of here wouldn't do. But that didn't mean I couldn't try. It would take some time and some careful planning though.

With that thought, I turned on my heel and made my way to the en suite bathroom. I turned on the showerhead and watched as the water cascaded down the tiles for a moment. As I undressed and stepped into the shower, the steam from the hot water enveloped me, wiping my stress away temporarily. This shower was heavenly and would be the only good memory I would have of this godforsaken place. Plus, I didn't have Soren staring at me this time.

Once I finished, I wrapped myself in a plush towel and returned to the bedroom. The air was cooler on my skin due to it being damp, so I quickly checked the drawers in the dresser for some clothes I could change into.

My mouth dropped open in shock when I opened the top drawer. It was full of underwear that were all my size. I opened the other drawers and then the closet, and I was truly flabbergasted. Everything from dresses to skirts and even blouses had been neatly arranged, I assumed for me.

For a brief moment, I wondered if these were Eden Marsden Grant's clothes, but while we might have looked alike, I had no idea if we were the same size. My question was answered when I found clothing tags hanging from the garments, confirming that these pieces were brand new. Unless she'd never worn them before.

The closet also contained various shoes that I could wear, but I immediately grabbed a pair of slippers and placed them on my feet. After that, I grabbed a pair of sneakers and placed them near my bed in case I had to make a run for it quickly as my escape plan came together.

Much like the baseball bat I'd bought to protect myself, I didn't know how much good it would do, but it provided a small level of comfort I couldn't describe. And that was all I could count on at the moment.

As I dressed in a pair of sweatpants and a T-shirt, I couldn't shake off the feeling of being watched. I scanned the room, but nothing stood out to me. Maybe it was just my imagination running wild.

I walked over to the desk and picked up the notebook that I had found earlier. Flipping through the pages, I realized it was brand new. Why was this in here? Was it for me to use?

It might come in handy for anything that I might find since I was without a phone or any other device. But I needed to be careful about what I wrote in case someone came across the notebook and read its contents.

As I closed the notebook, I heard a soft sound I thought came from the hallway. I turned my head to face the door, wondering if I would hear the sound again to confirm that I hadn't been hearing things.

I walked slowly toward the door and pressed my ear against it, straining to hear anything. At first, there was nothing but silence. Then I heard the soft rustling noise once more. I shifted my body so my hand was hovering over the doorknob.

Taking a deep breath, I turned the doorknob and cautiously opened the door. The hallway was empty. I stepped out of the room and closed the door quietly behind me.

As I stood in the hallway, the hairs on the back of my neck stood up as I scanned the area for any signs of life. I took a step forward as my heart pounded in my chest. Every inch of my body told me to turn back, to go back into my room and lock the door. But I couldn't shake the feeling that something was off, and I needed to investigate now.

I took a couple more steps and heard the soft rustling sound again, and I realized it was coming from a door diagonally across the hall from me. I had no business being interested in this door. This wasn't my home. It was my prison. Yet my curiosity had me drawn to it.

I walked to the door and reached for the doorknob. I had a second to turn back and ignore what I'd heard, but when I heard it again, something within me told me that I couldn't. The doorknob turned in my hand, but the door didn't move.

It was locked. But why?

I jiggled the doorknob again, but it wouldn't budge. It wasn't weird that someone would have a locked room in their home, but for some reason, Soren having one raised even more red flags.

The door was solid, with no visible cracks or seams. I pressed my ear against it, hoping to hear something, anything, that would give me a clue about what lay beyond the door.

I knocked softly, half expecting some sort of response. But the only thing I got was silence.

With a final glance at the door, I turned away. I walked back to my room, but my thoughts stayed on the locked door that was across the hall from me. What else did Soren have to hide?

13

IRIS

The next morning, I didn't want to open my eyes. There was no confusion about where I was or how I'd gotten here, but the thought of opening my eyes to view the world around me seemed to be more trouble than it was worth. The reality of me being forced to stay here surrounded me constantly. It had a choke hold on me that only seemed to grow tighter by the day.

But if I was looking at the positives, at least I'd been able to sleep in a very warm and comfortable bed for the night, helping with the soreness that seemed to be a permanent fixture in my body at this point. As I lay here, feeling torn between the urge to sink further into these blankets or confront whatever was going to happen next, a tear escaped, rolling down the curve of my cheek.

I could hear faint sounds in the distance, maybe coming from downstairs. It was probably Franklin moving around, doing his job. It was comforting in a way, knowing that there was at least someone else in this place, even if he barely spoke to me.

I sighed when I came to terms with the fact that staying in bed was useless. I opened my eyes and stared up at the ceiling. I couldn't stay in bed forever, nor did I want to in this house. The room was mostly dark, with a sliver of light peeking through the heavy curtains that covered the windows.

Pushing back the comforter, I swung my legs over the side of the bed and allowed my feet to touch the cool, hard wooden floor. For a moment, I just sat there, collecting my thoughts, bracing myself for the day ahead.

I slowly stood up and walked over to the window. I pulled back the curtain just a little, letting in the warmth of the sunlight. For being a cold December day, the sun was bright, but the grounds that this mansion sat on still had a creepy feel to them, one that I couldn't shake no matter how hard I tried.

I turned away from the window and walked into the bathroom. Visions of Soren staring at me while I fucked myself in the shower just a few feet away still haunted me as I picked up the toothbrush and began brushing my teeth. I washed my face before walking back out of the bathroom and toward the closet in the room.

I searched through the clothes that weren't mine, though they were the right size. Finally, I pulled out a simple navy sweater and a pair of black leggings. The clothes felt snug and warm, perfect for a day like this. They also served as armor of sorts, set to protect me from whatever Soren or his staff were going to throw at me.

Once I was dressed, I ran a brush through my hair as I walked over to the dresser in the room in an effort to make myself look more presentable. I hated that my once beautiful hair, including its purple ends, now looked dull. I found a hair tie that had been resting on the dresser top and put my hair into a messy bun, somewhat hiding the purple. Dying my hair was a symbol of me taking a bold step and doing something I wouldn't normally do, and I felt anything but courageous at the moment. As I took a step back to fix my hair, my stomach growled, signaling that I should eat something.

With one last glance at the mirror, I stepped out of the room and moved toward the staircase that would take me to the kitchen. I walked down the stairs and entered the dining area where I'd eaten meals with Soren. I glanced at the spot where he'd backed me into the wall and kissed me like his life depended on it, and I shivered at the memory. The kiss had been both terrifying and thrilling at the same time, and I still racked my brain as I tried to decide how I felt about it.

I continued walking until I reached the kitchen and I stopped suddenly. To my surprise, instead of Franklin, I'd found Molly. Then again, maybe it wasn't so surprising since this was her domain. Her eyes flickered up to meet mine and I could sense the hesitation between us.

"Good morning, Ms. Bennington," Molly murmured as if she was uncertain about speaking to me.

"Morning, Molly," I replied. If I was being honest, I wasn't sure how to approach this either. I couldn't help but wonder how she'd come to work for Soren.

I followed her hand as she gave me a plate filled with breakfast items, and I noticed she avoided making direct eye contact. "I hope you enjoy it."

"Thank you," I said as I took a seat at the bar top. It would have been easy for me to go into the dining room and eat alone, but for some reason, I didn't want to. As I ate, Molly stayed in the room, tidying up the already clean space.

Once I finished my meal, Molly snatched my plate without a word and began cleaning that too. I sat there awkwardly for a moment because I wasn't sure how to proceed. When Molly didn't say another word, I got up and thought of this as an opportunity to examine the house further and figure out an escape plan.

I began to stroll through the mansion's hallways as my mind worked hard to memorize each turn and where certain rooms were in an attempt to find potential escape routes. Exploring the place allowed me to not feel as creeped out by the mansion, even though it did look like something that could be a part of a haunted attraction at an amusement park.

I discovered windows that were too high for me to reach or too securely fastened for me to open and doors that were locked. As I rounded another corner, I collided with a solid figure, and it took everything in me to gasp instead of screaming in shock.

It was Franklin. It was probably the most grateful I'd been to see him since I'd been here.

"Ms. Bennington," he said in a monotone voice.

"I was... I got lost," I stammered, my mind scrambling for an excuse when he hadn't even asked what I was doing. "I was looking for the library."

Franklin's gaze didn't shift at all, and I wondered if he knew I was bullshitting. "The library is down the hall to your left."

"Thank you," I said, turning quickly and heading in the

direction he indicated without another word. If I stood there any longer, I was guaranteed to screw myself.

Franklin's stare was burning a hole through me as I walked toward the library. My heart was pounding in my chest, and as I entered the library, I took a deep breath in. I was greeted by slightly musty air, but at least I was alone.

I spent the majority of the day in the library, losing myself in the books that were in there. It seemed as if Soren took great care in having many different kinds of books, making it easy to get lost in mysterious worlds that were not my own.

The weight of everything seemed to lighten a tad as night fell over the mansion. I didn't move until my stomach growled, alerting me that it had been hours since I'd eaten. I made my way toward the kitchen, slightly wishing that I'd find it empty.

As I neared the kitchen, the gentle hum of a song reached my ears. I walked in and saw Molly busy cleaning the kitchen. Her hands were cleaning the countertops, and her eyes focused intently on her task. But it was the softness of her voice that caught me off guard. It sounded beautiful, and I tried hard to remember if I'd heard it before, but the melody wasn't ringing any bells.

Taking a hesitant step inside, I cleared my throat. Molly's song halted abruptly, and she looked up, a mix of surprise and unease flashing in her eyes.

"I didn't mean to startle you," I began. "I was just looking for something to eat."

Molly hesitated for a brief moment before her features softened. "It's alright, dear. Let me whip up something for you."

As she moved around, fetching ingredients and setting

them on the counter, I noticed there was an air of motherly warmth about her that I'd missed being away from Gran, especially during the holidays.

"You were humming," I said, attempting to forge a conversation. "I was trying to figure out if I knew the tune."

Molly's face lit up. "Been humming that one since I was a young girl. It's soothing."

We continued to chat, me leaning against the counter while she gathered some food for me. I felt awkward having her do this, but I wasn't about to stop her because she looked happy to do it. By the time she handed me a warm plate of food, the tension in the room had lightened considerably.

"Thank you, Molly," I said.

She nodded with a kind smile, "You're welcome, dear. If you need anything else, please let me know."

I ate quickly as we chatted some more. I felt guilty for having her stay in the kitchen longer than she'd planned. I offered to wash my own dish when I finished and Molly didn't give me an opportunity to. Soon, I decided the only place to go was back to the room I was staying in for the time being. I was grateful for the lights in the hallway that lit the way, or else I would have been completely fucked.

Upon reaching my room, I showered and changed into my nightclothes before I lay down on the bed, enjoying the feel of smooth sheets against my skin. I turned the lamp out in my room, settled under the covers and closed my eyes. For a moment, I enjoyed the silence around me, knowing that soon dawn would come, and then I would have to face another day here.

Just as I was falling asleep, soft voices reached my ears. My eyes snapped open, and I lay still, straining to hear what they were saying. The voices were coming from just outside my door, and a chill ran down my spine when I recognized who was speaking: Franklin and Soren.

What were they discussing? And why were they standing outside my door?

I slowly got out of bed and held my breath as I walked over to my door and pressed my ear against the wood.

I heard Franklin's voice first. "A decision will have to be made soon."

Soren responded, his voice low and serious. "I know. I'm waiting on some news before making any decisions."

"So, what do we do until then?"

"We wait. That's all we can do."

"Okay. And if something—"

"We'll deal with it if it comes to that. For now, we wait."

There was a finality to Soren's statement that I didn't like.

Then there was silence. Their footsteps moved away from the door, and I was left alone with the quiet and my racing thoughts.

What were they talking about? What were they waiting for? I didn't understand. It was obvious that I was missing some pieces of the puzzle and that was frustrating.

I walked back over to the bed and lay there, staring up at the ceiling. I was more lost and confused than ever. I wanted answers, but I didn't even know what questions to ask. All I could do was see what the morning would bring. With that, I drifted off to sleep.

14

SOREN

Everything around me was silent, just how I preferred it. Everyone had long since gone to bed, but as usual, I was still awake. The demons that haunted me had done a number on me tonight and I found the need to leave my room to quiet them for a little while. I could hear the sound of the wind blowing against the windows as I walked through my home.

Today had been slightly warmer, so instead of snow falling and painting the landscape white, we received rain. I stared at one of the many windows and watched as water droplets fell down on the glass, designing a pattern all its own. I hadn't bothered turning on any lights. I knew this place like the back of my hand, with or without anything illuminating the way, and the moonlight did its job of helping in that department.

My eyes had already adjusted to the darkness around me as I touched the knob and softly opened the door. I'd made sure before giving her this room that the hinges were well oiled, making it so I could easily slip in and out of her room as I wanted. With the moonlight's help, I immediately found her in bed asleep. But I couldn't say that her sleep was completely peaceful.

The ache in my chest became lighter as I stared at her, and before I knew it, I was walking toward her sleeping form. It was as if I couldn't help but get close to her. I clenched my fists in an effort to not reach out and touch her, especially with how close I was to her right now. The light streaming in through the crack in the curtains gave me the opportunity to study her. She seemed fragile and innocent, but I knew there was an underlying fiery strength within her, plotting how she was going to get out of here.

I slowly made my way to a chair that was near her bed. It was then that I realized this was the closest I'd been to her in days. I'd decided to keep my distance from her after I blew up at the mere mention of Eden. It was hard being away from her in general, but I thought putting distance between us and allowing her some more freedom in my home would help remove the guilt and lessen my desire for her.

I was wrong. I still wanted her badly, even though she was trying to destroy one of the most important things I was fighting to protect. As I observed her, I couldn't help but feel a connection to this woman who served as a reminder of something that I shouldn't want or have.

My gaze lingered on her as if I were frozen in place. Her hair lay slightly tangled across her pillow, and I assumed that was from tossing and turning at some point during the night. I watched as she slept, her breath coming in soft, even sighs. I could see the slight bags under eyes from the stress I'd caused. She needed this time to recover from everything.

She deserved so much more than I could give her, including being far away from this place. But I wasn't willing to let her go easily, and that was only going to be more challenging with Parker and the Chevaliers breathing down my neck.

My heart thudded in my chest as I watched a small hint of a smile appear on her face. I found myself wondering what put it there. At least, while she was asleep, something was able to make her happy. The happiness she couldn't find here in reality.

I didn't know how long I'd been sitting there, but it had been way longer than I'd planned. After all, there was still one more thing I needed to do before I would leave her alone for the night.

I quietly stood up and walked over to the bedroom lamp closest to Iris. I adjusted the lamp slightly so the camera I'd instructed to be built within the design was fixed on the object of my desire versus the wall. I knew she'd hit the lamp when she'd gone to bed tonight because I'd watched her do it before I ended up standing in front of her door, talking to Franklin about her.

I pulled out my phone and tapped on the app that would bring up the live feed. As I watched her on the screen, mirroring the image I saw in person, I confirmed my adjustments to the lamp were correct.

Did I feel guilty about watching her?

Nope. Not one bit.

If this was the only way I could currently be close to her, then so be it.

I turned off the feed and placed my phone back in my pocket, and darkness filled the room once more.

As I turned slightly to look back toward the bed, my gaze locked onto Iris's peaceful form once again. As if she knew I was looking at her, Iris stirred in her sleep, causing me to freeze in place. I hadn't expected her to wake or for her to know that I was in here, but if my secret was about to be uncovered, so be it. I watched as she rolled onto her side and pulled the covers up toward her neck. I waited to see if she would open her eyes, but she never did. When Iris's breathing returned to normal, the tension that filled my body slowly eased, but not once did I take my eyes off her.

Maybe this was my cue to leave while I still had the chance to allow her to rest. I allowed myself to look at her before I walked to the door just as quietly as I entered. After stealing one final glance, I slipped out the door and closed it softly behind me.

I was alone again as I made the trek back to my room. Although my thoughts were still on Iris, it was about time that I got some rest too.

I'd made sure to put her in the guest room that was farthest from my room to resist temptation, but it hadn't worked. I still managed to make my way to her even though I could see her on my phone. Nothing was going to stop me from saying good night in my own way.

I reached my room and opened the door, noticing my room was just as I left it. It was dark inside, but much like Iris's room, there was just a bit of moonlight coming through my window. I walked in and closed the door.

A small yawn left my lips as I thought about the fact that I had another early morning, once again putting distance between Iris and myself while she was awake. I was sure she wouldn't mind that, and I thought it was for the best. Well, for right now anyway.

With that, I climbed into bed and closed my eyes. As if my soul was at peace from seeing her, my body finally let the night take over, and I fell into a dreamless sleep.

15

IRIS

The pale morning light flowed through my window as I finished putting my hair into a ponytail to keep it off my shoulders. It was another day stuck in here with nothing to do but distract myself with books in the library. As I ran my hand down the front of my pale-blue sweatshirt, I nearly jumped in the air.

A sudden knock on my door had jolted me from my musings, sending my heart into a panic. I could have sworn the sound echoed throughout this whole building, even though I was positive it was an exaggeration. I took a deep breath and let it out before I said, "Come in."

I turned to the doorway as the door opened and Franklin stood outside the room. My heart skipped a beat and jumped back into rhythm as I stared at him. I tried to calm my nerves as I wondered why he would be standing at the door. The silence was awkward at best, weird at worst. I stood there waiting for him to do something. Anything.

Then he finally moved before he spoke. "Ms. Bennington," he said. "Breakfast has been served."

My heart leaped into my throat. I knew without a doubt what that meant. I was supposed to be eating with Soren this morning. Should I have been prepared for this? Yes. But I wasn't. I wasn't ready to face him again even though it had been days since the last incident.

"Is Soren already downstairs?" I couldn't stop the question from leaving my lips.

"Mr. Grant will not be joining you for breakfast. He had other business to attend to."

Relief was the only thing I could feel as I fought to keep my expression neutral. Soren's absence meant that I could relax slightly, away from his intense calculating gaze or hell, just from him in general.

"However," Franklin continued. "He has suggested that you enjoy your breakfast outside today."

I was completely confused, but I couldn't hide my excitement about having the opportunity to leave the mansion, even if it was to just sit right outside of it. But why would he want me to do that? Plus, it was December. Was the point of this to force me to freeze outside? Instead of complaining, I took it as a challenge. "That works, I guess. Thank you, Franklin."

"Breakfast will be out on the terrace just outside the kitchen." Without waiting for me to reply, he left the room, closing the door behind him. I could only wonder why Soren had made this suggestion. Was it another one of his twisted games?

I snatched off the sweatshirt I had on and put a long-sleeved shirt on first. Once I thought I had enough layers, I put the sweatshirt back on and headed toward the stairs. I walked through the empty kitchen and found the terrace.

As I stepped out onto the terrace, I was greeted by the brisk December air, a refreshing change from the mansion. But what I wasn't expecting was to have my mouth drop open at the sight in front of me.

The garden sprawled before me, its beauty slightly muted by the grayness of the winter sky. Despite how cool it was, there was a beautiful setup for breakfast waiting for me. There was a small table with a plate of pastries, a thick blanket draped over the chair, and an outdoor heater to provide warmth for me.

I walked over to the blanket and wrapped it around my shoulders before I settled down. I closed my eyes as I allowed the natural sounds of nature and the gentle hum of the heater to provide the soundtrack to this lovely winter morning.

"Good morning, Ms. Bennington," came a soft voice from behind me. I turned to see Molly approaching me with a smile on her face, carrying a basket of fresh fruit and a cup of coffee. "Mr. Grant thought you might enjoy this."

"Thank you," I replied, offering her a small smile in return. She chatted with me for a minute before disappearing back into the mansion, leaving me alone once again.

As I made my coffee how I preferred it and took the first glorious sip, I couldn't help but think about the contrast between this peaceful moment and the turmoil that had become my life since Soren Grant had entered it. This was the most at peace I'd felt since I was brought here, but I knew better than to let my guard down completely. I wasn't convinced he wasn't trying to break the walls I'd put up as a way to lessen my defenses and then strike me where it would hurt.

I served myself breakfast and immediately dug in, happy to be feeling the fresh air caressing my face. From what I'd seen, Molly was an excellent cook, but being outside and eating was pure bliss. I was allowed to temporarily ignore the trouble I was in and pretend that everything was normal.

There was no way I was rushing through this meal. Every bite I took brought me closer to having to return to the building behind me.

I savored each bite and allowed my thoughts to drift wherever they wanted to go. This area was peaceful, and the soft, warm light from the heater made the space feel extra cozy. I adjusted the blanket around my shoulders, and once again, I was feeling comfortable despite the chill in the air. Deep down, I hoped I would be able to do this more often. That is if I couldn't leave here altogether.

I noticed some birds flying around and I was slightly confused as to why they were still around. I'd figured most birds had flown south for the winter. Watching them soar freely in the air with nothing holding them back made me think about my own situation. For a brief moment, I wished I could be as free as them, back to the time when I hadn't been kidnapped, nor was I obsessed with trying to find out what I could about Eddison Payne.

Maybe then, things could have been different.

I shook my head because there was no way I could go back in time and change anything, so it felt foolish to even think about doing so.

As I was finishing my breakfast, I saw Molly approaching me out of the corner of my eye. I turned and saw that she had her hands tucked into her apron and I wondered if we were about to have another awkward moment.

"Do you need anything else, Ms. Bennington?" she asked with a gentle voice.

"No, thank you, Molly," I replied, giving her a small smile again. "Everything was delicious."

"Alright then." She nodded, turning to leave. "Let me know if you need anything."

I watched as she walked back toward the kitchen, leaving me alone again on the terrace. I sat there for a moment, turning my attention back to the birds, but I knew I couldn't stay out here forever.

Before I went back inside, I made sure to look around, mapping out a way I could get out of here. Sneaking out of the kitchen would be a good option, and if I could get back to training, I might be able to run it. But where was the nearest major road? Could I do something like this at night without alerting the house? Then again, I didn't know what or who might be around in the middle of the night either.

But it was still worth a shot even if I did get caught. There were a bunch of trees farther out, and if I could get there, it might make it harder to catch me. But that was if I made it there.

Damn it. Sitting out here gave me a taste of what freedom would be like again, and I wanted it. However, what would be the cost if I failed?

I'd known that this wouldn't be a straightforward answer unfortunately, but now it was even more complicated. With a heavy sigh, I stood up with the blanket still around my shoulders and left the tranquil scenery behind.

I stepped back inside and folded up the blanket before placing it across the back of one of the barstools in front of the counter. Although I tried to push aside my feelings, dread was growing inside of me. I was back under lock and key and escaping seemed almost as dangerous as staying here. But I needed to push those thoughts away. For now, I needed to focus on planning my next move and figuring out how the hell I was going to escape this hellhole I'd found myself in.

16

SOREN

I could hear the pulsating beat of the music even though I was sitting in VIP. I took another sip from my whiskey as an unusual knot settled in my stomach. I was sitting in the back of Elevate, an exclusive bar and sex club in New York City, which was owned by members of the Cross family, who were Chevaliers and one of the most powerful families in the state.

Thankfully, this part of the club wasn't crowded, giving me privacy that would have been impossible downstairs. It fit because I wasn't here to party or to go and play in the basement.

I was here to meet with Parker Townsend.

As I took another sip of my drink, the liquor felt strong on my tongue. A strange knot had settled in my stomach as I waited for him.

It wasn't usual for us to meet this often, which already had me on edge. This was unexpected, and I'd hired a driver to bring me all the way to the city to deal with it, not to mention he was now late.

I took another sip from my glass before I pulled out my phone. I checked the feed from one of the cameras in Iris's bedroom, and I found her writing in the notebook I'd had Franklin leave on the desk in the room. I couldn't help but stare at her.

What was she writing? And why did I want to know so badly?

Her profile was stunning and the light in the room did a wonderful job of highlighting her beauty. Her face was a picture of concentration as she moved the pen across the page.

I should feel guilty about spying on her this way, but I couldn't resist. I was determined to know everything about her to the point that I could predict her needs. I was getting close, but there was always something to learn.

Switching to one of the other cameras I set up in the room, I watched as she set down the pen and walked over to the window. What was she looking at out there?

I could practically hear her plotting her escape from my home and that was to be expected. Knowing that didn't make me feel any better about it, but knowing she couldn't leave brought me comfort. Something I hadn't had in a very long time.

Out of the corner of my eye, I saw someone walking up the stairs to VIP. I looked up and found Parker walking toward me, drink already in hand. I closed the app and slipped my phone back into my pocket as I prepared to give Parker my full and undivided attention.

"Soren," he said, nodding slightly. I returned the gesture and watched as he took a seat across from me. "Sorry for being late. Something came up last minute. You know how it is."

I did, and I didn't mind the opportunity to relax and have a drink. I would have preferred to do it at my house, where I could be closer to Iris, but it is what it is.

"Why did you want to meet with me urgently?"

"It's time for your next assignment." Parker slid a sealed envelope across the table between us.

"You don't usually give me files on whoever you want me to handle."

"This one's different."

I hesitated for a moment, eyes flicking between the envelope and Parker. "How so?"

Parker's fingers drummed against the envelope, but I couldn't hear it due to the music that surrounded us from every angle. "This one's delicate."

I didn't like the sound of that. Instead of responding, I raised an eyebrow, waiting for him to continue.

He leaned back into the plush leather seat, his eyes carefully observing the crowd below. "It involves someone you know well. That is, you did once upon a time. Don't open the envelope here. Wait until you're back in the privacy of your own home."

My grip tightened around my drink, and I could feel the ice cubes clinking softly against one another. I was stuck pondering the words he used as I tried to piece together what he was trying to tell me.

I tore my eyes away from him, choosing to stare at the envelope that sat between us. I placed my glass down and reached for it.

"Someone I knew well?"

He simply nodded and lifted his drink to his lips. He took another sip as my fingertips pulled it closer to me, but I didn't open it.

"I know you'll handle this professionally." Parker's voice broke through my thoughts. "Keep it clean, keep it quiet. And remember, your duty as a Chevalier comes above personal grievances."

It was a warning, a reminder of my loyalty to the organization, and I was confused about it. Why even say that? I'd never given him reason to question my loyalty to the Chevaliers, so why was he now?

Our conversation continued, and after about twenty minutes, I could sense that our discussion was winding down. I assumed the main reason why he wanted to meet in person was because he wanted to hand me this envelope. I sent a text message to my driver, letting him know I would be outside in the next five minutes or so.

"There's something else we need to talk about."

"Oh?"

"Don't go soft on Iris."

My jaw tightened at the mention of her name, although I'd expected him to say something about her. I thought about watching her in the guest room, writing in the notebook that had been left on her desk. I'd already known she was an obsession I couldn't afford, and yet I couldn't get enough of her. This meeting was starting to annoy me.

Looking Parker dead in his eyes, I replied, "Why would I? Your orders didn't call for me to change anything."

"I'm just making sure."

"You've never done that before. You used to trust that I would get the job done no matter what."

Parker ran a hand through his hair. "It's obvious how much she looks like—"

I knew what he was going to say before he said it, and I hated every minute of it. I was trying not to reach over and break his damn neck. At this point, I didn't care if he was chairman of the Chevaliers or not. "Don't you dare."

"I'm not treading into those waters, Soren, but I need to know that you can do the job if it comes down to it. You've been through a lot over the last couple of years, and if you need to, we can hand this off to someone else."

"Who? Like Ioan?" I snorted to punctuate the end of my sentence. He could never replace me. I thought about seeing him standing next to Parker just before I met Iris on West-wick University's campus. There's no way Parker thought that he could carry this out.

"It doesn't matter who."

I leaned forward and glared at him. "But it does, and you know it."

He looked down at his drink before he continued. "I watched you two when she ran into you. You couldn't take your eyes off her."

This conversation needed to end. Being under his scrutiny when I'd done nothing to warrant it did nothing but irritate me. "I've got the situation completely under control." I was lying and I knew it. Iris had somehow shaken me to my very core, and I didn't know what to do about it.

Instead, I stared back at him, daring him to call me out on my lie. I kept my emotions behind a mask I'd perfected because I didn't want to show him how much his words were getting to me.

"Excellent. Make sure it stays that way," Parker said. The words were wrapped in a bow disguised as a warning.

He finished the drink he'd been nursing. He stood up, and I expected him to stick out his hand for me to shake. When he didn't, it was a clue that he knew that something was up. Parker gave me a small head nod before he walked away. Instead of going down the way he came, he stepped past me and strolled down a dark hallway. Where he was going, I had no clue, and it wasn't my concern anyway.

I needed to follow his lead if I was going to get back to my home at a decent time. I threw my drink back before I stood up, grabbed the envelope, and left the VIP area. Once I'd walked outside, I was greeted by the cool December air, clearing my mind slightly.

I stared down at the file in my hand, wondering what it contained. But that would have to wait.

I quickly found my driver and slid into the back seat of his car. The ride back to the mansion was quiet, interrupted only by the low hum of the car's engine, the light jazz playing through the speakers, and the noises of city life before we left New York City behind. While I used my phone as a distraction by allowing me to reply to emails during the ride, all I could focus on was the sealed envelope sitting beside me.

Once we pulled up to my mansion, I wasted no time. I got out of the vehicle and gave Franklin a swift nod before heading straight to my office. I needed to open this envelope right now.

Everything else faded into the background as I closed and locked the door to my office behind me. The fireplace was already going, providing warmth and light to the dark space.

I approached my desk and took a seat before I allowed

myself to open the envelope. The sound of paper shifting filled the air as I pulled out the contents and spread them out on the desk. I took my time studying the photos and documents as I tried to piece together the picture that Parker had vaguely painted.

And then there it was.

A name.

A photo.

They all hit me in the face like a ton of bricks. Now Parker's words made sense. I slowly shook my head as my jaw tightened.

This was going to be worse than I'd thought.

17

IRIS

My feet slid into my slippers, finishing the outfit I planned to wear today as I spent another day under Soren's lock and key. Without a second thought, I walked to my door and opened it slowly, for what reason I wasn't sure. It might have become instinctual for me to be as quiet as possible for fear of getting caught, but it felt silly now. Even if someone did hear me opening the door, what did it matter? I was allowed to walk around the premises if I wanted to, and that was exactly what I intended to do.

Plot my escape out of this gilded cage.

The first door I stopped at was the door that had become my nemesis since Soren had removed the cuff on my ankle. I still heard noises coming from that room every so often, and it drove me nuts that I couldn't investigate what it was.

Or who was in there.

What was behind that door? A hidden part of the house? A secret room? Or was Soren keeping another person in the house, just like he'd done me? The thought sent a shiver down my spine. I reached out and touched the doorknob once more, but the knob didn't budge. Not that I was surprised.

That didn't lessen my frustration, however. My gaze drifted up and down the length of the door as I thought of ways to get into the room. I bent down slightly and found a small hole near the doorknob. It almost resembled a keyhole, but it seemed too small for a key to fit through. Was this an old-fashioned lock? Could I pick it open?

It wasn't something that I'd ever done before and if I got caught, the chances of a punishment were high, and I wasn't sure what Soren would have up his sleeve when it came to that.

Was it a risk I was willing to take? I did have a lot to lose if I were caught and shouldn't try if I wanted to do my best to stay on Soren's good side.

Above all else, I needed to find something to pick the lock with if it was something I was willing to do. I didn't know how many people tended to keep doors locked in their own home, but for some reason, not having a clue about what lay behind that door was almost tormenting my thoughts. However, I couldn't dwell here because I needed to remain inconspicuous in order to hide my plans.

As I moved on, I heard a loud bang come from downstairs. My hand swung up until it landed on my chest, and I froze in place.

What was that? And was anyone going to investigate what had fallen?

I wasn't sure where Franklin and Molly were in the house, and I didn't want them to question what I was doing if they did come across me. That was enough to force me to move, and I walked down the stairs as quickly as I could.

As my foot landed on the last step, the creaking of the wood made me pause as I waited to see if I heard anything else. When I didn't, I walked into the dining room and then into the kitchen, but no one was there.

And nothing looked to be disturbed, so I wasn't sure what had fallen over.

I could use this as my excuse to look around the rest of the house.

With that excuse in my back pocket, I walked down the hallway I recognized from my ventures to and from the basement. I glanced at the portraits that lined the hallway as I came up to the first door. Franklin hadn't bothered explaining to me what any of the doors in this hallway led to during the quick tour he gave me, so what better time than now to find out? Maybe there was a more discreet way of getting out of here that I could use.

Those thoughts didn't make navigating this hallway any less stressful. In fact, it felt as if the people in the portraits were staring at me, chastising the decisions I'd made.

I stopped at one door and gently knocked, waiting to see if someone would answer. When I didn't get a response, I opened the door and stepped inside.

I immediately regretted it.

It only took me a second of standing in this room to figure out it was Soren's office.

The office was a nice size, with huge bookshelves and a large desk in the room's center. On it sat a monitor and a laptop and I immediately thought of the laptop he bought for me. From where I was standing, it looked to be just as expensive, if not more so, and I found it quite ironic that he had such a high-powered device in this space, given the old, weathered aesthetic that was present throughout this house.

There was a large window to the left of the desk, which had similar curtains to the ones that hung in the guest room I was staying in. Because of that, the light from outside shone brightly in here, allowing me to see most of the room without having to turn on the lights. A fireplace was also in the room, and I could imagine the relaxing atmosphere it created when it was lit.

I took a step closer to the desk and noticed that there were a lot of personal items that made sense for him to have in his home, but still, it surprised me. It was obvious that Soren spent a lot of time here, and it was probably the place where he came to get away from the world.

And I was invading it.

Much like he'd invaded my life.

That helped my nerves settle down. If he could do this to me, I could do the same in return.

I shifted my body slightly and found a silver tray on the floor beside pieces of silverware and a shattered mug. I assumed the noise I'd heard was the tray and its contents crashing to the floor.

The question of how the tray had fallen circled my brain as I walked over to the accident, but I got distracted by a piece of paper sitting on the edge of the desk. It wasn't the paper itself that had attracted my attention, but the fact that Eddison Payne's name was written on the document. I guess it wouldn't be unheard of for Soren to have something with Payne's name on it, but I couldn't help but think this was not a coincidence. Then again, I rarely believed in them anyway.

I leaned forward to pick up the piece of paper so I could get a better look at it. I read all the words on the paper once and then twice.

Then, I concluded that nothing on it made any sense.

It was a scattering of words on a page that I couldn't piece together, which, given the fact that this note wasn't for me, probably didn't matter. But with Payne mentioned in the letter, I wanted to know what it was all about.

I wished I had my phone to take a picture of the piece of paper so that I could review it later. And snatching it was a bad idea because if Soren noticed it was gone, he would know something was up and that I, more than likely, was snooping around his office.

Against my better judgment, I put the piece of paper down and turned my attention back to the things that had crashed onto the floor. I debated whether I should clean it up when I heard a noise that sounded too close for comfort. It was in that moment that I considered myself to be royally fucked.

I needed to get out of here, but as I turned, the sound of footsteps getting closer to me sounded throughout the hall-way, causing me to freeze once more. Something clicked in my brain, and I was able to move my body until I slipped behind a tall bookcase, forcing me into the shadows of the room. It forced me to stand in front of a door that was partially hidden by the bookcase. For a split second, I couldn't help but wonder if that was done on purpose.

I heard the door open first and then, from my vantage point, I watched as Soren entered. His gaze swept the room, landing on the mess on the floor. I couldn't see his face, but he moved closer and examined the upturned tray and the disaster it had created.

Soren, leave so I can get the hell out of here.

I repeated the words to myself over and over again, hoping that someone, anyone, would be able to distract him to the point that he would leave this area. Then he rose and stood there silently as if he was listening for something. Whether he could hear me breathing or not crossed my mind.

The seconds felt like hours and the silence was deafening. My heart raced as I prayed he wouldn't find me. I could feel my body trembling, my palms were sweaty, and my mind was spinning with every possible outcome of this situation. What was he going to do if he found me? What would my punishment be? If he didn't see me, how long should I wait until I tried to leave? All these thoughts ran through my head at the speed of light.

I wished that I could see him. Get an idea of where he was in the room, but that might reveal where I was. All I could do was try desperately to remain still and silent. My panic only grew more intense as time passed, and I couldn't hear if he'd left the room.

When I heard him mumble something, I sucked in a deep breath, which, only a few seconds later, I was sure was one of the worst mistakes of my life.

"Iris." Soren's voice sounded rough yet smooth at the same time. "What are you doing in here?"

18

IRIS

I waited a beat, confused as to how he knew I was in there without him looking at me once. Or so I thought. I slowly stepped from behind the bookcase just as he turned to face me. His dark stare bore into me, causing me to fight the urge to squirm.

This was the worst-case scenario and that was before he stepped into my line of sight.

My heart raced as I tried to think of something to say, but my mind went blank. He'd literally rendered me speechless.

My throat tightened with dread and my stomach twisted with anxiety as, once again, potential outcomes raced through my mind. All the while, his piercing gaze never wavered, sending shivers down my spine as I wondered what he might do next.

"I was just. . . exploring the mansion," I said, trying to keep my tone casual despite the tremor that was shaking my entire body.

Soren took a step closer and said, "Curiosity isn't always a good thing. In fact, it can be very dangerous."

I took a slow step to my right, hoping to get closer to the door and away from Soren. His vague warning ran on repeat in my mind. *It can be very dangerous.*

But that didn't stop me from talking back to him. "I'm looking around because I wasn't given instructions not to. I have to do something to keep myself occupied when I have nothing to do here." I was proud of myself for keeping my emotions under control.

"This isn't a vacation, petal. You're being kept here until we figure out what to do with you."

I was taken aback by his words. "What do you mean what to do with me?"

"You thought that the Chevaliers wouldn't take any recourse when you stuck yourself somewhere you didn't belong?"

"This is such bullshit. All of this makes me think I was on the right track because why would you all be wasting your time on me if I hadn't been?"

Soren shrugged. "Maybe we're going to use you as an example."

I shook my head. "All because I wanted to find out the damn truth."

Soren's hand shot out and his fingers wrapped around my arm. "This isn't your truth."

I looked down at where his hand met mine, and it was as if a light switch had gone off inside of me. My anger no longer simmered beneath the surface. It was about to boil over and anyone in its path was going to feel my wrath. "No, it's not, but it sure as hell is Margaret Turner's. She deserves to have her truth made public and not buried because you all have your heads so far up your asses that you can't admit a woman helped with the founding of the Chevaliers."

Soren's gaze studied my lips as his grip on my wrist tightened. He was studying me as if I was a work of art, and it sent a shiver through me. I hated that, even when our anger was showing its claws, he could still have this effect on me.

"You shouldn't have come here."

"You didn't tell me I couldn't."

He knew I had a point, but that didn't stop him from saying something back. "Be quiet, Iris."

The words shot out of my mouth before I could control them. "Make. Me."

The tension between the two of us finally snapped. I could see when Soren threw caution to the wind because, within seconds, he'd captured my lips in a searing kiss. Everything around us stopped as all my attention was drawn to the connection we shared. Soren's fingers released my arm and moved to the sides of my face. Our kiss deepened, awakening the desire I felt for him that I'd tried to keep dormant because of what he'd done.

His hands began to wander as he continued to kiss me, exploring my body through the fabric of my clothes. His touch was firm, and I sighed into it. Every brush of his fingertips sent a spark through my body that was both comforting and exhilarating. His hands moved down to grasp my breasts through my shirt, and I moaned—against my better judgment. When he began to play with my nipples, I was pretty sure they hardened instantly under his touch. In my head, I was telling him to rip off my shirt so I could feel his mouth on them, but there was no way I was voicing that thought out loud.

When I heard the creaking of the floor just outside the room we were in, I froze. It was as if ice-cold water had been poured on me, and I needed to stop this before it continued.

I tore away from the kiss, my chest heaving. "I hate you."

"None of that felt like you hated me."

I almost gasped when I saw that Soren had a pleasant grin on his face. But that didn't last long because it soon turned wicked. He reached for me again, but I slapped his hand away.

"Don't fucking touch me!" I reached my hand up to slap him for having the audacity to think this would continue.

"What did I say about slapping me before, Iris?"

I swallowed hard as I recalled the moment when I almost slapped him in the abandoned classroom.

We don't hit people around here unless it's me slapping your ass. Got it?

"It seems as if you haven't learned your lesson."

"But I didn't slap you."

"The intention was clear."

Before I could respond, Soren pulled me forward and wrapped his hand around my wrist once more. He pulled me to his desk before forcing me to lean over it. His hands moved to the waistband of my leggings, and it took me a split second to realize what he meant to do.

"Look straight ahead," he said, and I did as I was told.

He moved out of my line of vision, and I hated that, despite everything he'd done, just the idea of what was about to come had me excited.

He pulled my pants and panties down, exposing my ass to his wicked gaze. I didn't have a moment to think before he brought his hand down on my ass with a loud smack.

My skin stung from the sudden contact, but I bit my lip hard instead of letting out a sound.

"You like that, petal?"

"No. I just want you to go to hell."

"Oh yeah? Well then, I'm taking you right along with me." He ended his sentence with another smack on my butt.

He continued to spank me until my skin was hot and red from his touch. Soren stopped smacking my ass temporarily and moved his fingers to my pussy. I jumped at his touch because I knew what he would find, but the only reaction I heard out of him was a sharp intake of breath. With that, he went back to slapping my butt.

After the last swat, he brought his hand back up and gently massaged away the sting, changing the mood between us. When he was done, he forced me to stand up straight. He grabbed hold of my ponytail and pulled, forcing my eyes to look at the ceiling.

"You enjoyed that immensely. You should have seen how wet you were for me."

"I hated every second of it."

He pulled on my hair a little harder before he said, "Don't lie to me. I wasn't holding a knife to your throat. You could have left at any point."

My heart pounded in my chest as I realized he was right. I had enjoyed it, but I wasn't about to give him the satisfaction of hearing those words come from my lips.

"Just because I didn't run away doesn't mean I liked it."

"The display in front of me says differently." He dropped the hold he had on my hair and stepped back. "Keep challenging me and the punishments will only get worse."

I moved immediately and grabbed my pants and panties, righting them as much as I could.

When I turned back to face Soren, he said, "Now get out of my office."

I didn't bother trying to argue with him after what just happened. I swiftly left his office, trying to come to terms with what I'd just experienced.

I couldn't believe I let him do that and that I enjoyed it. All this further proved that I needed to get out of this place, stat.

As I walked gingerly up the stairs, it dawned on me what the game we were playing was.

He was the predator, and I was the prey. He was playing with his food, but it was only a matter of time before the games would end. And I couldn't let that happen.

19

IRIS

I stumbled back into my room, allowing the door to click shut behind me. My heart thumped wildly in my chest, its rhythm echoing the heated words Soren had flung at me moments ago. I couldn't stay here any longer and that was final.

I needed to find a way out of here right now.

"I could try leaving at night, but which option would be the best? Through the kitchen and the terrace or through the front door?" I whispered, weighing my options out loud. Based on what I'd seen, it would be easier to leave through the front door, but the chances of it being guarded in some way were high. The terrace would be less protected, and I'd found myself studying the landscape while I'd eaten breakfast out there.

It made the most obvious choice. The terrace made the most sense in the dark.

The fact that I had a small plan forming gave me some newly found determination. I walked to the closet in the guest room and found a book bag that had been stored there.

With shaky hands, I began gathering what few belongings I had as I thought about what could happen after I left the mansion.

It would take me some time to gather everything I thought I might need, but it would be well worth it.

I waited a couple of hours before I made it down to the hallway just outside the kitchen. I waited to see if I heard someone in the kitchen, but when I didn't, I quickly entered. I didn't know how much time I would have.

I walked over to the pantry, my eyes darting from shelf to shelf in search of nonperishable food items that would sustain me when I left. I hastily stuffed packages of crackers, a couple of water bottles, and a small jar of peanut butter into my backpack. I also grabbed a can of vegetables and fruit just in case too. I didn't want to grab too much and risk making Molly suspicious, but hopefully, this would be enough to sustain me. I prayed that it wouldn't take much for me to find a neighboring home or town and to call the police.

My next stop was the kitchen drawers, where I searched for anything that could be used as a weapon. My heart raced as I searched, but I only found silverware and cooking utensils in the first two drawers.

But in the third drawer, I found what I had been looking for. A sturdy kitchen knife with a wooden handle and what looked to be a sharp blade.

I snatched it and tucked it into one of the pockets of my backpack before leaving the room.

I quickly made my way up the stairs and back to the guest room, closing the door a little louder than necessary and resting my back against the now-closed door.

I'd made it.

I almost ran over to the closet and stuffed the bag into the farthest corner away from the door in hopes that it would conceal it more.

With that, I was another step closer to getting out of captivity.

TWO DAYS LATER, I found myself staring up at the ceiling in the guest room, watching the shadows that danced along the wall. One deep breath and then another was the only thing that was keeping me somewhat calm as I prepared myself mentally for the hurdles that lay ahead. It would all end tonight. I just had to be patient.

My backpack of supplies was tucked away in the closet, away from prying eyes and ready for me when I decided to make my move. I'd been waiting for everyone in the house to go to bed before Operation Get the Fuck Out of Here was a go. I'd already mapped out a way to get out of here and there was no room for me to fail. If I did, I didn't know what Soren would do to me, and I didn't want to find out.

I pictured the route in my mind once more, and I knew I just needed to get to the woods, where I would have no issue disappearing, hopefully.

I turned over to my side as I tried to quiet my mind. I needed to conserve all my energy for the hurdles ahead. The anticipation of what was on the other side of this imprisonment was almost too much to bear. I knew my life as it was had ended, but at least I wouldn't be trapped under his thumb any longer.

With a deep sigh, I just reminded myself of what was at

stake here. Impatience was starting to win, but I just had to wait a little longer to throw my plan into action. I was only minutes away from being free, and I couldn't wait.

Not having access to the time made this extremely difficult to plan, but I was determined that wouldn't stop me. Sometime later, I moved as silently as possible as I slipped out from under the sheets and the comforter. I dressed myself in layers, making sure that all the clothes were dark so it would be easier to blend into the night. The pair of sneakers I'd been wearing to eat breakfast outside or walk around the grounds were broken in now, perfect for when I needed to run.

I walked over to the closet and opened it.

My backpack of supplies was ready and waiting. I threw one of the straps on my shoulder and walked over to my door. I rested my ear against it, straining to hear any noises in the mansion. All was still and quiet, just what I'd predicted.

Cracking open the bedroom door, I looked out cautiously before leaving my room. My pulse pounded as I slowly crept down the hallway, praying that I didn't step on a wooden plank that would creak under my weight.

Finally, I reached the top of the grand staircase. With a deep breath, I slowly made my way down, one step at a time.

When I reached the foyer undetected, I let out a shaky breath. My exit from this house was only feet away. Soon, I would feel that cool winter breeze on my skin as I took off into the night.

I continued to walk slowly toward the dining room and, from there, into the kitchen. No looking back now. I was getting out of this mansion tonight, even if it killed me.

As I walked through the dining room and into the

kitchen, I mentally checked off another piece of my plan. Once again, there was no one. I debated with myself about whether I needed to stick more food into the bag but decided not to. It would only serve as a distraction and lead to me spending more time here than necessary.

I reached the screen door that would lead out to the terrace. With trembling fingers, I unlocked the door and slowly eased it open. I peeked outside to see if I spotted anyone, but the only thing that greeted me was the sounds of nature.

I slipped through the gap that I'd created and eased the door shut behind me. The breeze that caressed my face was more than welcome, cooling down my already warm face. With one final mental push, I shoved my fear aside and took off running.

I pushed forward, my lungs burning as I raced across the lawn. All my focus was on making it to the woods so that I could disappear. I was so close that I could taste my freedom.

But then it felt as if my world ended. I was suddenly grabbed from behind, causing me to scream just before a hand covered my mouth.

I struggled against the grip, but it was no use. Whoever had their hands on me was strong and determined to not let me go. I screamed against the hand, trying to get someone's attention, but all my efforts were in vain. In fact, I now realized the irony of waiting until nighttime to avoid being seen by anyone when that environment meant no one would be able to hear me scream.

Fear and adrenaline took over as I tried to think of a way out. I kicked and thrashed, doing whatever I could to break free, but nothing worked. The person's grip only tightened, and I was beginning to think that there was no way out of this. Tears began to stream down my face as I realized my chance at escaping this hellhole had probably been taken away from me.

"Not so fast. Where do you think you're going?"

I froze at the sound, a chill racing down my spine that had nothing to do with the season. I don't know why I was surprised that he'd figured out my plan and found me.

"Let me go!" I yelled, but my voice was muffled against the hand that covered my lips.

"Now, why would I do that, especially when you can't seem to understand how to not disobey me?"

I was impressed he was able to make out what I said. Soren's words struck deep as I tried to stop the tears that were falling from my face.

He brought his lips close to my ear and said, "When will you get it through your head that you can never escape me? Do you know why?"

I hesitated before I shook my head. He chuckled in my ear before he said, "Because I won't allow it."

Soren's hand moved from my lips and turned me around so I could face him. My eyes widened in shock when I found that he had a mask on. If he'd had enough time to put it on, that must have meant he'd known I had this planned. Before I could say another word, his fingers moved to grip my chin, forcing me to look up at him. I almost closed my eyes to avoid looking into his because I was afraid of what I might see.

"How did you find me?" My voice shook as I asked the question.

"I have eyes all around this place, petal. You should have known better."

His other hand came up and started tracing the line of my jaw. I shuddered under his touch as I wondered what he was going to do next.

"Please," I whispered. The single word fell from my lips, and I waited with bated breath for his response.

Soren's mouth curved into a cruel smile, and I swallowed hard. "Petal, you're begging already? We've only just begun." He leaned in closer, fingers tightening on my chin. "Clearly, I've been too lenient with you, but now all of that changes. I can't wait to see the change in you once I'm through with you."

A whimper that had been caught in my throat made itself known. I squeezed my eyes shut, but it did nothing to hold back the tears that were now in free fall down my cheeks. Thoughts of what he could do to me now that he'd caught me again filled my mind.

"I won't do it again."

"I know because I'll make sure of it. It's time you understood that you can run all you want, petal. But I'll always be waiting in the shadows, ready to catch you."

I swallowed hard as Soren crowded me even more, forcing me deeper into the forest.

20

IRIS

S oren pushed me through the forest until my back ended up against the bark of a tree. His dark stare bore into mine, and I could see the pure evil within its depths.

"What I can't understand is why you fight me when you want this as much as I do."

I thought about spitting on him, but all it would do was land on the mask. I struggled against the grip he had on me as panic crashed through me.

He leaned in, his lips grazing my neck as he found a sensitive spot there. A shiver ran down my spine that had nothing to do with the cold. "Do you remember what your safe word is?"

"Yeah, it's fuck you," I said as I tried to fight against his hold. But my efforts were in vain. He was way too strong.

Soren tightened his grip, his eyes narrowing. "Cute, but insulting me won't save you."

If I'd had any faith that I might be able to get out of this, it would have dropped to negative numbers at this point. There was no way I was going to be able to get away from this monster. Having him admit that he would always be there to bring me back to him was frightening as hell because I believed every word. He would chase me to the ends of the earth if he had to, and clearly, he had nothing to lose.

As if he sensed the dilemma I was in, he was determined to erase it all. His lips once again claimed mine. I moved my leg to knee him in the dick and he immediately blocked my attempt. He growled against my lips before he broke away from me.

"What's your safe word, Iris?" His tone told me the wrong answer wouldn't be tolerated again.

"It's diary."

"Perfect," he said. Before I could blink, he'd taken full control.

My brain was telling me to push him away. Yet my body did the opposite. I found myself craving his touch as my hands roamed his body, matching his energy with my own.

All thoughts about how I shouldn't be doing this and how wrong this was fled my mind. Nothing but where and how he was touching me mattered anymore. His hands were every-where in his attempt to possess all of me, and I had no doubt in my mind that he would succeed. How was he able to light a fire in me with all these layers on? The thought left my mind as I moaned softly, arching into him as my pussy clenched because of his actions.

Soren slid his hands under the shirts I had on, roaming up my stomach in a slow caress. I gasped as the air rolled over my overheated skin, causing goose bumps to appear all over my body. Or they could have come about as a result of him inching higher and higher until he reached my breasts. His touch was far from gentle, showing me how much trouble I was in with him.

And I liked it.

Pleasure and pain came together because of our union, and what a beautiful combination it was. What I didn't expect was to want to see his face, which was still covered by the mask he wore. Then again, I could use his wearing a mask as a way to pretend that this wasn't happening with him. Although I was loving all of this at the moment, I knew I would regret it in the morning.

"Admit it," he growled, bringing my attention back to what he was doing to me. He continued to roll my nipple between his fingers, forcing me to release a deep sigh. "You need this. You want me to fuck you so hard that you scream."

I bit my lip as I tried to hold back a moan. I refused to give him the satisfaction. But we both knew the truth. The way my body was reacting to him was all the answer he needed.

He smiled and stuck my nipple into his mouth. His touch ignited my body as I gasped, my legs shaking violently.

"Say it," he commanded after he'd let my nipple go.

"Yes," I cried out. "I want you to fuck me. Hard."

"There. That wasn't so difficult, was it?"

I couldn't come up with an answer because words failed me. I was drowning, suffocating because of the sensations that were coursing through me.

It felt as if every nerve ending in my body was on fire. I gasped for air as my hands clenched the fabric of his coat, clinging to him as a wave of pleasure took over.

Soren sucked on my breasts before going back to attacking my nipple. I was pretty sure the skin near my nipple would be bruised in the morning, his way of marking and claiming me, but I couldn't care less at the moment.

I didn't want to fight him anymore if it meant avoiding this. The fact that we were outside doing this didn't matter. All I wanted was for him to fuck me in any way he would take me.

"Please," I said, not even sure what I was begging for.

"Patience," he mumbled against my skin before his hands landed on my waist as he ground against me.

I gasped as I felt him against my core. Because of his positioning, it forced my panties to rub against my pussy, showing how soaked I already was from his touch. I shut my eyes and leaned my head back against the tree bark, happy to allow the rest of my senses to take over.

He'd managed to command my body, and I responded to him without hesitation. I was completely under whatever spell he'd cast on me. I was sure of it.

He removed his hands from my waist, and I felt a sudden sense of loss. But before I could think about it too much, he pulled my top layers down before I felt his hands on my leggings, pulling them down as well.

He grabbed a handful of my ass before he yanked my panties down just before turning me around so that I faced the tree.

"Spread your legs," he said. I quickly moved my legs apart.

Soren chuckled and I wondered if it was because I moved so quickly. "Are you ready for me?" he asked, his whisper sending a chill down my spine.

I nodded, not trusting myself to speak. I looked over my shoulder at him as I watched him unzip his pants and pull his cock out. I'd wondered if he'd taken off the mask, but he still had it on. The thought of him fucking me with the mask on had now shifted from helping me to disassociate from this to turning me on even more. Was having a mask kink a thing?

The sound of Soren's laughter brought me from my thoughts just before I felt the head of his cock teasing my entrance. He pressed forward, pushing his dick inside of me.

The sensation felt different in the best way, and it took a second for me to realize that I hadn't heard the sound of a condom wrapper ripping.

"Are you fucking me without a condom?!" I exclaimed as I tried to look behind me at him.

"I am," he said as he began to pick up the pace.

"I didn't consent to this!"

"I know for a fact that you're on the shot, and we're both clean, so what's the point in denying us what we both want?"

I gasped at the fact that he was able to get my health information. Then again, should I have been surprised?

"Even if you weren't, I still would have fucked you bare."

That sent a tremble through my body. There was no way I wanted kids anytime soon, and I absolutely didn't want them with the man who had no issue with stalking and kidnapping me.

But none of that changed the way he made my body feel.

The sensations were overwhelming, and my body shuddered as he moved. I moaned loudly and Soren took that as a sign that I wanted more.

He wasn't wrong.

Soren grabbed my hips and pounded into me with an intensity that was both thrilling and terrifying. I squeezed my eyes shut as I felt my orgasm building. This was like nothing

I'd ever experienced before. I couldn't deny the pleasure his thrusts were bringing me, and soon enough, I was screaming out his name as I came undone.

My body was trembling as I tried to recover from the intense orgasm. Soren kept his pace, determined to get what he was looking for. I heard his deep groan as he found his own pleasure.

Feeling him come inside of me was one of the strangest feelings ever. I didn't know how to describe it, and there was no taking it back now.

He leaned forward, pressing his forehead into my hair as we both tried to catch our breath.

When Soren finally pulled back, I felt my legs give out, and I was forced to lean against the tree.

I felt his cum leaking out of me, and I suddenly felt exposed. I could feel his eyes on me, and I was willing to bet he was staring at the scene in front of him too.

I quickly reached down and pulled my panties and pants back up, deciding that I would take care of the situation that he'd left behind once I got back to the mansion.

I turned around and looked at the house over Soren's shoulder as dread crept through my body.

All of this was boiling down to the fact that my escape plan had been thwarted and that I would be marching right back up to that house to receive whatever punishments that Soren deemed appropriate to give out.

21

SOREN

I reached forward and tried to make sure that Iris's clothes were back to normal, but she sidestepped me. She walked away from me, following the path back to the mansion as I took off the mask that had covered my face during our entire encounter.

The cool air brushed against my skin, but the only thing that could ease the ache I was now feeling was having Iris again. I walked away from the spot we'd ended up in during our romp in the forest and found the bag Iris had packed; picking it up to bring it back to my home. I watched from a distance as Iris crossed my lawn and walked back into my house the way she'd come out.

I had no problem giving her some space as she reflected on the events that had just occurred and tried to come to terms with what was going on between us.

Fucking her in the forest hadn't been what I intended, but I didn't regret it for a second. The tension between us had reached an all-time high, and it was about time we did something about it. I walked back to the house, entered the kitchen through the terrace, and made sure to lock the door behind me.

I dropped the bag off in the kitchen and made a mental note to tell Franklin to take care of it in the morning. I strolled through the house and up the stairs. I debated whether I should stop by Iris's room to see how she was before deciding that I would give her more time alone. Instead, I decided to head toward my bedroom and into my bathroom.

Within a couple of minutes, steam filled the air as I stepped into the shower, letting it wash away my adventure outside. The hot water cascading down my body felt wonderful, but my mind drifted back to watching my cum drip out of Iris and wishing deep down that I could shove it back into her so she didn't lose a single drop.

I rinsed off my body, stepped out of the shower, and dried off. As I wrapped the towel around my waist, I caught a glimpse of myself in the mirror and saw a satisfied look on my face. I had made the right decision in watching Iris plan her "grand escape" and then foiling it before she could get too far.

I threw on a white T-shirt and some black sweatpants before leaving my room and ending up in front of hers. I opened the door and peered into the room. I found Iris sitting on the edge of the bed, her shoulders slumped forward. Her chest rose and fell with heavy breaths. She stared at the floor, her brown hair covering her face.

"Petal—"

Iris's head snapped up to look at me. "Get out."

I walked into the room. "I can help you by—"

"I don't need your help," she said, cutting me off again. "Haven't you done enough?"

I was caught slightly off guard by how her words made me feel.

"You're going to take a bath," I said as I walked toward her bathroom.

"Would it kill you to ask me if I wanted to do something versus demanding that I do so?"

I paused for a second in the doorway before I looked at her over my shoulder. "Would you like to take a bath?"

She hesitated for a moment before nodding her head.

I stepped into the bathroom and started running the bath. Steam from the hot water filled the room, and I used a vanilla-scented bubble bath to form some bubbles in the tub. I grabbed some white, fluffy towels and placed them on the countertop.

I walked into the bedroom and held out my hand for Iris to take, but she stood up without my help and walked past me.

I debated whether I should walk in there and watch her take her bath, much like I'd done when she'd had her first shower here, but would that push her too far over the edge?

I heard her step into the bathtub, and it took everything in me not to turn around. I didn't get a great look at her outside between being surrounded by darkness in the woods and having a mask on, so the urge to see her naked body was even stronger than normal. But I knew I needed to ease her into all of this versus coming on too strong. Switching up my strategy wouldn't be the worst thing I'd done.

"I'll leave you to your bath. If you need anything, I'm all the way at the other end of this hallway."

Iris didn't respond, but I was sure she'd heard me.

When I walked to the door, I heard Iris call out my name, so I retraced my steps and ended back in the doorway of the bathroom.

"You asked if there was anything I needed. Well, there is something."

"What is it?"

"The holidays are coming up and I want to see Gran. She's getting older, and I don't know how many more holidays I'll have with her."

I considered it for a moment and realized she was right. The holidays were fast approaching, a time meant for joy and being with family. It was something I hadn't thought about in a while, so the fact that it was that time of year had been lost on me.

"I'll see what I can do," I said before walking out of the room.

I couldn't stand to be in there after I'd given her a bullshit answer. At the snap of my fingers, I could allow her to see her grandmother by letting her go and taking her back to campus.

But I couldn't do that.

As I walked back to my room, I contemplated her wish. It was the last thing I'd expected her to ask for, the first being that I let her go. But she'd surprised me again. Her request had caught me off guard, to say the least. Letting her visit her grandmother for the holidays was a simple enough ask. But letting her leave would be a huge logistic challenge, and the chances of Parker finding out about it would be high.

I'd done my best to make Iris feel more at home here since I'd let her roam around the mansion, but she was still a prisoner of mine because of her digging into Chevalier affairs that she had no business looking into.

But the holidays were meant for family. Keeping Iris from the only person she had left was cruel, and it would be one more thing she'd hold against me.

I paused at the window in my bedroom, gazing out at the forest I'd just been in. Perhaps permitting this small kindness would be the start of me building something between us that wasn't based on our history.

Instead of standing near the window for a second more, I strolled over to my bed and settled under the covers. Sleep didn't come easy, but that wasn't a surprise because it never did. But I still couldn't get Iris's request out of my mind.

I reminded myself that it could be tabled until tomorrow. I closed my eyes and let myself finally surrender to my thoughts and dreams for the night.

22

IRIS

What the hell was wrong with me?

The morning after my failed escape, I rubbed a hand down my face as I looked down at the counter. I refused to look up at myself in the mirror for fear of what I would see.

I should be angry. Yet it had been one of the most thrilling moments of my life.

Chaotic thoughts churned in my mind as I thought of Soren. Everything about him was a walking contradiction.

What I also couldn't get out of my mind was the door that was slightly hidden by the bookcase in Soren's office. It could be a pure coincidence that the bookcase was positioned in such a way that it made it seem as if the door wasn't there.

But I rarely believed in coincidences.

With a heavy sigh, I left the bathroom without looking up at myself once. I paced the bedroom, listening to my steps echoing on the hardwood floor. Nothing could change the feeling that the walls were closing in on me.

Desperate for something to do, I walked toward the door

of the guest room. Maybe leaving this room was the only way to get away from the suffocating feeling that surrounded me. I tucked a piece of my hair behind my ear and opened the door before stepping out into the hallway. The slight change in scenery didn't do anything to help my state of mind, but I kept on walking.

I ended up walking down the steps to the main floor. My gaze was focused on the door ahead, the one leading to the outside, but I was convinced that before I even made an attempt at reaching the door, someone or something would yank me back into this place.

"Good afternoon, Ms. Bennington. Is there anything you want from the kitchen?"

I blinked, startled by the intrusion on my impulsive thoughts. Then again, it was probably for the best if I didn't want to incur Soren's wrath for the time being. I turned my head and my eyes landed on Molly. To be honest, I was slightly surprised by her friendliness. Normally, I wouldn't be questioning whether her smile was genuine or not, but given the circumstances, I wanted to be cautious.

I shook my head. "I'm good. Thank you."

"If there's anything you need, just say the word."

"Will do." I hesitated momentarily, but curiosity won in the end. "Molly, is Soren in?"

She quickly shook her head. "I think he has a meeting on campus."

That was interesting, given that we were on winter break, but she probably didn't know what it was about. It was time to shift my questioning. "This is going to sound random, but I was curious. How did you end up coming to work for Soren?"

Molly's eyes widened a smidge, probably because she

hadn't been expecting me to ask the question. That made two of us. Her expression shifted back into the small smile she'd had on her face when she greeted me. "Maybe, like, twenty-five years ago, I was hired by Mr. Grant's father after Mrs. Grant died. A friend of a friend mentioned that they knew someone who needed a cook. While I'm not classically trained, I was home-taught, so I figured, why not apply? I got it and have been here ever since. The only time I hadn't worked here was when Soren briefly dismissed and rehired both Franklin and I recently."

That was weird. "That's fascinating. What an amazing friend to have been looking out for you."

"Yes, I was so thankful for that and the opportunity to prove myself in this job. Then again, I can't help but wonder if the reason why I was hired was because..." Molly's voice trailed off as she looked away, and I wondered if she would say anything at all. Instead of interrupting her, I decided the best course of action was to be patient with her and let her tell me in her own way and time. "Mr. Grant wanted a motherly figure to help with his son."

"I could only imagine," I whispered as thoughts about what it was like to lose my parents wandered to the surface.

Molly nodded and continued. "Through it all, both Mr. Grants have been great employers. They've compensated me well, and I could tell they appreciate the meals I cooked for them and Franklin. We've never spoken much about what had happened to his mother or his wife, but it was clear that Soren was still grieving. The change that I see in him from before his wife's death until now has been a complete one-eighty."

I narrowed my eyes as I tried to make sense of her words.

"What do you mean?"

Molly sighed before she began to explain. "Mr. Grant stayed home a lot after her death, not that I blamed him. It's only been in the last few months that he started going out more, sometimes coming home when I would be waking up to start prepping for breakfast."

I bit my lower lip as I tried to process this new information about Soren's life after his wife's death. I couldn't help but wonder what caused the shift in his schedule. It made sense for him to want to stay home and grieve the loss of someone he loved, but him leaving and staying out later the last few months likely meant. . . he'd changed his routine when we ran into each other on Westwick University's campus.

"That's interesting. Maybe that was his way of starting to heal."

"Maybe so. Anyway, I should probably get in the kitchen and get back to prepping things for lunch."

I nodded. "I don't want to keep you."

Molly gave me another smile. "You're not. Feel free to stop in the kitchen whenever to chat more. It can get awfully quiet in here."

Didn't I know it. "Will do. Let me know if I can help or anything."

"You're too kind."

Molly walked away, and I was left standing in the foyer, running through the information I'd just heard and debating if it was wise to enter Soren's office.

Shoving my conversation with Molly aside, I approached Soren's office as my heart thumped out of control. I needed to do this and be fast, just in case Soren came back soon.

I looked around the hallway to see if Molly might have come back to talk to me or if Franklin was wandering around. Seeing neither, I turned the doorknob and stepped into the room.

Soren's office looked similar to how it had when he'd caught me in there a few days ago. The only thing that seemed to be missing was the silver tray and its contents, which had been knocked over and scattered all over the floor.

My heart was thumping against my ribs as I stepped farther into the office after making sure to close the door behind me. Instead of taking in his office, all my focus was on the corner where I'd hidden several days ago. I quickly walked over to the bookcase and stood in front of one of the doors in this house that had perplexed me since I'd come across it. Without a second thought, because there was no time to waste, I grasped the knob before turning it, and instead of being greeted by a locked door, it opened with ease.

The first thing I was greeted with was the smell of dust and neglect. It was obvious that this room hadn't been cleaned in a while and I couldn't help but wonder why. But that was the only thing I knew because I could barely see in there. Figuring that the most likely place for me to find a light was along the wall, I shifted inch by inch along it. Creeping forward and staying close to the wall, I hoped I wouldn't end up falling flat on my face or tripping over something.

I paused for a split second when I found the switch. With a flick of my wrist, light filled the room, illuminating every corner. My pulse pounded in my ears as a gasp slipped past my lips.

23

IRIS

As the room flooded with light, the first thing my eyes landed on was a portrait in the center of the room. The resemblance was uncanny—same hair color, the same face shape, even the same piercing blue gaze that seemed to look right through me. If I hadn't known the truth, for a moment, I might have believed I was looking into a mirror rather than at a painting. However, this wasn't me, but I had no doubts about who it was.

Eden Marsden Grant.

The fact that she looked so similar to me when my hair was my natural color tripped me up once more. Her dark hair was pulled into an updo and there was a hint of a smile on her face. The portrait showed Eden's back, with her looking over her shoulder at the person painting the picture. The background was a lighthouse and the cliff that it sat on, looking over the water below.

So many questions floated through my mind as I looked at the painting that was almost a mirror image of me. A chill that settled into my bones made me shiver as I took in the painting. I couldn't take my eyes off it.

I took one step and then another and another until I was standing directly in front of the portrait. I knew she didn't have the answers to the questions I was seeking, but I was still drawn to the display in front of me.

My fingers trembled in the air, hovering a few inches away from the canvas. It almost felt as if there was this magnetic pull between it and me, one that I don't think I'd ever be able to explain. The silence in the room vanished. I swear I could hear the crashing of the waves against the cliff, feel the spray of salt water on my face, and see the light coming from the lighthouse as it shined through the darkness.

I traced the outline of the frame, being careful not to touch the actual artwork itself. I couldn't help but wonder how long it had been back there, given that there was no show of wear and tear on the portrait.

My lip trembled as I stopped myself from talking to the painting and, therefore, talking to myself. I wished she was here to give me some insight on Soren and how the hell I could get out of this prison, but all she could do was stare at me with her crystal-blue eyes forever in that painting.

I shook my head as if to remove the trance the painting had put me in from my brain. I only had a limited time back there and needed to use it wisely. Having no idea when Soren left nor when he was planning to return, I needed to get a move on looking around, stat.

I turned away from the portrait, allowing my gaze to sweep over the room. Boxes were all around, and I covered my mouth as I sneezed from all the dust. When I sneezed again, I froze. Could someone have heard all the commotion?

I froze in place, listening to see if I could hear any footsteps indicating that someone was coming closer to where I was. Seconds felt like years as I waited to be caught once more, and all I could think about was that I must have a death wish if I couldn't control my desire to investigate things like this. But when no one showed up, I was able to breathe again, dust-filled air and all.

My heart raced as I approached several of the boxes. There had to be something here, some sort of clue in all this clutter. I refused to leave this room empty-handed without an idea about how to escape this house or something that might give a hint as to where Eddison Payne's documents were. I sifted through the contents, trying to pinpoint if any of the things I was looking at could be another piece of the overall puzzle.

I was about to give up hope when a folder tucked in one of the boxes caught my eye. It was odd to me because it was the only folder in that box, and it was surrounded by what appeared to be old books and notebook paper that had been ripped in half. With trembling fingers, I grabbed the folder and then opened it. A single piece of white printer paper was inside. After I skimmed the contents, my mouth dropped open in shock.

It was a document that talked about the history of the Chevaliers Headquarters, including mentioning that their most important documents were being held there. Could this be where they kept all the documents related to their founding?

I slammed the folder closed and growled in frustration.

Had I been looking in the wrong place the entire time?

My mind raced with possibilities of how I could sneak into the headquarters without getting caught. After a few seconds, I came up with a plan that sounded like it belonged in a B-rated action flick versus something that I could achieve in real life, and I quickly shoved the idea aside because I didn't have time to think about this now when I still needed to escape this mansion in order to be able to somehow travel from here to New York City to the Chevaliers Headquarters.

As I put the folder back where I found it, one of the other pieces of paper caught my attention. I picked it up and noticed the very neat handwriting of the person who wrote it. After skimming the words and trying to piece together which half went with which, it didn't take me long to discover it was part of a long letter that Eden had written for Soren.

Dear Soren,

I know you're going to tease me about writing a letter to you versus just telling you this, but I figured this could be a way to memorialize our friendship forever. However, I've been sitting here for a while, trying to find the right words to write to express what I want to say. It's kind of funny how sometimes words can't capture everything you're feeling, right? But I'll give it a go.

First and foremost, I want to say thank you. Given everything you've done to help me throughout the years, the sentiment seems so small in comparison, but I hope you truly understand the magnitude of what you've done. By marrying me, you saved my life, and I don't think it's something I'll ever be able to pay back, but damn it, I'll try.

Even if I can't repay you, I promise to be there for you whenever you need me. That's outside of the fact that you're now stuck with me as your WIFE.

Love you loads (even if that sometimes annoys you),
Eden

My fingers tightened around the pieces of paper as I devoured each word once more. There was no way this could be true, was there?

I walked backward until my back hit a wall. The Soren Eden had described was unrecognizable compared to the man that I knew. I couldn't help but wonder if she was the reason he'd become the way he was. If all of this was a result of a wound that was too deep to heal.

If what I'd put together was accurate, it made me see Soren in a slightly different light. That made the picture of the monster in my mind more convoluted, but I didn't have time to process it. I needed to get out of here as soon as possible for fear of facing Soren's wrath. I put the papers back where they belonged and quickly left the hidden room.

Once I was back in Soren's study, I ran over to the door that would lead me to the hallway and paused for a moment to see if I heard any indication someone was nearby.

Fortunately, I couldn't hear anything, so I opened the door slowly. I stepped out into the hallway and looked around to make sure that no one was there. I could feel my heart racing as I made my way toward the stairwell.

It was a delicate balance trying to look as if I hadn't been snooping around the house, but I didn't want to risk anyone questioning me about where I'd been.

I kept my eyes peeled for any sign of movement while trying to be as quiet as possible. Soon, I reached the stairs and began walking up. I continued to remind myself that I couldn't run because it might draw attention to me.

After a few more seconds, I reached the guest room

without any incident. As soon as I shut the door behind me, I leaned against it and all my muscles seemed to relax simultaneously. For a moment, it felt like this whole ordeal had been nothing but a dream.

But that was only until reality sank in again with a jolt and reminded me of everything that had just happened. In order not to draw any suspicion from Soren or anyone else in the mansion, it was important for me to act normal despite all these thoughts running through my mind.

24

IRIS

Exhaling a heavy breath, I ran my hands down my face as I stepped away from the guest room door. Each step meant that I was farther away from what I'd discovered in the small room next to Soren's office. As I pulled on the chair sitting in front of the desk, it creaked softly, something I'd grown used to, given how much I found myself doing this exact same motion. Sitting down, I took a moment to pause. This room was the only place in this house where I could feel slightly settled, beyond the chaos that seemed to surround me with every step I took here. I took a moment to gather my thoughts and feelings.

Once that was done, I reached for the notebook that I'd been using to process what had been happening here. It opened with ease, used to my constant use, and flipped to a new page. I picked up the pen that had been resting beside it, and soon, the words began to flow from my mind and onto the pages below.

Much like the times I'd written in the book before, I made sure to be careful about what I was writing because I didn't want to reveal everything I knew. I didn't know who might be reading this, and I didn't trust Soren as far as I could throw him. And he'd already mentioned having watched me, so I'd been especially careful since that night he'd found and fucked me in the forest. Thinking about that made me shiver for a second and I hated myself for wishing something like that would happen again.

I was willing to say that nothing here was as it seemed. It never really had been. It was difficult to tell what was steeped in reality and what was a complete lie. I had to question everything and the answers that I found only led to more questions. It was as if the answers I'd found in my search were like a key that opened one door, but once I'd stepped inside, I was confronted by a hallway with more locked doors with no way to escape. Fitting, given the door near the very room I was in that I still hadn't managed to get into. I continued writing, enjoying the ability to somewhat put what I was thinking on paper. It gave me the opportunity to dissect my thoughts a bit and untangle the items that I could.

When I was done, I tossed the pen down and closed my eyes, choosing to take time to rub my temples to ease the tension that was growing in my head. My fingers moved in gentle circles, attempting to soothe the dull pain.

No matter what, everything circled back to Soren, no matter how much I tried to not think about him. There were so many things that only he knew the answers to, and I wasn't sure if I'd ever get the answers to all of my questions.

When the door to the guest room creaked open, I tensed. I cracked my eyes open slightly and bit back a big sigh. He must have known that I was thinking about him and decided to grace me with his presence.

Soren was standing at the threshold. Holy shit. I'd just managed to get out of Soren's study before he got home. Did he know that I was in there? He waited until I'd given him my full and undivided attention before he strolled into the room. "I have an update on your request to see your grandmother."

If all my focus hadn't been on him before, it definitely was now. "Yes?"

"I can't let you see her in person, given the circumstances we are under."

My heart dropped to my feet. I wasn't sure how to feel about this news, and because of everything I'd just experienced, my emotions froze.

"But we can set up a video call so that you can talk to and see her."

I nodded slowly, feeling a mix of disappointment and relief. "Okay," I said, trying to keep my voice steady. "When can we have the call?"

"Tonight," Soren replied, his eyes never leaving mine. "I've arranged for a secure video call to be set up in my office in thirty minutes. I'll come up and get you and will be with you the entire time. By the way, your grandmother thinks that you've been studying abroad, so keep up that lie. Got it?"

I nodded again, feeling a sense of gratitude toward Soren for making this happen, even if it wasn't exactly what I wanted. Having him there was annoying, but from his perspective, it made sense. This wasn't something worth arguing about, especially given what I'd just found out. "Thank you," I said quietly.

Soren nodded his head once in acknowledgment before turning to leave the room, closing the door behind him. As he walked away, I couldn't help but watch him, my eyes tracing the lines of his broad shoulders and the way his suit hugged his muscular frame.

I shook my head, trying to clear my thoughts. This was not the time or place to be distracted by the fact I was attracted to my stalker turned professor turned kidnapper. I had more important things to focus on, like talking to Gran.

I stood up from the desk and my nerves got to me. I was going to see Gran for the first time since I'd gotten kidnapped, and I wasn't sure what to expect. I would love to find a way to let her know that I was in trouble here, but I didn't know how I was going to be able to do it on a secure video call with Soren staring at me, watching my every move.

Fuck.

This could be either a disaster or the one thing I needed to survive in this shit. I looked down at what I had on and decided to freshen up and change before the call. As I headed toward the bathroom, I wondered what Gran would say. Would she suspect something was wrong?

I thought about that as I quickly showered and changed into something more presentable than my usual attire. I took a few extra moments to brush my hair and put on some light makeup. I thought showing up like I'd just rolled out of bed would leave Gran questioning things, and I didn't know how to answer those questions with Soren breathing down my neck.

Just as I finished getting ready, Soren walked into the room without knocking once again. He gave me an approving nod before leading me down the stairs to his office. We walked in silence, but it wasn't uncomfortable or awkward, thankfully.

Once we entered his office, I asked him, "How does Gran know that we are having a call?"

"She was informed," he said without further explaining himself.

Soren showed me how to use the laptop he had set up for the call with Gran. He then stepped back and gave me some space so that I could have my conversation with her without her knowing he was there.

I got comfortable in Soren's chair behind his desk while he stood in the corner and leaned against his bookcase, staring me down.

I took a deep breath before clicking on the link that would connect me to Gran. A couple of minutes later, her face appeared on the screen, and my heart melted at the sight of her.

"Hi, honey! It's so good to see you! How are you? How is your time in Greece?" she asked in her gentle voice as she stared at me with loving eyes, unaware of what had been going on with me since I last saw her.

My throat tightened as tears welled up in my eyes, but I managed to keep myself together. "I'm doing okay, Gran. It's so lovely to see you."

"You look tired. Is everything okay?"

I could feel Soren's eyes on me and knew I had to be careful with my words. I couldn't tell her the truth, so instead, I focused on what she did know. "Yes, everything is great. The time zone difference has me a little tired."

We took a moment just to look at each other before Gran spoke again. "Tell me all about Greece! It must be incredible experiencing a whole new culture and studying abroad."

I glanced down because I hated to lie to her, but I painted

a picture of what I thought Greece was like, hoping it didn't sound forced.

Gran's eyes lit up with excitement as if she was living through the experience with me. "Oh, and the food! Have you tried any local dishes?"

I hesitated for a split second. "Yes, and all of them have been spectacular."

Her eyes twinkled. "That sounds delightful! I'm so proud of you for taking this opportunity to learn and explore. Remember to soak in every moment." She paused for a moment. "I wish you were home for the holidays, but don't take that to mean that I'm trying to force you to come home early."

I bit my lip to keep from crying. "I know, and I will, Gran, I promise."

Out of the corner of my eye, I saw Soren shift and my eyes darted to the right to watch him for a second, but his expression remained blank. I blew out a deep breath as I thought about the lies that I'd told her, even though she didn't seem to suspect a thing.

Gran smiled. "Just promise me you'll stay safe, alright?"

How ironic was that question? "I promise, Gran," I whispered.

The conversation went on for a couple more minutes before I said goodbye and the call ended.

Soren walked over from where he was standing and said, "Good job not telling her where you are or what was going on."

"Thank you?" I said, confused about his half-assed compliment. "Do I get a reward for it?"

"Your sarcasm is cute, but if you really want a reward, I'd be happy to give you one."

I swallowed hard and shook my head quickly. I didn't want to spend any more time with Soren tonight. Hell, I didn't want to be around anyone after the day I'd had. "I think I'm just going to go to bed. Alone."

Before he could respond, I jumped up from the chair and left the room, happy to have some space between Soren and me.

I hadn't ever been more thankful that he hadn't tried to follow me than I was this time.

25

SOREN

The golden glow from the flames in my fireplace provided a peaceful backdrop as I sat leaning over my desk. It was doing its best to keep the chill in the air at bay, but given how late it was, there was still a small draft in the house due to the drop in temperature. None of that meant anything to me as my pen flew across the page, detailing the plan that I intended to carry out.

Once I finished what I needed to write, I leaned back and allowed myself to scan what I'd written down. It was a lot to pull off in less than twenty-four hours, but none of that mattered. This would go off without a hitch if it was the last thing I did.

I reached for my phone and called the last number I'd spoken to. I tapped my fingers on the desk, each beat echoing the urgency of what was going on. We needed to act, and we needed to act fast.

"Hello?" The voice on the other end was barely audible.

"I'm calling to make sure everything will be ready to go by sunrise," I said.

"Of course, Mr. Grant," he replied. "We have everything ready and will be at your house shortly."

"Everything has to be perfect." My voice was low and thinly veiled with a warning. If they fucked this up, I'd be sure to make their lives a living hell.

This was my attempt at turning a page, and it must be executed to perfection.

"Understood," he said, his tone clipped and professional. "We won't let you down."

"See that you don't," I replied, ending the call abruptly.

The moment I hung up the phone, a satisfied smirk played on my lips. The wheels were in motion, and everything would go according to plan. I stood up and strode to the door and flung it open. There stood Franklin as if he knew I was about to go search for him. If it were anyone else, I'm sure they would have been scared to have Franklin standing there. But I was so used to him doing this it didn't faze me.

"Ah," I said, my voice low and deliberate. "Just the man I needed to see."

"Mr. Grant," he said as he stepped into the room, careful not to make a sound. I closed the door behind him before I spoke.

"Everything is in place," I informed him. "They should be arriving here within the hour."

"Very good, sir," he murmured. "I'll keep watch and will let them in when they arrive."

"Thank you," I said before Franklin gave me a sharp nod and exited the room as quietly as he entered it.

Alone again, I began to pace the length of the room, my footsteps echoing softly with each step I took. This was an excellent plan and I knew it.

This would be perfect for Iris, and I couldn't wait to see her face when she saw it.

I was finally embracing what Eden wanted for me all along. Not isolating myself any longer and leaning into finding everlasting love.

26

IRIS

The next morning, I woke up feeling slightly groggy, and I struggled to open my eyes. It was as if something was weighing them down. When I could finally commit to doing so, my eyes landed on a cloudy sky outside of my window. I stared at the variations of gray that somewhat swirled together as I tried to clear the mental fog.

I stretched and turned over, but confusion still filled my brain. There was a light streaming into the room from under the door, and curiosity got the best of me. Rubbing the sleep from my eyes, I slowly got out of my bed, giving myself a chance to wake up more before I walked toward the door and turned the doorknob.

As the door opened, my mouth dropped open in awe. The once gloomy hallway outside of this room had been transformed into a winter wonderland, lit by strands of twinkling lights, small, decorated trees, and garland. Fake snow on the floor completed the look, and it almost looked as beautiful as the snow that I'd noticed when I'd eaten out on the terrace, which unfortunately didn't last long.

The sight before me took my breath away. My first emotion was confusion as I took it in, but that quickly turned into joy, something I hadn't been expecting while I'd been forced to stay here. This looked like something out of a movie or a fairy tale. What the heck was this all about?

Obviously, this was a project that Soren had ordered to happen. First of all, how did I sleep through the noise that this would have caused? Also, when did Soren have time to plan all of this?

I shook off my questions, deciding that I needed to enjoy this moment instead of wondering how this all came to be. As I wandered through the hallway, I couldn't help but admire the decorations because not only did they evoke nostalgia and the holiday season, but they also brightened this place considerably. The soft music from a piano drifted to my ears, and I couldn't help but smile.

For a brief moment, I could pretend this was a normal holiday season. That I was home with Gran instead of staying in the mansion of a man who had no issue with stalking or kidnapping me. While I didn't think he'd done all of this himself, the fact that he'd gone out of his way to do all of this after I'd mentioned feeling upset about not being with Gran for the holidays made me feel warm inside.

I never thought I would describe something Soren had done as sweet, yet here I was, swooning over what he'd done in his house. What was wrong with me? I let out an audible gasp when I saw a massive tree in the foyer, filled with lights and ornaments.

The coldness around my heart softened at the sight. It was stunning, and I was in complete shock.

A floorboard creaked behind me, shattering my focus on

the scene in front of me. I whirled around to find Soren leaning against the wall, a weird expression on his face.

"It's lovely, isn't it?"

I hesitated, wondering how to interpret all this along with the man in front of me. "Yes, it's absolutely beautiful."

The corner of his mouth forced his lips into a smirk. "I'm glad you like it." He walked toward me and offered me his arm. "I have something else I want to show you."

The change that I was seeing in him had me wondering if I was in a fever dream. But I still found myself staring at his arm before I looped my own through his, allowing him to lead me into the living room.

"Holy—"

My words died on my lips. The living room and dining room had also been decorated festively and I swore I'd stepped onto the set of a family sitcom or into a magazine for a department store. Both had been transformed into a winter wonderland, adorned from floor to ceiling in shimmering icicles and silvery garlands. I quickly walked over and grabbed a sugar cookie that had been set on the coffee table in the living room before I turned and smiled at Soren.

He looked to be in shock at the look on my face, but then his face became more relaxed as a small smile appeared on his lips.

This was absolutely perfect. I cleared my throat and then said, "Soren, why did you decide to put so much effort into decorating for the holidays? You never gave any indication that this is what you wanted to do."

He looked at me as if he was debating how much he wanted to share. After a few moments, he shrugged and said, "It was a nice thing to do."

There was doing something nice, but there was doing this. What had happened here was a transformation.

"What made you do it?"

"I was inspired."

That made me raise an eyebrow. Sure, he could have found inspiration anywhere, but the timing of this was suspicious.

Right after I was upset about not spending the holidays with Gran, he decided to hire people to do all this decorating?

"It's interesting what you can come up with when inspired to do something good versus something bad."

I saw Soren do a double take before he responded. "What are you talking about?"

"I assumed you were inspired to hunt me down for some reason, so shifting your attention to this was a good choice."

Soren snorted, actually snorted. "I make whatever decisions that I want to make, and I do it when I want to make them."

I couldn't help but roll my eyes. Of course he wouldn't admit to anything. I shrugged it off and decided to enjoy the moment, letting go of my suspicions for now. "Well, it's beautiful. Thank you, Soren."

He nodded in response before gesturing to the couch. "Sit. I have something else to show you."

I did as I was told, and my attention was drawn to the fireplace and all the decorations around it. All the holiday decor softened this home as a whole and brightened up every room I'd been in so far. I looked up when I saw Soren returning, and when he stopped in front of me, he handed me a neatly wrapped package, and I just stared at the gold ribbon that shimmered in the light.

"This is for me?" The question was ridiculous because he was handing it *to* me, but I couldn't believe it.

"Yes, it is," was all he said with all the patience in the world. His confidence was somewhat annoying, given how nervous I was about this whole exchange, but there wasn't much I could do about that.

I carefully pulled apart the ribbon and unwrapped the package. I was stunned to find a journal, or maybe it was a diary. It had a deep-blue leather cover and a beautiful, intricate design on it with sapphires embedded in it. My mouth dropped open as I opened it and turned the pages, and I was surprised to find that the pages had gold edges. It looked to be handmade.

My eyes darted to Soren. "This is. . . I mean, it must've cost a small fortune!"

A faint smile tugged at his lips. "The artisan crafts only a handful each year. I knew you would love it."

That made me do a double take. "How did you know I would love it?" It was a silly question given he'd stalked me, but besides jotting down notes in the notebook in my room, I didn't think I'd written in a real journal unless it was for school since he'd entered my life.

Soren cleared his throat as he sat down next to me. "I suspected it might be something you'd enjoy after you made it your safe word, and that was why I made sure that I had something for you to write in when you moved to that room. I wanted to give you something more beautiful to write your thoughts down in."

The words that came out of his mouth were sweet, but it also sounded like something he made up on the spot. I raised an eyebrow at him before my eyes landed back on the journal. I ran my fingers over the cool sapphires, the weight of the gesture sinking in. "Thank you," I murmured, genuinely moved by what he'd done. "It's truly magnificent. I can't believe how beautiful it is."

I couldn't help but stare at the journal. It was a beautiful gift, but I also felt guilty about it. I knew he must have spent a lot of money on something like this. Then again, after what he'd put me through, why was I concerned? But I couldn't shake the feeling.

"Soren, this is too much," I said softly.

"It's nothing."

"No," I said, "it's not nothing and you and I know it."

His fingers brushed my cheek, pushing back a stray strand of hair that had fallen in front of my face. "It's a gift that I wanted to give to you. If you absolutely hate it, I'll get rid of it."

I quickly shook my head. "No! I love it." With a heavy sigh, I said, "Thank you."

"Now that is more like it."

27

SOREN

I couldn't help but stare as Iris's face lit up as she continued to take in all of the efforts of the team I hired to perform this miracle in the middle of the night.

My gaze lingered on her smile, a glimpse of joy that I'd rarely seen on her face since I walked into her life. In this moment, she looked young, carefree, and happy to be here with me. It sent warmth through my body, having a much bigger effect on me than I thought it would, stirring something in me that awakened a part of me that I thought was dead.

Iris turned to look at me again. "When did you have time to do all this?"

I shrugged. "It all happened last night when you were asleep."

"I didn't hear a thing..." Her voice trailed off as if she was trying to figure out how she slept through it when I knew exactly how we managed to create this miracle.

I'd made sure to put a sedative in the tea she'd asked Molly to prepare for her last night to ensure that she went into a deep sleep so they could work. They tried to be as quiet as possible, but the sleeping medicine gave us some more reassurance. Had I taken it a step too far by ensuring that she was knocked out? Sure, but it wouldn't be the first time I went above and beyond what was required of me.

"You didn't have to go to so much trouble," Iris said softly.

Trouble was an understatement. I had moved heaven and earth to give her this one perfect moment, and I would do it again in a heartbeat.

"It's the least I could do," I said. And that was the honest truth.

Iris laughed, the sound light and airy and something that I could get used to. "Well, you've outdone yourself." She paused, glancing around once more at the winter wonderland I had created just for her. "Thanks again, Soren. It's perfect."

"You're welcome... again."

Iris shook her head at me, and I could see that she was fighting the urge to smile. Together, we spent time chatting and staring at the holiday decorations until a delicious smell caused both of us to look in the direction of the kitchen.

"That would be brunch," I murmured, more to myself. I stood up and held out my arm for Iris to grab. She adjusted her new journal so that she could carry it and loop her arm through mine, and together, we walked into the dining room.

The table was already set and contained two extra spaces for Franklin and Molly. There was a beautiful arrangement of winter flowers in the center of the table, and serving platters with fluffy pancakes, scrambled eggs, bacon, and fresh fruit had already been set out.

As we approached our seats, Franklin walked out of the

kitchen with a pot of coffee in his hands and said, "I was just about to come get you, Mr. Grant."

"No need. We smelled the food from the living room," I replied.

It took a few moments for us to get settled, and soon, we were all eating and engaging in light conversation about the holidays. Even Franklin, who was a man of few words normally, was talking more than I'd seen him talk in all the years that he had worked for me.

The rest of the day ended up being very quiet, and I think everyone appreciated that. About an hour after dinner, I walked into the living room and found Iris sitting by the fireplace and writing in the journal I bought for her. She didn't look up as I walked into the room, so I softly said something in hopes of not scaring her. "I'm glad you're enjoying your gift."

She stopped writing and looked up, a slightly startled look on her face before she relaxed. "I am. It doesn't get much better than sitting in front of a fireplace and getting a quiet moment to enjoy the festive cheer."

I didn't know much about that until today, but it felt foolish to admit those words out loud.

Instead, I took a seat next to Iris and pulled her closer to me. Having her in my arms, just like this, was pleasing to my soul. Another thing to add to the list of things I hadn't expected.

When she laid her head on my shoulder, I couldn't help but lean over and kiss her forehead. It felt like the most natural thing in the world. But even as I thought about how relaxed I was in this scenario, the ugly black cloud that hung over us through the entire time that we'd known one another was still present and well.

"When are you going to let me go, Soren? When can I go back to my normal life?"

Her words cut through the air like a knife, immediately altering the calm atmosphere that had existed between us. It was as if she'd known what I'd been thinking about but had the courage to utter the words out loud.

"I haven't gotten word on what is supposed to happen to you," and that was the honest truth. However, a nagging suspicion that she might not believe that did bother me.

"Oh. Okay," she said, and I could hear the disappointment in her voice. Unfortunately, it was the only answer I currently had.

This was because the best decision here was not to bother Parker about an answer now. I knew the man well enough to know that pressuring him on anything wouldn't end well. If he put out the call to end Iris's life, then that was it. If I didn't do what he asked, then he would send someone else after her to finish the deal, and she'd be living the rest of her life having to constantly look over her shoulder. That would be a shitty way to live.

This all could have been avoided if she hadn't practically wanted to dig up Eddison Payne's remains to prove a point that has been passed down as a fact in her family for who knows how long at this point.

All my thoughts about us came to an end when Iris jumped slightly as the buzzing of my phone interrupted us. The warmth in my chest faded because I was pissed about the intrusion. I mumbled a few cuss words under my breath as I pulled out one of my burner phones and looked at the screen, alerting me to who was calling.

"I need to take this," I said as I stood up.

She nodded but didn't look up at me, instead choosing to focus on her new journal. I ran a hand through my hair and turned away from her. I walked out into the foyer and answered the call.

"What is it?" I asked in a loud whisper, irritated that I'd been interrupted during a sweet moment with Iris.

"You need to perform your assignment tonight." The voice on the other end was curt and unapologetic. "We'll have more information for you this evening."

I gritted my teeth, taking a few steps toward the living room so I could look back at Iris. She was still sitting in front of the fireplace, staring at the journal I'd given her. Her fingertips softly brushed the leather cover as if she was still amazed that she had it in her hand.

With effort, I tore my gaze away from her. "I'll be there tonight."

The call ended abruptly. I took a deep breath as I stared at the phone. I squared my shoulders as I turned to face Iris again. As I walked back into the room, her eyes met mine and I could see all the questions she wanted to ask but didn't.

"Just something for work I have to take care of later today." That wasn't exactly a lie, but hopefully, this would be the last job I'd have to perform for a while.

I rarely, if ever, felt conflicted. When I came to a decision, I followed it through wholeheartedly because I knew I'd made the right choice. But this one had me puzzled.

"That sucks, given the holiday."

I shrugged. "Duty calls and never sleeps."

"Kind of like New York City, right?"

I nodded, confused as to why she'd brought the city up. "Sure, kind of like New York City."

LATER THAT NIGHT, I walked to my car, my boots crunching in the freshly fallen snow. When my mind should have been on the assignment I needed to complete and the anger that I was feeling at the moment, I'd done my best to force myself to think of a happier time, like the time I spent with Iris all of today.

But now was the time to get back down to business.

I let out a deep breath and noticed that it was cold enough for me to see it in front of me. It had been foolish to ignore what was going on in the outside world today and pretend that our lives were simple.

I climbed into my car and started it up, enjoying the soft purr of my engine as it roared to life. I put my destination into my GPS and pulled out of my long driveway.

As the minutes ticked by, my anger slowly grew. Everything was finally coming to a head, and I couldn't wait to get this over with.

It would soon be showtime.

28

SOREN

Part of me couldn't believe that I was about to have the opportunity to do what I wanted to do. What I needed to do.

Gripping the steering wheel tighter, I pressed the gas pedal down farther. The deep hum of the engine matched the adrenaline racing through me as I sped toward the location that was blinking on my GPS.

I had to find him and make him pay for what he did. There would be no more hiding. It had taken two years to get to this point, and I wasn't about to lose the opportunity presented to me.

I only slowed down when I noticed how close I was to my destination. Up ahead, a narrow driveway cut through the trees, barely visible in the darkness. There was a worn sign that read "Private Property" as I turned sharply onto the dirt road. My car's tires crunched over gravel as I approached the isolated cabin deep in the woods.

I turned off my headlights in an effort to sneak up to the building in hopes of still having the element of surprise on my side. Thankfully, the cabin was surrounded by the forest, making it easier for me to hide my car. I parked my car and stepped out as quietly as possible. I walked toward the cabin and stopped only when I was a few feet away.

I looked through one of the windows and I could see a faint light coming from inside. What was it coming from? Crouching down low, I crept around to the other side of the building and tried to look inside again.

Shifting where I was standing did give me a better viewpoint, and it was then that I realized the light was coming from inside another room. Based on the blueprints that I had of the cottage, I suspected it was from the bathroom.

Perfect.

With him occupied in the bathroom, it was easy for me to break into his home. When the lock on the front door clicked softly, I knew I'd gotten in. I pushed the door gently and was pleased that there was not a sound from the hinges.

The sounds of a shower occurring made this all the better, muffling any noise I made. It was pure luck that he would be taking a shower this late. I knew it was a sign that I was doing the right thing. Since I didn't know when he stepped into the shower, I knew I had to act quickly.

As the sound of water splashing played in the background, I moved toward the bedroom. I wasn't surprised to find rustic furnishings in there, and there weren't many personal items for the man of the hour. I suspected it was because he'd been on the run now for years. There was one chair in the corner of the room, near a standing lamp, that gave me the perfect spot to wait.

I sat down in the chair and began tapping my finger on

the arm, waiting patiently for him to walk out of the only place keeping him alive at the moment.

But then, the sound of water falling from the showerhead ceased. It was replaced by the light echo of the dripping water and the movement of someone preparing to exit the shower.

I checked my watch, 2:56 a.m.

I planned on being out of here by 3:10 at the latest. While he deserved to suffer the highest form of torture known to mankind, I didn't want to waste more time here than I needed to.

Finally, there was silence, but I didn't move a muscle.

The door opened part of the way to reveal an older man standing in the doorway, wearing nothing but a pair of black sweatpants. I was pleased that it wasn't a towel because, while it would help with cleanup, it would make things messier with the plan I'd come up with on the way here. Before he could turn off the light, he spotted me. His eyes went wide at the sight, his already pale face growing paler by the second.

"Y-you..." His voice shook. "How did you find me?"

"Does it really matter? The point is that I finally fucking found you."

I stood up and took a step forward, and he followed by taking a step back. Our dance continued until he was backed into a corner on the opposite side of the room.

"How did you find me?"

I shrugged. "You decided that now was the time to stick your name into some Chevalier business and were trying to hunt down someone." I was referring to the intel that we received that he was trying to be the middleman and handle the deal of snatching Iris Bennington because our enemies thought she might have information about us.

"Please. . ." he whimpered while he held up a trembling, scared hand. "I don't want any trouble."

"Trouble?" I growled. The fucking audacity. "You don't know the meaning of the word because what I'm about to do is anything but trouble."

I got as close to him as I dared, easily towering over him, and before I realized it, my hands were clenched into fists. How satisfying it would feel to grab his neck and squeeze until I watched the life drain from his eyes. It would bring me so much joy.

I punched him in the face and made quick work of tying his hands behind his back with a zip tie.

"Over the years, I tried to come to terms with what must have been going through your mind when you made the decision you did, but nothing, and I truly mean nothing, can excuse what you did."

"But she disobeyed—"

"She was your daughter!" My shout echoed around the room. "Your own flesh and blood, and you tried to sell her to the highest bidder."

His eyes darted all over the room as I stared him down. When he focused a little too long on the door, my rage increased tenfold. There was nowhere to run. Nowhere to hide from what he'd done.

I was determined to make him pay.

"You sold your daughter's hand in marriage, causing her to be so desperate that we agreed to get married to keep her other marriage from happening."

"And a whole lot of good that did me."

I slammed my fist into the wooden wall just above his head. "Your daughter was murdered because she married me instead of whoever the fuck you sold her to!"

This time, his eyes cut to look straight at me, almost as if he was shooting daggers out of his eyes. "It was your job to protect her. She died on your watch."

"Don't you dare attempt to put this on me. You should have never put her in that position to begin with."

He shrank back from me, and I enjoyed the slight power struggle going on between us. If he thought he was getting out of this alive, he had another thing coming.

I was tired of this. I pulled out my knife and watched his eyes widen in fear as he realized what was about to happen.

"Nothing I say to you or to anyone else will bring her back or erase the guilt I felt seeing my best friend die in front of my eyes. But, fuck, seeing you bleed out on this floor would still be worth it."

I pressed the blade to his throat as a warning, and he visibly swallowed hard. His eyes were glued to mine, and I could see all the guilt, shame, and regret in them.

My grip tightened around the knife handle as I stared him down. He knew what was coming.

But he didn't know how I was going to do it until I made my move. And this wasn't going to be an easy, quick death.

I slashed the blade across his midsection and smirked when he screamed in agony as the blood started to flow from his body. I didn't stop there though; I continued to slice and stab him until he was left a bloody mess on the floor.

I wanted him to suffer for what he had done, so I made sure that death would be a slow and agonizing process for him. He deserved nothing less than that for what he had done.

When it was finally over, I stepped back and watched as his blood seeped out of him onto the cold hardwood floors. Once I made sure that he was indeed dead, I made my way to the front of the cabin.

As I stepped out of the building, I checked my watch to see the time: 3:05 a.m.

Perfect.

I completed my assignment five minutes early.

I took off my bloody clothes and dumped them into a garbage bag in the trunk of my car. The scene I'd left at the cabin had been a bit bloodier than I thought it would be and it was something I would have to live with. I didn't mean for my emotions to spiral, but they had.

The drive back to my home was in complete silence. The only thing keeping me occupied was my thoughts. I slipped back into my home, and as quietly as possible, I made my way upstairs to my room, where I quickly stripped out of my clothes.

Once under the hot spray of my shower, I tried to decrease my adrenaline, but nothing was working. I stood there for what felt like an eternity, letting the warm water cascade over my body.

Finally, I started to feel a sense of peace wash over me. Satisfaction settled within me as I came to terms with taking another life, but it was one that needed to be taken in order for justice to be served.

Once I finished, I stepped out of my shower feeling refreshed, and the only thing I could think of was pulling Iris into my arms and going to sleep.

It had been the first time in a long time that I felt the desire to sleep beside someone in bed. Although I wanted to bring her into my room so that she could sleep in my bed, I didn't want to disturb her rest. Instead, I walked into my bedroom, threw on what I planned on wearing to bed, and walked into the hallway.

My eyes were zeroed in on Iris's door as I strolled down the hallway, and before I knew it, I was opening her door and stepping inside.

The room was dark, lit only by the dim light coming from the window. Dawn would soon be here, but I was willing to take the few hours that I could have her in my arms versus not having her there at all. I walked over to her bed and gently pulled back the covers.

Before getting in, I took a few moments to look at her sleeping form. She looked so peaceful and beautiful as she lay there, almost as if she was an angel sent down from heaven. Her long brown hair cascaded over her pillow, and her face had an expression of contentment that I'd only recently gotten to see on her face when she was awake.

Finally, I got into bed next to her and pulled her close to me so that I could feel the warmth of her body against mine. She shifted slightly until she found a comfortable position. With Iris in my arms, everything I'd been thinking about or had done disappeared as I drifted off into a deep sleep.

29

IRIS

As I rested my head on Soren's chest, I closed my eyes, allowing the rhythmic beat of his heart to relax me. The way his chest moved up and down was soothing in a way I hadn't been expecting. It was how we woke up this morning, and I was completely confused about how we ended up in that position.

I'd gone to bed alone last night but woken up in his arms this morning. It was strange because it was the first time we'd ever slept in the same bed, and I thought, given how much I hated him and with him not attempting to force me into his bed so far, it meant that was something he wouldn't do.

Once again, this was an instance when I had more questions than answers.

When Soren stirred, I waited to see if he would wake. His eyes met mine briefly before he shut them again. "Good morning," he murmured, his voice thick with sleep.

"Morning. Why are you here?" I blurted out.

"I wanted to sleep here with you, so I did." He said it so matter-of-factly.

I was still in shock, trying to comprehend why he wanted to do that. This change in him was new, too new, if I was being honest with myself. He must have seen the confusion on my face because he began to explain.

"I know it may seem strange, but I just wanted to be close to you. Nothing more, nothing less." His voice was sincere yet still contained the hardness that it usually had.

There had never been a doubt in my mind that he wanted to be near me, given how he'd stalked me, but this all felt weird. I swallowed hard as I thought about how I still wanted to leave here as soon as possible. A pang of guilt hit my stomach even though I knew I shouldn't feel that way. After all, I had been kidnapped by Soren and was being held here against my will.

I sat up and watched Soren get up from the bed. I couldn't help but follow him with my eyes as I saw each muscle shift with his movements.

"I'm going to get ready, and you should do the same," he said.

"Why? What's going on?"

"Nothing. It's just time for breakfast."

This whole exchange had me questioning everything as I stared at him before he turned on his heel and left the room. I didn't move from that spot for several seconds, still confused about what had just occurred.

After getting ready for the day and eating breakfast, Soren and I decided to sit in the living room and enjoy the holiday scenery that still dressed the living room. Soren's hands made their way to my hair and gently played with my strands. I could fall asleep right now because I was so comfortable.

Never in a million years would I have thought I would be in this position and content, but here I was.

As my eyes closed, the chiming of a doorbell slashed through the silence we were sharing. I jumped slightly and I lifted my head to look at Soren. Was he expecting someone and hadn't mentioned it?

I sat up on the couch and allowed Soren to move. He quickly walked to the window and looked outside. I stood up too and watched as Franklin was about to open the door when Soren said, "Wait."

Everyone froze.

Soren's face turned to me. "Go upstairs and hide. Now," he demanded, grabbing my arm and taking me toward the stairs.

I ran up the steps, confused about what was going on. "Who's there?"

"Just do as I say and hide," he said, leaving no room for argument.

I reached the top step and walked far enough back that I couldn't be seen and waited for Soren or Franklin to open the door.

"Parker, what a surprise," Soren said. "How can I help you?"

"We have a problem, and I need to speak to you in private immediately. I brought my sister along with me, but this will only take a minute."

"Okay, come into my office."

What the hell?

I waited until I heard their footsteps retreating, wishing that I could get near Soren's office to hear what they were talking about. I heard Franklin talking to someone, and then things went silent. After waiting a few seconds, I walked toward the stairs and my mouth dropped open in shock.

Aria stood alone in the foyer. She was someone I'd hung out with on occasion and who lived in the same dormitory as me on Westwick University's campus. Why was she here?

Then again, that wasn't the question I should be asking.

I crept down the stairs until Aria spotted me, and she and I shared mirroring expressions.

"I'm so happy to see you," I said before lowering the volume of my voice. "We don't have much time, but you have to help me."

It took Aria a second to respond. "What are you doing here?"

"I was kidnapped by Soren."

Aria did a double take. "You were what?"

"Yes, and I need your help in getting me out of here before they get back."

Aria hesitated, her gaze dropping to the floor. I could see the wheels in her head turning as she weighed her options. The longer she stayed quiet, the more my hopes of getting away vanished.

Finally, after what felt like an eternity, Aria spoke up. "I don't know if I can do this," she said slowly. "There are some things you don't know about Soren and my brother, and getting on their bad side could be detrimental to both of us."

I bit my lip and ran my hands through my hair, trying to think of something that would convince Aria to help me. I knew how dangerous Soren was, and if he found out that Aria had helped me escape, all hell would break loose. But she was my only hope.

"Please," I begged, my voice barely above a whisper. "I

know you're scared, but so am I. You're the only one who knows I'm here, and if you don't help me, then there's no hope for me." Tears grew in the corner of my eyes as desperation took over. When she didn't answer right away, I decided to come clean.

"I was looking for something related to the Chevaliers, and Soren didn't want me to find it, so he brought me here."

"The Chevaliers?" Aria asked and I nodded quickly. "Parker is their leader."

I could have sworn right then and there that my soul left my body. Aria's brother was Parker, the leader of the Chevaliers, the organization that was the reason I'd been kidnapped.

And that's when it dawned on me why Soren wanted me to hide. It was because he didn't want Parker to see me.

I was convinced that there was no way she was going to help me now.

Aria's gaze shifted from me to the hallway Soren and Parker had walked down. I could tell she was torn between helping me and going against her brother.

I knew if I didn't come up with a way to convince her, Aria would turn away and leave me here to fend for myself or tell her brother what I'd told her.

I took a deep breath and tried to think of something that would make her help me.

"Aria, I'm begging you," I said, my voice shaking slightly. "Please help me. What I could find if I'm out of here could shake the world, and being here any longer than necessary is threatening my life."

I hadn't felt that way around Soren in a while, but if it was a way to get me out of here, I was willing to take it.

I took a deep breath before continuing. "You're my only hope right now."

My words hung in the air as Aria looked at me with an expression filled with uncertainty. After a few moments, she finally spoke up again.

"Okay," she said quietly but firmly. "I'll help you but know you are putting me in danger if this ever gets back to Parker. No one should be held against their will."

Both relief and surprise flooded through me. After being rejected before, I was shocked she'd agreed. I couldn't stop the tears that fell from my eyes. Part of me wanted to question it because I wasn't sure I believed it, but I didn't want her to change her mind.

"Thank you," I said just before I swallowed hard.

Aria gave me a small smile and nodded her head. "But we need to make sure that we have a way to communicate."

I watched as she dug into her pocket and produced a smartphone that looked to be only a couple of months old.

"Take my phone," she said. "I'll get another one, and I'll text this number. I hope that we can get you out of here quickly. Given how old this house is, there might be some public records that indicate whether there are other exits that will help make this even easier so that you don't have to... I don't know... walk out the front door."

I held the device in my hand as if it were a foreign object, something I'd never seen before. This was now my lifeline.

Just then, I heard a noise and thought it was Soren and Parker returning. Aria immediately tensed up while I froze, unsure of what to do. I should have expected that this would happen, but my body still didn't know how to act.

"You need to get out of here before they come back," she said.

I nodded quickly and moved toward the staircase that would take me upstairs. Each step that I took caused my heart to pound, and I could only pray that Soren didn't realize what I'd done.

When I finally reached the guest room, I stopped for a moment and glanced over my shoulder to look down the hall. Seeing nothing, I quickly slipped into the room and closed the door behind me.

30

SOREN

I gestured for Parker to enter my office and closed the door behind us. His showing up without contacting me first had me on edge, and I wasn't in the happiest mood about the intrusion. Plus, he'd interrupted the time I was trying to spend with Iris.

"You were messier this time around. Made it more difficult to clean up everything," Parker said as he took the chair across from my desk.

I sat down in my chair and stared right at him.

"I did what I wanted to do, and he deserved every second of what I put him through."

"I'm not judging how you killed him."

"It sounded as if you were," I replied.

For a moment, Parker just stared at me, probably wondering where this conversation was going. I was wondering the same thing.

"This wasn't the reason why I stopped by."

Finally, we were getting to the reason. "Aria needed to stop by her dorm to get something, so we were already in the area and I figured it wouldn't hurt to stop by for a couple of minutes before I took her home. We need to talk about Iris."

I folded my arms across my chest, trying to maintain my composure. "Okay."

"Is everything going fine with her still?"

"Yes. She's still tied up in the basement."

Parker nodded. "Excellent. I need you to deliver Iris to me by the end of the week."

It took everything in me to not launch myself over my desk and attack him. The fact that he came to this decision without mentioning a word to me pissed me off, not to mention what he was requesting me to do.

He must have noticed my silence because he continued on, "She needs to pay for what she's done. Trying to find out information about us and rock the foundation of our organization. We can't allow this to get out and we've killed people for less."

I kept my mouth shut, trying to think of a way to protect Iris. There was no way I was going to let him harm a hair on her head, the Chevaliers be damned.

I thought about all the ways I could keep her safe. Options like taking her far away from here, hiding her in a secret location, or maybe even faking her death were on the table. However, none of them seemed like they would work long term. If Parker found out I lied, he wouldn't stop until both Iris and I were dead and buried.

Shit.

Instead of focusing my attention on why Parker was doing what he was doing, I shifted tactics. I wanted to appear to be ambivalent to his next moves, to hopefully remove any suspicions that he might have in regard to me and my relationship with her.

"What are you planning on doing to her? And what do you need me to do?"

Parker leaned back in the chair and grinned. "Torture is definitely on the table."

My blood boiled. There was no way I was going to just roll over and let this happen. But I needed to keep my cards close to my chest. While I wanted to open up a negotiation with Parker to save her, letting him in on my feelings for her would be detrimental.

"Just keep her here until the end of the week and then drop her off with me as planned. I'll send you an address when I have it. I'll take everything from there."

I nodded my head slowly, trying to think of a way that I could keep Iris safe while still abiding by Parker's wishes.

"I understand," I said calmly, but I was anything but. In fact, the longer I stayed in Parker's presence, the more pissed I became.

We spoke about several other matters, but I barely paid attention. The only thing that I could think about was the impending deadline in regard to Iris and what I needed to do to stop it.

Finally, after what felt like an eternity, Parker got up from his chair.

"I'll be in touch," he said as he stood up, and I followed suit. We both walked to the door, and he opened it.

I followed him out of my office, continuing to try and maintain my composure. I led him to the foyer of my home, where he and his sister, Aria, were reunited. I glanced upstairs briefly before I turned back to the two people in front of me. Thankfully, it seemed as if Iris was nowhere in the area, keeping our secret between us. I walked them to the front door, and before I knew it, the two of them were getting in Parker's car and pulling off.

Once I confirmed they were gone, I closed the door and walked upstairs to Iris's room. I paused in front of her door in an effort to maintain my composure behind the mask I was wearing, but my adrenaline was threatening to boil over. Without another thought, I twisted the doorknob and opened Iris's door.

When I entered, Iris glanced up from her journal that she'd been busy writing in at the desk in the room. The expression on her face confused me because I couldn't figure out what it meant.

I scrutinized her face for much longer than I'd planned. "What's wrong, Iris? Are you keeping something from me?"

Shock registered first before she made her face expressionless. Her lips twitched, and a bitter smile that didn't quite reach her eyes appeared on her face. "No more than usual."

I didn't know what game she was playing, but I couldn't deny that the thought excited me. I stalked toward her before caging her between my arms. She shrank back for a moment before straightening her posture in order to not appear intimidated even as color rose in her cheeks. "Careful, petal. You don't want to piss me off."

"I don't appreciate being threatened."

"Then tell me what you're hiding."

This time, she had no tells that showed me that she was lying. "I'm not hiding a thing."

I lunged forward and grabbed her wrist, pulling her so that she ended up against me. Watching her blue eyes stare into mine was like staring into the ocean. If she was lying to me, she was hiding it well. From what I knew about her, she wasn't the best liar. Still, I couldn't ignore the doubt in my mind.

But there was something else between us, something that I couldn't deny. She'd had this pull on me that I didn't think I could describe, and it wasn't something I ever wanted to walk away from.

I stared down at her and kissed her hard. Her lips were soft against mine and reminded me of the differences in our bodies. Where she was soft, I was hard. Our differences brought us together in ways I never expected, and it only made me want to explore whatever this was that we were doing further.

I felt her body go lax in my arms as she melted into me. It was like the world around us had stopped spinning and all that mattered was us.

The kiss intensified as I deepened it, exploring her mouth with my tongue. Her hands tangled in my hair, and I pulled her closer to me. She gasped into my mouth, and I could feel every inch of her body pressing against mine, igniting something inside of me that released the primal desire that I had for her.

She was mine.

I let my hands wander down her body, exploring every inch of her. She shivered under my touch as my hands roamed over her skin, sending a thrill through me that made my heart race.

I could feel the heat radiating from her skin and it only made me want more of her. My primal need for her was too strong to ignore, and I fucking needed her now.

It pained me to pull away from her for even a moment, but it was time to step things up a notch.

"What's your safe word?"

Her mouth opened and then shut before she opened it to speak again. "Diary."

"Do you understand when you're supposed to use it?"

She nodded. "If I want to stop any activity or action that we are doing, all I have to do is use it and everything ends."

"Good job, petal. Keep that in mind as I tell you what's coming next. I want you to listen to me closely. Change into some of the lingerie pieces that I bought for you, and then come into my bedroom. You'll close the door and then get on your knees, where you'll wait for my next command."

31

IRIS

Excitement filled me as I replayed Soren's words over and over again in my mind. My mouth opened and closed and then opened once more before I was able to form the words to speak. "I understand."

Soren nodded and said, "You have ten minutes." With one final glance, he walked out of the room, leaving me alone to digest the things he'd said. It took me a second to process what was going on before I sprang into action.

I first walked to the closet and found all the lingerie he'd purchased for me. When I'd seen it initially, I thought it was oddly presumptuous of him to think that this would ever be used, but now I was grateful that he'd been prepared. All the pieces were beautiful.

I quickly freshened up in the bathroom. I made sure to brush my teeth and my hair, removing any of the snags that had been in it to help it lay loosely down my back. I carefully slipped into a dark-purple lingerie set that I found and adjusted it so that my tits and ass looked even more phenomenal in it. I grasped my breasts, enjoying the way the fabric felt in my hands, and when my eyes landed on my face once again, I realized that I didn't recognize myself.

What had the woman in the mirror turned into? I wasn't quite sure and the thought of not knowing who I was scared me. But right now, I was just wasting time.

With one final glance at myself, I knew I made the right decision. I turned on my heel and walked as fast as I could to Soren's bedroom. When I opened the door, there was no one there, leaving me in a state of confusion.

Soren wasn't there.

Although I thought it was strange, I still did as Soren said. I closed the door behind me and then got on my knees in the middle of the room. I waited for what felt like an eternity before I heard a noise coming from outside his bedroom door.

My breath caught in my throat as the door opened and Soren stepped into the room. I couldn't see his face because I was looking at the ground, but I could feel his stare. "Aren't you quite the good girl, petal?"

It felt as if all my senses were on fire. I didn't know what he was going to do, and the thought was both frightening and thrilling.

"Let's see how long you stay *good*."

I swallowed hard as I heard the creaking of the floorboards under his weight. Then I saw his shoes appear in my peripheral as he walked closer to me, one step at a time.

The only thing that I could hear between the two of us was the sound of him walking around me, inspecting every inch of me and my breathing, the harshness of which was grating to my ears.

His hand gently caressed the side of my face, and I found

myself instinctively leaning into his touch. I wasn't sure what had gotten into me, but I was willing to see where all of this would go.

Every second that passed when he didn't make a move made my nerves kick things up another notch. His hand drifted away as he walked around me before he left my field of vision. I heard the sound of his mattress dipping under his weight, or so I assumed.

"What was one of the first things I told you that you were going to do when I locked you in my basement?"

The question stumped me. I tried to bring up every memory of my time in captivity to figure out what he was talking about, but came up empty. "I don't remember."

"Try again. It was the reason why I handcuffed your ankle to the wall and not your wrist."

I licked my lips as I tried hard to think about it. When it came to me, it hit me like a semitruck. "You wanted me to crawl to you and beg you to let me go."

"Excellent. That's what you're going to do now. However, you'll be begging me to let you come. Crawl to me, Iris."

That hadn't been what I was expecting him to say, but then again, Soren didn't tend to act like everyone else.

And what was my response to his demand?

My body moved as if caught in a trance as I assumed the position necessary to crawl toward him. I lifted my head slightly and my eyes met his. His gaze was intense as he watched every move I made, and I only grew more excited.

I finally reached him and stopped at his feet. My eyes never left his as I waited for what he had in store for me next. He used his fingers to grab my chin and tilted my head up.

"Undo my pants and pull out my cock." His voice was commanding, but there was a touch of gentleness.

I took a deep breath before I got up on my knees and my hands made their way to his belt.

My fingers trembled as I undid his belt and unzipped his pants. I made sure to take my time because it was obvious how hard he was. I continued moving as gently as I could until I was holding his dick in my hands. My fingers wrapped around him, and I smiled when I heard his sharp intake of air.

He moaned softly in pleasure as I stroked him, and when I moved my hand faster, the sounds from his lips grew louder.

And that was before I took him in my mouth.

I shifted my body and allowed my tongue to run up and down his shaft. When I looked up to see the effect I was having on him, I couldn't help but smile as I watched him crumble in front of me.

When his hands got tangled in my hair, I knew it was time to up the ante. I opened my mouth to take him in. I could feel my pulse race when he mumbled several cuss words under his breath.

I moved my head back and forth slowly, bobbing as the sounds of what I was doing and his reaction to it filled the air around us. His hands tugged at my hair every time I increased the intensity of my movements.

I temporarily stopped my motions when I gagged on his cock, but it didn't ruin the mood at all. When I thought he might ask me if I was alright, I went back to the task at hand and his questioning gaze quickly disappeared.

"Petal. . ." his tone sounded as if he was issuing a warning to me, but he didn't elaborate. So I kept doing what I was doing. His words would also be my undoing because the more I sucked his cock, the wetter I became. I didn't know that pleasuring someone else would get me into this state, but I wasn't upset about it. At all.

I kept going, my mouth and hands working together in sync. When I let his cock drop from my lips, I took in several deep breaths as my gaze moved from his face to his dick. I bit my lip as I checked out the work I'd done. Soren took this as an opportunity to stand up, and I moved back to adjust for him.

"I'm going to fuck your face. If you have an issue with that, use your safe word."

All I did was nod my head, keeping my eyes on him as I took him back into my mouth.

His hips began to move as if the lower half of his body had a mind of its own. His breathing grew shallow, and his hands managed to find my head again. I could tell he was coming closer to the edge.

Through his groans and grunts, Soren managed to say, "If you don't want my cum dripping down your throat, then let go of my dick."

I took it as a challenge. I sucked him harder.

He started to thrust faster, his breathing becoming more erratic with each passing second. His hands tightened in my hair as he let out a strangled moan. I could feel his cock swell in my mouth, and I knew he was close.

When I felt his body tense up, I knew the game was over. I moved my head away and sat back slightly with my mouth wide open.

He let out a deep growl just before I felt his cum cascading down my throat.

When he was done, I watched as he walked into another

room and came back out with his pants zipped up again and with a towel. He gently wiped my face, making sure to take his time cleaning me up.

Once he'd finished, he tossed the towel to the side, turned back to me, and gave me a wicked smirk.

"Don't think you're getting off too easy, petal, just because you let me fuck your face. This is just getting started."

32

IRIS

Soren's gaze on me was so intense that I wasn't sure how to react. I couldn't help but stare back at him as I waited for his next directive. I didn't have to wait long because he moved closer, his eyes never leaving my face as he reached out and touched my cheek tenderly with his finger, replacing where the towel had touched me only moments ago.

He then moved his hand and held it out to me. Once I placed my hand in his, he helped me off the floor, and I quickly stretched my legs, given the position I had been in for quite some time. After I finished adjusting myself, he leaned closer to me, and naturally, my eyes drifted shut. He wasted no time, and before I could take my next breath, I felt his lips land on mine in a passionate kiss.

As we explored each other's mouths, I wondered if he tasted his cum on my lips. It made me grow warmer at the thought, but it was obvious that he didn't give a fuck because our kiss deepened. His hands moved to my waist, and he used it as an opportunity to turn us around before he pushed me onto the bed.

He stared at me for a moment before he said, "You sucking on my cock is the sexiest thing I've ever seen. Plus, you looked so beautiful with my come dripping down your mouth."

It looked as if I wasn't the only one thinking about me sucking him off when we were kissing.

"Move up the bed until your head is lying on the pillows."

I hesitated for a moment before I said, "No."

"Excuse me?"

I raised an eyebrow at him before I replied. "I said no."

Soren's eyes narrowed at me. "You've been such a good girl, and now you're going to throw it all away?"

I shrugged. "I know this is going to lead to me having to beg you to make me come and I refuse to do so."

"But you've already crawled to me, so what's the point in denying me the rest of my prophecy?"

"I'm not making this easy for you."

"None of this has been easy, petal."

I could sense the double meaning in his words, but I still looked up at him defiantly. It would be very easy to do what he wanted me to do, but the thrill of defying him was enough to make me combust.

Soren cleared his throat. "If you're going to act like a brat, then I'll treat you like one."

It was as if something inside of him snapped because before I could blink, he was climbing on top of me and dragging my lips into another punishing kiss.

His hands moved down my body and his fingers tugged at the fabric of my lacy, dark-purple bra. He, painstakingly slowly, I might add, pushed down the straps and then the cups of the bra without undoing it.

He played with my nipples, rolling one between his fingers before he moved to the next breast. Soren made sure to give each breast equal attention by sucking and licking each one until I was trembling beneath him as I tried to anticipate what he was going to do next.

His fingers trailed down my stomach while he played with my tits, causing my breath to catch in my throat. I knew that he was going to where I wanted him most. He reached the hem of my panties and gently ran a finger along it, leaving featherlight touches that made goose bumps appear on my skin.

"Please," I mumbled under my breath, but it was enough to garner Soren's attention.

"What was that?"

"Nothing," I said quickly. "I didn't mean to distract you." My words came out breathier than anticipated and I felt a blush creeping up on my cheeks.

Soren chuckled and slipped his fingers underneath the fabric of my underwear. He didn't even bother taking them off, instead pushing them aside so that he could access my pussy.

He used his fingers to tease me, and my body lost all sense of decorum the more he kept me on edge. He knew I wanted him to slip his finger inside of me, but he continued to circle around my clit.

I arched my body in an effort to get closer to him, to convince him to give me what I wanted, what I needed. When he finally did, I groaned loudly as his finger started to move inside of me. He added another finger and that only increased the pleasure. He started to move faster, pushing deeper inside of me until I was trembling.

The moans were fleeing my mouth at such a rapid pace that it almost sounded like a song. His fingers moved quicker and at an angle that hit all the right spots inside of me.

Before I could blink, he shifted his body so that he was in a better position, and he was kneeling between my legs. His thumb found its way to my clit as he continued to stroke deep within me. The pressure inside of me was so close to erupting that I was pretty sure I was going to combust from the inside out. I was so close to coming that it took all my strength not to scream out his name as he pleasured me like this.

"I-I'm going—"

The words were there, but I couldn't release them. That could have also been because Soren almost came to a halt, causing the trip I'd been on to stop in its tracks.

He looked up at me and I wanted to smack the smile off his face.

"You need to say the words, petal. I won't let you come otherwise." His words were commanding, and if I hadn't been soaked before, I was now.

I took in a sharp breath and said, "P-please, Soren. Let me come. And I want it to be all over your mouth."

Shock registered on his face for a split second before the smirk returned. "Well, that was easy." I guess he'd expected me to put up more of a fight due to my bratty attitude earlier, but it was the furthest thing from my mind. I needed this orgasm like I needed my next breath, and I was determined to get it by any means necessary.

He moved his head until it was right at my pussy and licked along my slit until he reached my clit.

"Fucking mine," I heard him mumble before he did the same motion one more time and wrapped his lips around my clit, which was just what I needed to get me to the finish line.

Everything in my body went rigid as I screamed out in bliss. He didn't stop until every last drop had been wrung from my body. It was only then that he finally slowed down and withdrew his hand and mouth from between my legs.

I took a few seconds to catch my breath as Soren stared me down. His gaze drifted up and down my body as he undressed, but the blank expression on his face meant I had no idea what the hell he was thinking.

But then everything changed in the blink of an eye. He flipped me over and it took my brain a second to process what was happening.

"Get to your hands and knees, petal, so that I can fuck you properly."

He didn't need to say the words twice.

As soon as I'd assumed the position, he slammed his cock into me. My eyes widened in surprise as he filled me to the brink. I couldn't control the shudder that passed through my body.

"Oh my—"

"But he's not here, baby."

He said it so nonchalantly that I questioned whether I'd heard him at all. I clenched the sheets between my fingers as I cried out, happy that things had gotten to this point. I knew I was guaranteed at least another orgasm, maybe more, because it was him and how sensitive I still was.

My body moved with his, creating a rhythm that only we knew, and it was perfect. He grabbed my hips and used them as an anchor before slamming back into me again.

My brain was scrambled. Each thrust into my body increased the fire until the intensity became too much to bear. I groaned loudly as another round of orgasmic bliss sailed through me.

But that didn't stop him. "One fucking more," he said, and it almost sounded like a growl.

And I was determined to give it to him.

How he had enough energy to pick up the pace again, I'd never know. I used my body to match his rhythm until I couldn't do it anymore. Then I gave him what he wanted. I exploded.

I would have fallen forward onto my face if Soren wasn't holding my waist as he pounded into me. When I heard a guttural groan leave his lips over the rushing of blood in my ears, he, too, went over the edge before collapsing on top of me.

Soren made sure not to completely crush me as we both tried to catch our breath and process what just occurred.

"Fuck," Soren said as he ran a hand down my spine, making me shiver in response. He removed himself from me, and I immediately felt a sense of loss. I watched through tired eyes as he walked into his bathroom and returned with a washcloth that appeared to be wet and a dry towel.

He kneeled down between my legs and started to clean me off slowly and delicately. He took his time as he cleaned up all the evidence from our fucking before drying me off with the towel. Then he cleaned himself up.

Once he was done, he undid the lingerie I had on, leaving me as naked as him before he pulled me close to him so that I was resting against his chest. For a few minutes, we just stayed there while our bodies tried to recover from the intensity of what had just happened.

As I listened to the beating of his heart, I couldn't help but think about how happy I'd been in his arms. However, in the back of my mind, I was waiting for the other shoe to drop.

33

IRIS

A couple of hours later, I stepped out of the shower, but I couldn't convince myself to finish drying off and move on with my day. I tightened the towel wrapped around me and rolled my eyes at myself for lingering in the bathroom. I tapped my fingers along the cool marble countertop, fighting the urge to open the drawer.

That drawer contained Aria's phone, and I'd been checking it multiple times a day since she'd given it to me to see if there was an update on how we could get me out of here, but there never was. Now, it felt as if I was only setting myself up for disappointment.

The thought of opening the drawer filled me with a mix of dread and excitement. On one hand, I was scared of what I would find when I looked at the phone—or rather, what I wouldn't find. But on the other hand, it felt like maybe this time something would be different.

I let out a sigh as I weighed my options. The desire to look was growing stronger by the second, but at the same time, I knew it would only lead to disappointment and frustration if there wasn't a new message there.

But if I checked it, ripping the Band-Aid off, then I could move along with my day instead of thinking about it.

That was a lie. The only time I wasn't thinking about Aria contacting me was when Soren was fucking me.

This wasn't one of those times, and it was why the urge to look was too strong.

Over the last few days, I told myself I'd made the right decision in telling Aria about what had happened. But deep down, I was worried she might tell her brother, whom I had no doubt she had more allegiance to than she did to me.

I took a deep breath and finally made the decision to check Aria's phone. I pulled it out of the drawer, feeling my heart race as I turned it on and unlocked it. I'd been doing my damnedest to save the battery as much as I could because I didn't have a charger for it. I scanned the notifications, but there was nothing new. No messages from her, but there were a few from other people I didn't know.

I sighed and put the phone down, disappointment washing over me like a wave. I was a fool for getting my hopes up again. As I was about to turn the phone off and put it back in its hiding space, something made me look at the screen a second time and I saw it.

A new text notification appeared on the screen from an unknown number.

I was shaking so hard I needed to put the phone down so I didn't drop it and potentially bring more attention to myself from someone in this house. I typed in her passcode and read the message on the screen.

My heart jumped into my throat as I reread what I'd just seen because I didn't believe it to be true. I glanced over my shoulder, half expecting Soren to walk into the room. But I was alone. I hesitated for a moment as I thought about what had been evolving between Soren and me. With a deep breath, I quickly typed back a response.

I double-checked that the bathroom door was locked and waited for Aria to type back to me.

I put Aria's phone away for now, making sure to turn it off and hide it again in case Soren or Franklin did come in here looking around. I grabbed my toothbrush and let it run under the faucet. After I put toothpaste on it, my hand shook as I brought it to my mouth. My mind twisted and turned as I tried to come to terms with what I was doing and how it was going to change everything. I didn't know what waited for me on the other side of this because this could be choosing life or death for me and Gran, not to mention what Soren would do when he found out.

Spitting into the sink, I rinsed my mouth and splashed cold water on my face. When I looked up, my reflection stared back at me, and my thoughts weren't any clearer.

With a sigh, I ran a hand through my hair and unlocked the bathroom door, but I froze midstep.

Soren was standing there, just outside the bathroom. To say I was shocked would be an understatement.

He raised an eyebrow, an amused smile tugging at the corners of his lips. "You seem surprised to see me."

I swallowed, struggling to find my voice. "I. . . wasn't expecting you."

"I just wanted to check in on you."

The thought was sweet, but I didn't know if he'd question why I'd had the door closed. "I was just, uh, brushing my teeth." I pointed to the toothbrush on the counter as proof. "I was getting ready for bed."

"I didn't think you. . ." His voice trailed off and I began to wonder if I overdid it.

Soren stepped aside so I could walk past him, letting me out of the bathroom.

"I want you in my bed tonight," he said.

That made me do another double take. I hadn't slept in his room the entire time I'd been here, but now he wanted me to on the evening I was planning my big escape. "Why?"

"What do you mean why?"

I adjusted my stance in an effort to not appear nervous or show that I was getting annoyed with his questioning. I needed to remain neutral if I wanted to keep my little secret to myself.

"Because you've never wanted me with you in it before. Outside of. . . you know."

"What is it, Iris? I want you to say the entire sentence."

"Outside of when we fucked."

"Good girl." Soren's face softened slightly, and he stepped closer to me. He brushed a strand of hair away from my face, his fingertips gently grazing my cheek. "That changes tonight."

"Why?" I asked again, trying to think of an excuse about why we couldn't do it. Being alone in my own room would be required if I was escaping tonight, and this was throwing a wrench in my plans.

He ran his fingers through his hair and sighed before speaking again. "Because that's where you belong. In my arms," he said finally.

"But I was planning to sleep in here tonight."

He tilted his head slightly, studying my face. "You don't trust me," he noted, more as a statement than a question.

That was an ironic statement, given everything I'd been through. "It's not that. I was just hoping for more time to process everything. The past few days have been a huge shift in... whatever this is, after all."

Soren raised an eyebrow at me. "Is that why you really want to be alone tonight?"

Fuck. Did he suspect something, or was this his way of trying to keep the conversation going?

"Seriously. It's just that I wanted time to think about everything."

"You can think about it in my bed."

Soren wasn't relenting and I wasn't sure what to do about it. I didn't want this to continue going on and have him get even more suspicious.

"Fine. I'll sleep in your bed tonight."

"Excellent and I'll have Franklin move your things into my room tomorrow."

"Sounds. . . great." A small smile appeared on my face, but I was anything but happy.

Now things were way more complicated, and I had to find a way to sneak out of his bedroom tonight.

34

IRIS

The soft, rhythmic sound of Soren's breathing was all I could hear as I lay in his arms. It was a stark contrast to the frantic beating of my own heart. It was strange seeing him so at peace.

I lifted my head from his chest and my gaze landed on the digital clock on his nightstand. The red numbers displayed 2:30 a.m. I needed to be out of here by 3:15 a.m., according to Aria's last text. Yet I still hadn't figured out a way of getting out of here without waking him.

Just as I was building up the courage to slide out of bed, the shrill ring of a phone sliced through the room's quietness. My body went rigid, and panic was the only emotion I felt. But as Soren's hand shot out to grab the phone, I pretended to be half-asleep, filled with grogginess. I turned to him and forced a yawn that almost sounded real.

He glanced at me before trying to read the phone's screen. He sighed and said, "I have to take this."

I made a sleepy murmur, acting the part of someone who was woken up suddenly.

Soren answered the call. "Hello?" His voice, though low, sounded very irritated because he'd been disturbed at this hour.

I forced my breathing to remain even while straining to catch snippets of the conversation.

"Yes? Now? Understood." There was a pause, and he sighed. "I'll be there."

Hanging up, he turned to face me, the lines of his face hardened with resolve. "I have an assignment I need to complete. Hopefully this is the last one I have to do for a while. I'll be back soon," he whispered, pressing a gentle kiss to my forehead.

"Why do you have to go? Can someone else do it?" I had to say I was impressed with my acting skills because, while I did want him to leave to make this easy on me, I was doing a pretty good job of pretending I didn't want him to.

Or maybe some part of me didn't want him to go.

"It's something only I can do."

I nodded slowly. "Okay. Be safe." I could lie and say that I was pretending to be concerned, but I was genuinely worried about him. I wasn't sure when that feeling had come to be, but here it was.

"Always," he replied.

I watched through barely parted eyelids as he swiftly dressed and left the room.

The door clicked shut, and I let out a deep breath. Things were going to be very different when he returned.

Silence surrounded me as I waited, choosing to watch the clock to make sure that Soren was actually gone and not coming back for a little while. When I heard the house creak from old age or settling, it did make me nervous because each sound seemed more magnified than normal.

When the clock struck 2:50 a.m., I whipped the covers off my body and left Soren's bedroom. I did my best not to make a sound as I walked down the hallway, grateful that the holiday lights were still up, giving me more light than I normally would have had.

I dashed into the guest bedroom and ran into the bathroom, where I quickly opened the drawer that held Aria's phone. Sure enough, there was a new message from her.

> Unknown Number: Everything's a go. Follow the path I sent you, and you'll get out of that mansion without a hitch. You'll need to walk a bit, but I'm parked right between Soren's place and the closest neighbor's house. We can do this.

My lip trembled slightly as I was overcome with emotion about what was happening. There was no way I was going to be able to repay her for this. Ever.

Once again, I found myself dressing in dark clothes and layers to help protect me against the cold. It was also to make it harder for anyone to see me in case Soren had increased his level of security around the place due to when I tried to escape the first time. I eyed my black gown that I'd tossed on the floor of the closet after I'd been shown this room and thought about how far I'd come since Soren had kidnapped me.

But I was determined to look forward and not back. I had some things I needed to accomplish, and I needed to do so.

I made sure to grab the phone and place it in the pocket of my hoodie for safekeeping. I also had my wallet and credit cards that Soren had given me back, as well. Once I was ready to go, I cautiously opened the bedroom door and slipped out into the hallway.

Instead of heading toward the main staircase, I walked back toward Soren's room, but before getting to his doorway, I opened a door that was just to the left. It was pitch black, so I took the phone out and used it as a flashlight to guide me down the stairs. According to Aria's text, this was the back stairway that would lead me to what would essentially be another part of the basement, hopefully without being seen.

With every step I took, the wood creaked under my feet, making me cringe at the sound. I could only hope that, with how late it was, no one in the house could hear me. I hoped that I wasn't making the wrong move.

Once I'd reached the base of the stairs, I found myself in an unfamiliar hallway. Large wooden doors lined one side, but I wasn't sure where it led. I double-checked Aria's text messages and I turned to my right, where I could make out the faint outline of a larger door. Aria told me to go through this door, so I did.

I used my phone to shine light onto the new area and found myself in a wine cellar. Rows upon rows of wooden racks filled with bottles of wine stretched out before me. Soren had never mentioned he had one, and I wondered if that was purposefully left out to avoid having me ask to explore it. After all, if Aria was right, I might have discovered how to get out of here.

Using my makeshift flashlight, I tried to find another door to go through to get out of here. I walked around the room until I found another wooden door with rust on it. Aria's message told me to walk down the long hallway on the other side, and within a couple of minutes, I should be able to make my way outside. It was time to see if she was right.

I breathed a sigh of relief when the door opened without issue, and I stepped inside. It was very clear that this hallway wasn't nearly as well kept as the rest of Soren's mansion because it was filled with spiderwebs and who knows what else. But if this was the way that I was going to get to freedom, then so be it.

As I walked through the corridor, I tried not to think of what could be hanging around here. I turned when I heard the sound of liquid dripping down from a leak, but I refused to investigate. I jogged the last few steps and blew out a stream of air when I'd made it to the other side of the hallway.

I opened another door and climbed a few more stairs that led to a hatch. I used the phone to find the lock and I pushed once and then twice before the doors flew open and a rush of cool air ran across my face.

I was outside, and from the looks of it, I was all alone.

Holy shit. I'd done it.

I was free.

I climbed out and closed the doors behind me, not worried if the sons of bitches flew open after I was gone.

A gust of wind blew past my face as I turned around and saw just how far Soren's home was from where I was currently standing. I was still apparently on his property, but I was a decent distance away from his house now. However, I needed to keep going.

I checked Aria's phone once more before I started jogging in the direction I thought she wanted me to go. I could see that I was coming up on a major road, and that only encour-aged me to push myself harder.

I didn't know how long I'd been traveling, but I did know that I was moving farther away from Soren's mansion, and it wasn't until I saw a dark sedan sitting in the distance that I allowed myself to fully embrace the idea that I was getting out of here.

The moment our eyes met through the windshield, I felt a complex mixture of emotions well up inside me. Relief washed over me like a huge wave, crashing against the other emotions in my body.

Aria leaned across the console to throw the door open, and I got into the passenger seat of her car. I swear I didn't breathe until Aria turned the car on and pulled away from her parking spot. My chest tightened as I glanced out the window, watching as Soren's mansion faded into the background.

It took me a moment to gather my bearings so that I was finally able to speak. "Thank you... for everything," I said quietly, turning to face her.

"You're welcome. But you have a lot of explaining to do, Iris," she replied, her eyes flickering over to meet mine for a brief moment before returning to the road ahead.

35

IRIS

The car ride quickly devolved into an awkward moment as silence passed between Aria and me. She continued driving to who knew where while my leg bobbed up and down because I was nervous as hell.

"Where are we going? I assume not back to Westwick's campus. Then we can talk about all of this." She gestured to me, and I sighed.

I was thankful that Aria chose to speak instead of waiting for me because we would probably still be sitting here in silence.

"Nope. There's nothing for me there right now."

A part of me wanted to tell her to take me to Gran's, so I could see and explain everything to her, but that wasn't possible or safe. Right now, time was precious, and we only had a limited window to do what we needed to do.

That is, if Aria was willing to do so.

"I want to go to the Chevalier Headquarters in New York City," I said, looking in her direction.

"Is something wrong with you? You can't just demand to

go there. Well, you could, but you can't just waltz up there and demand entry!"

This was along the lines of what I'd expected her reaction to be, so I wasn't surprised.

"I know, which is why I'll need you to help me with that too. I know I'm asking a lot of you, but—"

"You know, yet you continue to do so?" Aria asked, cutting me off. The anger in her voice was beginning to rise, and I didn't blame her. "Also, how do you know I can get in there?"

I wasn't sure the best way to try to explain myself to Aria, so I just blurted out the first thing I had in mind. "There's a lot that you don't know."

"Well then, you better get to talking."

"Where do I begin..." I trailed off, mostly talking to myself. Before Aria could form a response, I said, "I think my ancestor was involved in the founding of the Chevaliers."

Aria's eyes cut over to me before she turned back to the road. "You can't be serious."

"She was cut out of getting recognition, and I'm determined to prove that. But the Chevaliers don't want this information getting out."

"My brother is trying to keep this information secret?"

"Yes, but it's not just your brother. All the members of the Chevaliers are trying to keep this information a secret, including Soren. It was why he kidnapped me. I don't know why they are doing so, but they are. And I am not sure what they would eventually have done to me."

Aria sighed and shook her head in disbelief. "If I were to help you, what would you want to do?"

I hoped this was a good sign and meant that she was considering my plan. I took a deep breath before I spoke again. "We need to get into the Chevalier Headquarters and find out more information about Eddison Payne and some of the letters he wrote to Margaret Turner. We can use that to prove she was involved in the founding of the Chevaliers, and then we can make sure her name is recognized. As it should be."

"I'm going to get into so much trouble with this. Parker isn't going to speak to me again."

"Just say I held you at gunpoint and you're doing all of this because I made you do it."

Aria groaned and rolled her eyes. "You won't have to do that, but we'll need a plan. And we need one fast because we have to do this tonight."

"First of all, can you get us into the Chevalier Headquarters? That would change things significantly."

Aria thought for a moment. "I can't get us directly in there, but there might be a way around it. I can get into Parker's office after hours, and it's in the same building."

"That would be amazing. I assume what I'm looking for would be in some sort of archives or, at this point, it could also be stored digitally too."

Aria tapped her fingers on the steering wheel before she responded. "There's a chance that if the letters were put into a digital format, Parker has access to them from his computer. It would make sense, being that they are in the same building, for him to be able to connect to whatever he needs at any given time."

That was a good point. So if our search of the Chevalier Headquarters came up empty, or we weren't able to get in at all, then that could be our next step.

"Maybe this will work after all," I murmured more to

myself than Aria.

"I can't believe I'm doing this," Aria said before she glanced at me. "You need to explain everything to me."

I thought about what she said for a moment, debating what I was going to say next. "I will once you answer a few of my questions."

"I hardly think you're in a position to negotiate, Iris."

I raised an eyebrow at her. "Even if I think that you know more about this situation than you're letting on?"

Aria's grip on the steering wheel tightened, but she said nothing. Every so often, her eyes shifted to the rearview mirror, not checking for cars but seemingly lost in thought. There was no doubt in my mind that I'd hit a nerve.

"Just spill it," she finally said.

"Was our meeting at the beginning of the school year a setup?"

"No," she said confidently. I didn't have a reason to believe that she was lying.

"Did you start hanging out with me because I was hunting down information about Eddison Payne?"

"Sort of."

Her response caused me to look at her so fast I should have gotten a case of whiplash. "So you did know about what I was doing?"

"Not fully. Parker asked me to look out for you and to see if I could piece together what you were up to. This was after we'd already met, but it was the reason why I asked to get lunch with you."

"So if our friendship is your brother's doing, why did you help me tonight?"

Aria spared a glance at me. "Because no one should be

kidnapped and imprisoned, and I felt a little guilty about the role I played in this. For that, I do apologize, Iris."

I nodded because I accepted her apology and didn't plan on holding a grudge. "If your brother is one of the leaders of the Chevaliers, why couldn't you score an invite to the party?"

Aria sighed. "I found out last minute that Parker made sure I didn't get an invite. It's also probably part of the reason I'm doing this too. I was pissed I didn't get an opportunity to go, so on that account, he can fuck all the way off."

Angry energy jumped off her, but I didn't blame her. I couldn't help but wonder if she wasn't invited because Parker was trying to keep the number of potential witnesses who knew me down the night I was kidnapped.

"And you're okay with pissing him off again by helping me?"

"Wholeheartedly. He's done his share of pissing me off, so I'm ready to give him the same treatment. Plus, this isn't the only reason I'm doing this."

"What's the other reason?"

"Oddly enough, it's a similar reason to yours. It's bullshit that women can't join the organization and I did the things that Parker wanted me to do when it came to you in hopes that it would lead to a change. But it didn't."

I leaned back in my seat as I thought about what Aria said. Maybe I did make the right decision by letting her in on some of the things I knew, with plans for us to have a more in-depth conversation while she was driving me to New York.

This was probably going to be one of the longest drives of my life. However, I knew it was going to be therapeutic to finally tell someone all the things I'd been holding in for so long.

36

ARIA

Although I was sitting inside my car, my body had gone as cold as if I was standing in a frozen tundra as I thought about what I'd done. Saving Iris was going to directly affect my relationship with my brother Parker.

My reasons for doing it weren't just to help her, although I couldn't bear to see someone being held against their will. Becoming a member of the Chevaliers has been a goal of mine for years, and I was over being told no. The memories that I had came flooding back, some of the conversations that I heard that weren't meant for me. Times when I'd overheard bits and pieces, not enough to understand what was going on, but enough to know that there was something serious happening.

The radio played softly in the background, but I barely registered the upbeat tunes. I was so caught up in my own thoughts that nothing else could get through. All I could think of was the look that would be on Parker's face when he found out what I'd done.

I glanced over at Iris. She looked to be deep in thought too, probably wondering what would come next. We were in this together now, a hot mess of a team. But I couldn't help but wonder if I'd just traded my family's loyalty for a friend's trust.

A sigh escaped my lips, and I loosened my grip on the steering wheel briefly to flex my hands. My gaze landed on New York City's skyline, which stood tall against the night sky. More questions about why I was doing this floated to the surface. Next to me, Iris shifted in her seat, bringing me back to reality. "We're almost there," she said, stating the obvious.

I let out a shaky breath. "I know. And I'm not sure I'm ready for it all."

"I'm not either, if I'm being honest."

I carefully navigated my way through the streets of Manhattan, even though it was late enough that there was much less traffic on the road. It wasn't long before I recognized the streets leading up to where Parker's office and the Chevalier Headquarters were located.

Iris shifted her body as I slowed down in front of a building. "That's the place, huh?"

I nodded, running a hand through my curly hair. "Yeah, that's it. We've made it."

"Are you ready?" Iris's question was a loaded one.

"Nope, and yet here I am."

"Your brother is going to be so pissed," Iris warned, her blue eyes searching mine for any sign of hesitation. She was right of course. Parker would see this as a betrayal against him. But there was something about Iris's story that drew me in, and I couldn't shake it.

"There's nothing I can do about it now," I said, finally meeting Iris's gaze.

Nerves filled my body as I found a place to park my car on a side street. We both got out and I shivered in the cold night air. Iris looked up at the towering skyscraper before she glanced at me. "Hopefully this is it."

I looked at her, admiring her bravery. "I hope so too." I wasn't prepared to face whatever consequences that would be coming my way, but I had no choice now. I was in too deep and wanted to see this to the end.

Together, we made our way to the back of the building, and I couldn't help but wonder if we were truly prepared for what lay ahead.

"Stay close," I whispered to Iris. "There shouldn't be anyone to question us, but just in case, it wouldn't hurt."

We slipped into the building without seeing anyone and made our way to Parker's office.

We eventually reached his office door, which was closed but not locked. We entered the room, and nothing looked different from the last time I'd been here, but I watched as Iris took it all in.

"I think the first place we should check would be those cabinets over there and maybe his computer? If we can't find anything there, we should find a way to get downstairs into the Chevalier Headquarters."

I couldn't believe I was sitting here spitballing a plan that would put me in direct opposition to my brother. Something was seriously wrong with me.

Iris began searching through the cabinets while I managed to log on to Parker's computer, using the random password generator he'd given me access to when I was desperate to get on the internet for a school project in high school. We were looking for anything that might give us a clue as to where Eddison Payne's documents and letters might be.

After a few minutes, I sat back in Parker's chair and looked at Iris. "I think what we're looking for must be downstairs. I'm not finding anything to indicate that Parker has any of Eddison's stuff up here."

Iris turned to me and asked, "Have you found anything about Margaret Turner?"

I shook my head. "Nothing so far."

We both sighed heavily, knowing that the only way to get answers was to make our way to the Chevalier Headquarters and attempt to gain entry.

I made sure we left everything the way it was before I said, "I'm pretty sure the way down to the headquarters from in here is somewhere around here..."

My voice trailed off as I tried to look around his desk, looking for something, anything that would indicate a way to get downstairs. It was then that I had a memory about a book falling on a panel on Parker's desk and triggering the bookcase to move to reveal another door. That door opened into a short hallway, and I was pretty sure that was where the elevator was.

But the question was, where did the book fall? I did my best to not mess up Parker's desk while moving papers around as Iris walked up to stand next to me.

"What are you doing?" she asked.

"Finding a way for us to get downstairs," I said without looking in her direction. I didn't need the distraction because I was trying to search without disturbing anything. That was until I saw a little latch on the surface of his desk, and I gave it a small nod because I'd found what I was looking for. I pulled on the latch and pressed the small button inside of it.

Soon, we were staring at a private elevator with a single call button.

Iris's eyes widened. "Is this how we're getting down there?"

I nodded as guilt weighed heavily on me because we were only digging a deeper hole with every step we took. Pressing the call button, the elevator doors slid open silently. We stepped inside. As the doors closed, I noticed that instead of buttons next to floor numbers, the control panel had a single unmarked button.

Without a second thought, I pressed it. The elevator began its descent, its movement so fluid that it felt like we were floating on a cloud. It didn't take long, thankfully. Iris and I only had a couple of moments to share a glance with one another before the elevator came to a gentle stop.

While it felt as if we were going into a supervillain's lair as we stepped out of the elevator, it looked anything but. It was more old-fashioned in a way, reminding me of Westwick's campus more than some high-tech business center.

"I'm not sure where we should go, but I also don't want to split up either," I said as I walked out of the elevator with Iris trailing behind me.

"I don't want to either, but we need to move fast."

"Without a doubt," I said.

Just as I was about to turn and walk to my left, a sudden noise caused us both to freeze. It was the soft sound of a shoe squeaking against the polished marble floor. Iris and I exchanged panicked glances. We weren't alone.

37

LANDON

I fought a yawn that begged me to let it loose as I tried to get comfortable in my car. It was way too damn early to be awake, yet here I was, on alert as I waited for my target to make her next move.

Aria had left her house in the dead of night and parked her car near Soren Grant's home. To say that was strange was an understatement.

What the hell was she doing here?

I had a small inkling about why she might be here, but I wanted to be absolutely sure that was what was occurring. Then I saw a figure dressed all in black hop into Aria's car, and they took off down the street.

This was the last thing I'd expected her to do, and her brother was going to be pissed.

I pulled away from the side of the road, making sure to keep enough distance between me and Aria so she wouldn't suspect anything. I used my dashboard to call Parker. He was going to be pissed about me calling him this late at night, but he told me to call him at any time, so here we are.

Once I found Parker's number, I clicked send and the phone rang and rang. This more than likely meant Parker was either asleep or in the middle of fucking someone, but I was just doing my job.

Finally, I heard someone answer the phone, but it took another couple of seconds before a groggy voice broke through the silence. "Do you know what time it is?"

"I do. But you told me to call whenever I had an important update on Aria."

"I suspect you do then?"

"I do. She's just helped Iris escape Soren's home."

Silence followed my comment, and for a second, I wondered if he'd fallen back to sleep.

"She. Did. What?"

"Yep. You heard me correctly."

"There's no way she would have done that. Aria knows better."

I cleared my throat. "I swear I saw it with my own two eyes. Based on where we are headed now, I think they might be driving to the city."

There was another pause, filled only with Parker's heavy breathing. I hoped he wasn't having a heart attack because that would be shitty on so many different levels. "Where are they now? Are you following them?"

"Yes," I said as I cleared my throat. "Keeping a safe distance. They haven't noticed me."

"Keep it that way," Parker ordered. "Stay on them. Update me with their every move. Do not let them get away."

"I don't plan on it."

Parker hung up on me, and I put all my attention back on driving.

I kept a steady distance from Aria's car, making sure that I remained just out of her rearview mirror so she wouldn't get suspicious. I wished there were more cars on the road because it would be easier to blend in, but there was nothing I could do about that.

A text message appeared on my console, and I saw that it was from Parker.

Parker: Are there any changes?

I used voice to text to send a message back.

Me: Still on the same route, heading closer to the city.

Parker: I'm also in the city, so I can meet you wherever as soon as possible.

That was good to know.

Before I could respond, Parker sent another text message.

Parker: Soren is also aware. He is already near NYC because of another assignment.

Aria's car maneuvered effortlessly along the road and then through the city streets. The closer we got, the more I was convinced that I knew exactly where she was going. I kept my distance, blending in with other vehicles while ensuring I never lost sight of her.

Aria turned down the street I thought she would and slowed down in front of a building. I wondered if she was debating her choices and deciding whether she was going to follow through with whatever her plan was.

But then I saw her park the car.

I watched from the shadows of my vehicle as Aria and Iris walked into the building that held Parker's office and the Chevalier Headquarters. My job wasn't to follow them into the building because it would be too easy for me to be seen.

While I waited, I thought about this assignment. I'd been following Aria for a while.

Parker had called me into his office before a meeting with some of the top leaders in the Chevaliers and explained to me what my next assignment would be.

"Landon," he'd begun, looking out of the tall windows of his office, "I need you to watch Aria and report back to me what you find. Make sure you do it discreetly." It had been the last thing I'd thought he'd ask me to do after I finished the job following Nash and Bianca Henson. Watching your boss's sister wasn't just any assignment, especially when that boss was Parker, and he was in charge of one of the most powerful organizations in the world.

It wasn't easy to track Aria. She moved unpredictably, which made sense given that she was a college student, but it had been easier now she was on winter break. Aria barely left her parents' home unless she was with them or Parker.

Until tonight.

I hadn't been sure what she was doing tonight until the last minute. The only red flag was that she'd recently bought a new cell phone, and I now assumed that was how she'd planned this with Iris. But that hadn't been something I was aware of until tonight.

Sometimes, I wondered if she knew I was there, tailing her, but she never acknowledged it. That was how I liked to keep it.

I rolled down my window, turned off the engine and allowed the city's sounds to be the soundtrack to this scene that would be unfolding in front of me. Once Parker and Soren arrived, the games would begin.

38

SOREN

I fought the urge to push the gas pedal down harder because getting stopped by the police was the last thing on my mind. The city lights swirled around me as I drove through the night, but I was barely paying attention. The only thing that mattered to me was getting to the Chevalier Headquarters as soon as possible.

Parker's call had pissed me off on a multitude of levels. As he described what Iris and Aria had done, I couldn't help but see red as Iris's betrayal became more apparent. She slipped through my fingers despite my warnings and threats. I had Franklin double-checking how she'd done it, and although I was angry, I couldn't deny being impressed by her ability to do so. However, her desire to disobey me at every turn had put her in more danger than she realized because now she'd further pissed off the head of the Chevaliers.

But above all else, I'd let my guard down. I'd thought we'd moved past everything that had happened and were in a better place, but then she pulled this damn stunt.

I'd already told her that no matter where she ran, I would

be right there, ready to snatch her back in an instant. So, if I was being honest, it was almost funny that she even tried.

And then they decided to go to the Chevalier Headquarters in New York City, which was strange unless they thought they could get in and out without someone catching them.

No matter what the reason was, Iris had caused a mess, and I would be forced to clean it up for her.

Because that is what I would always do for her.

Parker's voice ran through my mind, his anger at Iris for bringing his sister into this. He was also going to be pissed at me because she slipped out of my custody when I promised that I would make sure she didn't.

While he didn't know the extent to which I had disobeyed his direct orders, I knew that there would be a lot of questions coming my way that I would need to answer.

That all had to wait for now.

What I did know was that I had to get to the Chevalier Headquarters and Iris as soon as possible.

The closer I got to the building, the more I began to wonder if Iris's behavior over the last few days was because she was plotting this. The change in her attitude toward me had been significant. Now, I wondered if she'd done this to lull me into a false sense of security with this idea sitting in the back of her mind.

But if she really wanted to get away, why come here? She must have known that she would be caught, but she still came anyway.

My eyes darted to my left before focusing back on the road ahead. There was a hidden agenda afoot here, and I think I might have figured it out.

She was still determined to prove that her ancestor was a founder of the Chevaliers.

To be honest, that made me proud of what she was doing even though I was still angry with her.

I had no plan, no leverage in any of this. Just a desperate need to protect a woman who should mean nothing to me. But for some absurd reason, she meant everything instead.

I was in love with Iris.

The realization hit me like a ton of bricks, and if I weren't racing to get to her, I would have had to pull the car over to the side of the road to process the thought. I'd been trying to deny my feelings for her for so long, but there was no use in that anymore.

This was why I was willing to put everything on the line to protect and be with her. And this was what tonight was all boiling down to.

Finally, I parked outside the Chevalier Headquarters. While everything in my mind encouraged me to break out into a run to get to Iris as quickly as possible, I maintained the poise that people were accustomed to seeing from me. It was then that I came across Landon sitting in a vehicle nearby. His eyes met mine and we gave each other a small nod, my way of acknowledging that I was thankful for his work in finding my girl.

There had been a few times I've been to the Chevalier Headquarters in the middle of the night. Silence was a virtue I embraced, but I could see how many people could find this creepy.

I used my badge to get into the building and used the same badge to get on an elevator to head downstairs. I reached the entrance, and as I pushed open the heavy double doors, the darkness that filled the building consumed me. I glanced at the security guard that stood in there, who'd also known what was happening and let Iris and Aria get as far as they did without stopping them. He gave me a small wave once he recognized me, and I did the same in return.

The Chevalier Headquarters reflected my place more than I liked to admit. Both looked to belong in another era with their heavy emphasis on wood and stone. Its darkness matched my energy, and it only increased as I stepped further into what was the proverbial lion's den.

The place was almost too quiet, understandable, given what time of day it was. However, it made the sound of my footsteps seem louder, announcing my arrival to anyone in the area. I stood still for a moment, trying to hear which way I needed to go, and then I heard it. Faint whispering that then turned into yelling.

It didn't take long for me to find them in the middle of "The Chamber," a special meeting place where we held some meetings at headquarters. No one who wasn't a member of the Chevaliers should be in this room, yet we had two nonmembers standing across from the chairman of the entire New York chapter.

I decided to stay in the shadows and listen versus jumping out and causing even more mayhem. It took everything within me to not go out there without a care and grab Iris.

"Aria, how could you do this?! Betraying your own family for someone you barely know?" I could hear the strain in Parker's voice. He wasn't used to having his authority disobeyed by anyone, let alone by his own sister.

"How do you know how well I know Iris? And I couldn't

let you keep her locked in someone's basement for who knows how long until you decided what punishment best suited her. How fucked up is that?"

"It was none of your business," Parker said. "And you just had to insert yourself into this. Now I have to make a decision."

"What decision?" Iris asked, speaking for the first time since I'd arrived. Her voice sounded strong, and I was proud of her. Even after everything that had happened, I was proud of her for being brave throughout all of this.

I stayed hidden in the shadows and shifted my body so I could watch everything unfold. Parker looked pissed, more so than I've ever seen, as he stood in front of Iris and Aria. His body was tense like he was ready to do something drastic at any second. His voice was sharp and loud as he spoke to them. "Whether or not I'm going to kill you right here."

From my hidden spot, I could see Iris and Aria standing together. They didn't look scared, even though Parker was pretty intimidating. Iris glanced at Aria, and they shared a look. It was like they were having a whole conversation without saying a word.

I moved quickly, stepping out from where I was hiding. Before Parker could turn back around, I had his arm twisted behind his back. "Enough," I said quietly but firmly. "You're out of line."

Parker struggled a bit, but I held on tight. I could tell by the look on Iris and Aria's faces that they were surprised to see me. But they also seemed relieved. Especially Iris.

Keeping my grip firm on Parker, I could feel the way he tensed up under my hold. He hadn't expected me to step in, not like this. "What do you think you're doing, Soren?" he grunted, trying to look over his shoulder at me, but I didn't let him. His voice was a mix of confusion and annoyance, but I didn't care.

"I'm putting an end to this, Parker," I replied, my voice steady. I knew I had to keep control of the situation. Parker was ready to go off at any moment, and I would fucking kill him before he hurt a hair on Iris's head.

I glanced over at Iris and Aria. Their faces were a mix of emotions now—relief, shock, and there was some worry there too. I gave them a quick, reassuring nod, trying to tell them without words that they were safe now. It was more for Iris because I was pretty confident Parker wouldn't harm his sister. But I knew he wouldn't have an issue with pulling the trigger on Iris.

Parker was still trying to wriggle out of my grip, but I refused to loosen my hold on him. "I don't want to hurt you, but I will if I have to."

For a moment, there was a standstill. Then Parker stopped struggling, and the four of us just stood there. It was like the whole world was holding its breath, waiting to see what would happen with this tense exchange in the Chevalier Headquarters.

Then, without warning, Parker's composure shattered. With a sudden, fierce jerk, he twisted in my grip, his elbow catching me off guard and striking me in the ribs. The force of the blow made me stagger back, loosening my hold just enough for him to break free.

In an instant, he was lunging toward Iris, his movements fueled by rage. "How fucking dare you!" he spat at her.

Acting on pure instinct, I lunged after him, tackling him to the ground. We hit the floor with a thud, and someone screamed, but I couldn't tell who. "Parker, stop!" I yelled, trying to pin him down, but he was like a wild animal.

The altercation was a blur of motion and noise, a physical struggle that meant so much more. It was a clash of wills because there was no way that I was going to let him hurt the woman I loved.

Finally, I managed to get a firm hold on Parker once more, my arms locked around his chest, pulling him away from Iris. "Enough!" I shouted, my voice echoing down the hallway. "If you hurt her, I'll kill you."

Slowly, the fight seemed to drain out of Parker. This isn't how I wanted things to end up, but that's where we were at this point. "I need you to promise me something." I waited a beat, ensuring I had his attention. "Promise me you won't try to hurt Iris, and I'll let you go."

There was a pause, a brief moment where the only sound was our collective breathing, heavy and uneven. For a second, I wondered if he would refuse my request. If he would let his anger take over once more. But then he nodded, his voice a hoarse whisper as he said, "Okay. . . I promise."

I hesitated as I tried to gauge the sincerity behind those words. This was a gamble, but I needed to de-escalate this situation. Slowly, I loosened my grip, ready to react if he decided to go against what he'd said.

As I released him, Parker stayed still for a moment, then pushed himself up to a sitting position. He didn't look at me, his gaze fixed on the floor, making it so that I couldn't see his expression.

I stood up, keeping a cautious distance, my stare focused on him. "We need to talk."

Parker just nodded again, silently acknowledging my words. It was all that I could ask for at the moment,

As the tension in the hallway began to dissipate, Iris stepped forward. How I wished that her eyes were on me, but they were fixed on Parker. She stopped a short distance away as Parker, who was still sitting on the floor, collected himself.

"Parker," Iris's voice cut through the lingering silence. "Was Margaret Turner one of the founders of the Chevaliers?"

The question hung in the air. Parker, who had been looking down, lifted his gaze to meet Iris's. For a moment, Parker seemed to weigh his response, his eyes searching Iris's face as he decided how to answer her question.

Finally, with a slow exhale, Parker nodded. "Yes," he admitted, his voice low. "Margaret Turner was one of the founders."

Iris's reaction was a mixture of emotions—vindication, surprise, and a deeper curiosity. This revelation was the single most significant piece of the puzzle she was trying to piece together and now, at last, an answer had been given.

39

IRIS

My lip trembled as the words circled around my head on repeat.

Margaret Turner was one of the founders.

The silence in the room surrounded us, suffocating all its occupants, including me. It almost felt as if the room was closing in on me, which was the opposite of the reaction I thought I would have to this news. I couldn't shift my gaze from Parker's face. Finally, I spoke. "Tell me what you know about Margaret Turner and the Chevaliers. I need to know everything."

"Margaret Turner was an intricate part of the founding of the Chevaliers. Back when the Chevaliers began, things were different, especially for women," Parker said. "They were often pushed into the background, no matter how brilliant they were."

I braced myself, not knowing if I was prepared for what he was about to say next.

"All of the credit for the Chevaliers went to Eddison Payne, Theodore Cyrus, and Otto Frederick," Parker continued. "But, in reality, a lot of their foundational work, the core ideas and principles, they were all because of Margaret."

I didn't expect to feel the amount of anger that I felt, having confirmed what I'd been told by Gran. The Chevaliers had been built on Margaret's ideas, and she got none of the credit, nor were women allowed to join the organization. "So, you're telling me the Chevaliers are more Margaret Turner's brainchild than Payne's, and he, Theodore Cyrus, and Otto Frederick are the ones who got all the glory?"

Parker nodded and sighed. "Exactly. Only a handful of us know just how much Margaret shaped this organization. Her thoughts were revolutionary, but the world just wasn't ready for a woman like her."

This was more than just some forgotten history. It was a massive injustice. Margaret Turner had been the real driving force behind an entire organization, and history had erased her. Well, more like buried her.

I let out a shaky breath, trying to calm my emotions the best I could. Rage filled me because of everything that happened. "The Chevaliers owe her big time, and it's about time you recognized that. Not to mention that women also belong in this organization. And you know it."

"You're not going to tell me what the Chevaliers need to do."

Parker's words were filled with warning, but I didn't care. I took a step forward and said, "Yes, I am. And you're going to reform your admission standards to allow women to have a chance at being admitted too."

I could see the wheels in Parker's head turning and that what I'd said had done anything but make him happy.

"You want me to change the way the Chevaliers do things?

You think it's that easy?" he said, his expression becoming more irritated the longer he stared at me. "You know it's not going to be that easy. We've been around for decades, and this isn't something we can just change overnight."

He crossed his arms over his chest and glared at me. I could feel Aria and Soren staring holes into me, probably wondering where this was going to end up. What I did know was that I refused to back down.

"Margaret Turner deserves recognition for what she did, and women deserve a chance to join this organization too," I said.

"No." Parker's response was swift, but I refused to be deterred.

"Then I guess I'm going to the media. That includes social media as well," I replied.

Parker shared a look with Soren before turning his attention back to me, and he looked as if he might come toward me. I pushed away from Aria slightly so that she would be blocked from anything he might do and to show I wasn't afraid of him, Soren, or his organization anymore. "You don't actually think I told you all of that so that you can tell it to everyone you fucking know, right? There is no way that this news is getting out."

"I will have no problem slitting your fucking throat if you lay a hand on her. Don't fucking test me. I have no problem tearing this whole damn world down to avenge even a small prick on her skin."

I glanced at Soren but shifted my gaze so that my focus remained on Parker. I would deal with Soren later.

It was obvious to me that Parker was caught between a rock and a hard place. Soren probably knew way more about where the proverbial and actual bodies were buried and seemed hell-bent on doing what he could to protect me. Parker would have to take out both of us and potentially his sister in order to maintain the status quo he was so desperate to keep.

Parker sighed heavily and looked away from me. "Fine," he said, and I knew it took every bit of willpower in him to finally say it. "We'll change the admission standards for the Chevaliers to allow women in. It won't happen overnight, but I'll make sure it happens."

I narrowed my eyes at him, not quite believing it was that easy. "And you will recognize Margaret Turner for her accomplishments?"

Parker nodded slowly as if he knew there was no other option. "Yes, we will recognize Margaret Turner and give her proper credit for her work in helping to develop this organization into what it is today."

I could feel the tension in the room start to dissipate as Parker finally conceded and agreed to do what needed to be done. The pressure had lifted off my shoulders. It felt as if I could finally breathe for the first time in days.

"And I'm supposed to believe that you will keep your word?"

"He will," Soren said as I felt the heat of his gaze on me.

Parker seemed resigned to his fate, and I felt a sense of satisfaction that justice had been served in some small way. Whether or not this would lead to real change remained to be seen, but at least I had taken a stand, and at this moment, I'd won.

I released a deep breath, feeling exhausted from the confrontation and. . . from everything that happened. All I wanted to do was go home and be with Gran. "I want to go home now."

"I'll take you," Soren said. It's something I knew he would offer, but I didn't want to hear it.

"Do you think I would ever want to be in the same building as you, let alone in a car where you can dictate where I'm going or what I'm doing, ever again? I don't want to ever see you again."

I could see that Soren wanted to argue with me, but my glare persuaded him not to. I hated that the turning point of our relationship had happened under such dark circumstances, but it was what it was.

Aria stepped forward and cleared her throat. "I can drive you to your house," she said quietly.

"No, you must be tired. Why don't I drive your car to my house, and you rest before driving yourself home? I do have my driver's license on me."

"That would be great," she said, and I could see the exhaustion settling into her eyes. Hell, she could sleep in the car on the way back for all I cared. Plus, it would give me the opportunity to be with just my thoughts outside of the confinement of Soren's home.

When I looked at Aria, she gave me a small nod and I turned to the two men in the room. "We would like for you to show us out."

Soren gave me a look as if he wanted to say something but decided against it. I was glad he didn't because I wasn't sure what I would have done if he had tried to talk to me at that point. Soren turned and began walking, and I quickly followed, with Aria walking behind me. I assumed Parker was bringing up the rear, but I refused to look behind me to verify. We all walked in silence as we reached the entrance of the building. Without saying another word, I stepped out of the building with Aria standing next to me.

The cold air hit me like a wave of relief, and I couldn't help but smile as the sun was starting to rise. For a moment, everything felt right in the world again. As we made our way to Aria's car, I silently thanked Soren and Parker for finally doing the right thing, even though it had taken far too long for them or anyone else to do so.

Would I ever verbalize my thanks? That remained to be seen after everything that had happened.

Aria handed me her keys and I unlocked the car as we approached it. I quickly got into the driver's seat and waited as Aria and Parker talked outside of the car. Soren stood several feet away, and I felt the weight of his stare, but I refused to give him the satisfaction of looking his way.

Finally, Aria and Parker said their goodbyes, and I started the car. Once Aria was settled, I drove away from the building. I felt a strange sense of peace wash over me. Despite all the darkness that had surrounded me for months, I was finally on my way home.

It didn't take long for Aria to fall asleep in the car, just as I suspected she might do. I couldn't help but look over at the sun as I drove along the highway, casting a warm orange glow across the horizon. Gone were the leaves on the trees, but the branches still swayed with the wind from the cool winter air.

I glanced in the rearview mirror and my eyes landed on Soren, driving what looked to be a fancy sports car. It seemed as if he was following us to make sure that we arrived at our destination safely because he could have easily stopped this whole excursion if he wanted to.

But he hadn't. He was letting me return home to Gran.

The only thing that kept me company on the drive was the sounds of soft pop and rock tunes that helped the time pass. The sun moved higher in the sky the closer I got to Gran's home. A few hours later, I pulled into Gran's driveway and turned the car engine off. Aria was still asleep, and I waited a moment before waking her. I watched as Soren parked his vehicle and noticed another black SUV pull in behind him. I couldn't see the driver, but for some reason, I didn't think that was a coincidence.

"Hey, Aria. We're at my house," I said as I unbuckled the seat belt.

She immediately stirred and it took her a few seconds to remember where she was. She undid the seat belt before she said, "That was a good nap, but I am surprised I was able to fall asleep at all. On second thought, I think I'll just drive back home from here right now."

I turned to look at her. "Are you sure?"

She nodded. "Yeah. My parents might be wondering where the hell I am anyway, and I'm not sure what Parker might have told them, so I should probably go and take care of that as soon as possible."

"Okay. Well. . . I guess the only thing that I can say is thank you. I'm so grateful for everything you've done for me."

I could see tears forming in her eyes. There was no way I was going to be able to avoid them either. Aria opened her arms and pulled me into an awkward hug due to us being in the car. I double-checked that I had everything I'd stored in the pockets of my hoodie before I exited the vehicle.

Aria followed my lead, and we gave each other another hug before we separated. I walked up to Gran's porch and stood there as I watched Aria settle back into the driver's seat of her car. She gave me a small wave just before she pulled out of the driveway, and then she took off down the street. My eyes landed on Soren's car once she was gone, but then I noticed the SUV that had been parked behind Soren had pulled out and left too. That was when I knew that none of this was a coincidence, but I didn't know what it was about.

"Iris?"

The question caused me to do a one-eighty and run into the arms of the only family I had left.

"I'm so happy to see you, but what are you doing here? I thought you were studying abroad?"

Hearing her repeat that lie caused the dam that was holding all of my emotions together to break. I began to sob uncontrollably.

"Oh my goodness, Iris, let's get you into the house."

I nodded quickly, to the point that I knew I probably looked like an upset bobblehead figurine. But I managed to get a few words out before the tears descended even more. "Gran, there's so much I have to tell you, but I did it. Margaret Turner will no longer be forgotten."

40

SOREN

The gravel crunched beneath the tires of my Porsche as I parked it in front of my home.

My mind was in a whirlwind as I replayed what happened at the Chevalier Headquarters. I stepped out of my car and into the chilly embrace of the winter morning. I walked toward the entrance of the Gothic mansion, feeling slightly numb as the heavy door creaked open, revealing the dimly lit interior of my home.

Franklin nodded at me as he took my coat but didn't say a word. It was as if he could sense I didn't want to talk, and I appreciated that about him.

My footsteps echoed through the halls as I made my way to my office. Once I was seated behind my massive dark desk, I tried to focus on the work that lay before me that needed to get done, but my thoughts inevitably drifted back to Iris.

"Fuck," I muttered under my breath. She was a force to be reckoned with, her fiery determination igniting something within me that I hadn't felt in years, and now I missed her being here with me.

As I sat there, I couldn't shake the image of Iris from my mind—her piercing blue eyes that seemed to see straight through me, her soft, dark-brown hair that I ran my fingers through while she was sleeping. She was the embodiment of all that I had tried to suppress within me when Eden died. She was a living reminder of the man I once was before my best friend was murdered by the man her father promised her to in front of me. Now, both of them wouldn't live to see another day.

Suddenly, there was a loud noise from what sounded like the front of the house. Muffled voices filled the room, and I couldn't help but wonder what was going on. My curiosity piqued, I rose from my chair as irritation flooded through me because of the unwelcome interruption.

As I approached the foyer, I could hear the conversation that was occurring between Franklin and my unexpected guests.

"Where is Iris Bennington?"

Silence filled the room before another question was asked.

"Where is Iris?" the woman in my foyer spoke again.

"And who are you?" Franklin asked.

"Take me to her. Now," the same voice said, and I could hear her anger in every syllable.

"Bianca—" A male voice said this time, but it wasn't Franklin. If Bianca was the Bianca I thought she was, then it seemed as if Iris's best friend had finally come to pay me a visit.

"Please, come in," Franklin said.

I waited until I heard the heavy front door shut before I

walked out of the shadows that my home did an excellent job of creating.

"What are you doing here? Don't you know it's rude to show up unannounced at someone's home?" My voice boomed, bouncing off the walls, but Bianca barely flinched. I watched as the man I could now confirm as her boyfriend, Easton, tried to get between her and me as I approached, but Bianca wouldn't let him.

"Where is she, Soren? Where is Iris?" Bianca demanded, her voice trembling with anger and fear. "Tell us where she is, or I'll search this damn place myself!"

Her piercing gaze burned a hole into me, demanding an answer. While I understood where she was coming from, the audacity of her to do such a thing added to everything that had happened today was pissing me off.

"You aren't going to waltz into my house and demand answers from me, and if either of you knew any better, you would watch your tone because you have no idea what I'm capable of."

The mask of bravery slipped slightly, although I could still feel Bianca's anger radiating from her body. She took a step forward, her eyes never leaving mine as she challenged me.

"You're not going to intimidate me, and I will get the answers that I want. Tell me where she is."

I had to say, I admired her courage. She had to know that she was walking into the lion's den. Even though it was two on one, it would have been easy for me to take them both down in my domain, but she wasn't cowering in fear. The determination I saw in her, I also saw in Iris. As well as knowing that Bianca's brother, Nash, possessed it, leading to him becoming the leader of the Brentson chapter of the Chevaliers.

Her boyfriend stepped between us once again, trying to defuse the situation before it got out of hand. But the Band-Aid had already been ripped off.

"Iris is not here," I said firmly. "And even if she were, why would I tell you?"

My admission caused Bianca and Easton to pause for a second as they processed what I said. "What do you mean she isn't here?" This time, it was Easton asking the questions.

"Just what I said. Iris isn't here. In fact, I would suggest you go and check her grandmother's house. That was her last known location."

Bianca's eyes narrowed on me. "You expect us to believe that? After everything you've done? I don't believe you for a second."

"Believe what you will because I don't care. But Iris isn't in my home." It took everything in me to make sure that I said my home and not our home. As much as I wanted it to be, that wasn't the reality I was currently living in.

Bianca's eyes flashed and I could read the suspicion in them. "And why should we trust anything you say?"

"To be honest, I don't give a fuck what you think." I could tell that my comment took Bianca off guard. I didn't wait for her to reply before I spoke again. "Franklin, can you bring me Iris's phone?"

With a short nod, Franklin left us in the foyer, moving silently as he did so. Maybe by giving them this, it would be enough to show them I was telling the truth. I was ready to get them both off my property and get back to the work I needed to do.

"Why wouldn't Iris contact me as soon as she got back to her Gran's house if you're telling the truth?"

It took everything in me not to roll my eyes. "Because she doesn't have her phone?"

The statement hung in the air, and I let the two young adults before me sit in the awkwardness of their own making. If they'd listened to me the first time, they could have already been on their way to Iris's grandmother's home.

Easton seemed to soften slightly. "We'll check her grandmother's place." Bianca didn't bother speaking, choosing instead to shoot daggers at me with her stare. It was a worthwhile price to pay as long as it resulted in her leaving my house.

It was then that Franklin returned with the phone in hand, and I couldn't have been happier that this conversation was ending. I'd given Bianca and Easton more grace with their questions than I had with most people, but this ended right now.

As they turned to leave, Franklin stepped forward. "Should I show them out, Mr. Grant?"

I nodded. "Yes, Franklin, thank you."

Bianca turned to look at me and I knew that she had to get one last parting shot in. "If she's not there, we're coming back here tonight to finish this. And I fucking mean that with every fiber of my being."

"You won't be back here tonight."

Once they had left, the foyer felt eerily silent. I stood there for a moment, lost in thought, with Franklin, who was just staring at me.

Finally, when I moved, Franklin spoke. "Is there anything I can get for you, sir?

"I'm fine." But I was lying to both of us because I really wasn't.

With a heavy sigh, I left the foyer and made my way back to my office. Every step felt heavier, no matter how much energy I exerted. Each step was a reminder of the distance between Iris and me that occurred inside of this house and outside of it. Sitting at my desk, I looked at the empty chair across from me, imagining Iris sitting there, her eyes filled with that fiery determination I had fallen for.

I leaned back, closing my eyes. The image of Iris standing up to Parker remained in the forefront of my mind, no matter how much I tried to push it out.

But one thing was clear in my mind: there was no getting rid of Iris from my brain, at least not anytime soon. Everything within me had decided that I needed to see her, to try and mend the hatred she obviously had for me. Not that those feelings weren't warranted because she had every reason to hate me.

I turned on my laptop and began to type. There were calls to make, people to contact, and a plan to formulate. I would stay away from her for the time being, but what she didn't know was that I would move heaven and earth to be with her. This time, the game I was playing was for keeps, no matter how long it took for me to win.

41

IRIS

The brisk chill of the morning air that wrapped around me was more than unwelcome as I stepped out of Payne Hall. Things were much different since the last time I'd been on campus. Since the turmoil at the Chevalier Headquarters, my life had fallen back into some version of normalcy.

I'd spent the rest of the winter break at home with Gran and enjoyed every moment with her. I enjoyed soaking up her hugs and homemade food. It was wonderful to be with her after everything that happened. To tell her what I had found out and what I'd forced the chairman of the Chevaliers to promise he would do.

She was overjoyed because I'd kept most of the dark and sinister things that I'd gone through to myself. I didn't want to cause her to worry any more than she already did, but even I could sense that she knew that something had changed within me. Everything had shifted.

I found my thoughts drifting toward Soren more often than I'd like. He loomed in my mind like a shadow, even though I hadn't seen him since he'd followed me to Gran's house after the showdown at the Chevalier Headquarters. It was a welcome reprieve, but there was still something missing in my life that only he filled. Deep down, I knew I needed to find someone who could help me work through all of the emotions and trauma I'd gone through, but I hadn't made the leap to do so yet.

Reflecting on everything that had transpired, I realized how these events had reshaped me. I was not the same person who had walked these halls at the start of the school year. The innocent belief I had about how I was going to find Eddison Payne's papers and prove that my ancestor, Margaret Turner, was involved in the founding of the Chevaliers seemed like a distant memory. I had been transformed and been through an awakening of who I was as a person that I didn't expect.

I yanked my coat tighter, wishing I'd remembered to wrap a scarf around my neck. There wasn't much of a need to worry about it though, because soon I was going to be in the warmth of another academic building, settling down before the start of my first class for the day. Other students rushed past me, their expressions showing their focus on where they needed to be.

"Miss Bennington."

My heart stuttered at the sound of his voice, but it wasn't from fear. Soren stood several feet in front of me, and it immediately reminded me of when we met for the first time. His presence commanded attention, and I could see some people glancing at him as they walked by the two of us. His dark-brown hair was tousled, and the darkness that made up his eyes held an unfamiliar vulnerability. The sight of him stirred something deep within me, but I couldn't pinpoint what it was.

"Professor Grant," I said, proud of myself for getting over the shock as quick as I did. I decided to keep it professional on Westwick's campus, just in case anyone was listening to us talk. Was he even still a professor here? "What are you doing here?"

"I wanted to talk to you."

Of course he didn't ask to talk to me. It was as if he was demanding that I did. I couldn't help but roll my eyes. "Hell of a time you picked; I'm on my way to my first class," I said as I made up the distance between us and walked past him. He didn't waste any time in catching up with me, matching his stride with mine.

I scanned the area to see if anyone was paying attention to us, but everyone seemed to be focused on themselves. Even in the crowd, turmoil grew inside of me the longer I was in his presence. Part of me wanted to tell him to fuck all the way off and leave me alone, but the other part was curious about what he wanted to say.

"You're going to have to speak quickly because I'm on my way to class and refuse to be late because of... this." There was an edge to my voice that wasn't normally there, but I didn't care. Soren approached me without giving me any warning, so he was going to get whatever version of me that he was going to get.

He hesitated for a moment before he spoke to me. "I wanted to apologize for everything because I want to move forward."

"Move forward? Apologize?" My pulse quickened, and I

couldn't stop the bitter laugh that escaped my lips. "For what exactly? Stalking me? Kidnapping me?"

"Please, petal." His voice was low but stern. I could hear the beginnings of a plea in his tone, but it wasn't quite there. "I need you to understand—"

His using the nickname he'd given me was almost my undoing, but I managed to keep it together. "Understand?" My tone was sharp, biting. "You can't be serious right now."

"I know I have no right to ask for your forgiveness, but I need you to know how deeply sorry I am for what I've done, although I don't regret a second of it. I know the trauma it caused you, but there were numerous reasons why I did what I did. If the circumstances were the same, I would do it again. I'm hoping that by confessing this and apologizing, we can start fresh."

His words struck me like a blow, stirring up memories I had tried so hard to bury. Images of him breaking into my room, me walking into one of my classes and discovering that he was now my professor, seeing him at Chevalier Manor and him kidnapping me and taking me to his house. More importantly, the time things shifted between us over the holidays. But the latter memories were tainted by the things he'd done to manipulate me to do what he wanted during this situationship.

"Start fresh?" I echoed bitterly, my voice barely audible. "How can we have a fresh start when everything between us is built on lies?"

Soren's jaw clenched, and for a moment, I thought he would argue. Instead, he let out a shaky breath, and it was the first time I'd ever noticed him seeming unsure of himself. "I don't expect you to trust me right away or to accept my apology. But give me a chance to prove myself to you."

This sounded ridiculous. "Prove yourself? Soren, do you even understand what you're asking for?" Any sense of professionalism had gone out the window. The words that were sitting on the tip of my tongue were going to hurt him more than they could ever hurt me. Because now, I was speaking my truth. "Do you not understand how many times you violated me? All you cared about was getting your way and what you wanted. Nothing about me. And I deserve to have someone who will give me that and more. You haven't shown through your actions that you will be able to do that, and that's not even counting the heinous things you've done to me."

Before Soren could utter another word, I released a big sigh and turned to face him, stopping us both in our tracks. "I've seen sides of you that I can't just forget. You've hurt me, and it's not something that can be erased with a few apologies or promises to do better."

He nodded, seeming to accept my words, but I wasn't sure what to believe. "Even if you don't forgive me, I can't stand the thought of not trying to make things right. Not when I care about you as much as I do."

His admission hung between us, and I wasn't sure what to think of it. Once again, I thought about everything he'd done to make me feel more at home during what should have been a time I would have been spending with Gran, but it wasn't enough. Too much had happened for me to sweep it under the rug, even though a part of me wanted to see where this might go with him.

"Care about me?" I questioned, a hint of sarcasm creeping

into my voice. "Soren, caring about someone means respecting them, understanding them, listening to what they want and need. Can you honestly say you've done that?"

He looked at me, and for a moment, I saw a flicker of regret before he hid it behind the mask that he always wore. "No, but I want to. I want to be someone who deserves you, Iris."

My heart skipped a beat at his words. It was the kind of declaration I might have once dreamed of hearing from him if things had been different between us.

"No," I said finally, my voice barely above a whisper. "I don't accept your apology and I would appreciate it if you left me alone."

As I turned to walk away, I felt his gaze on my back and I wanted to turn and look back at him, but I forced myself to keep marching forward. I needed to leave Soren in the rearview mirror if I wanted to move on with my life, and I was determined to do so.

The rest of the day passed by relatively fast. Later that evening, the quiet hum of my laptop filled my dorm room as I brought a cup of decaf coffee to my lips. I was mentally preparing to settle in for an evening of study. Despite the distractions of the day, I was determined to focus on the homework I needed to get done. I glanced at my phone to see if I had a text message from Bianca. Seeing none, I placed the screen face down on my desk before a small chime forced my eyes back to my laptop.

It was an alert, signaling that I'd gotten an email sent to my school account. I switched browsers and scanned through the list of new messages. One subject line caught my eye: "Special Lecture Series in Economics."

Curious, I opened the email. It was an announcement for a series of guest lectures in the economics department. My eyes scanned the details until they landed on a name that made me pause—Soren's. He was listed as one of the guest lecturers. Shock made my mouth drop open. I knew Professor Hamby had returned, so Soren's continued involvement in the department seemed weird.

The email detailed the schedule and topics of the lectures. Soren's session was on media economics—a direct overlap with what I'd begun focusing on at Westwick. It was almost too coincidental, and I wondered if I was being paranoid.

I leaned back in my chair as confusion swirled within me because I found myself in a conundrum. On one hand, Soren's expertise in economics could offer valuable insights for my studies. But on the other, attending his lecture meant facing him again, something I didn't want to do.

I closed the tab, deciding that would be enough to put the issue at hand out of my mind, but it didn't. At least for now, I didn't have to worry about this because the lecture was a couple of months away.

For now, I would focus on the work that I needed to get done, and Soren would just have to be placed on the back burner.

42

IRIS

My dorm room was only lit by the soft glow coming from my laptop. With the snow falling peacefully outside, it provided a beautiful, cozy atmosphere as I wrapped myself in a thick quilt and streamed a show before bed.

I tucked back a piece of my hair that really needed to see the salon behind my ear as I settled into my pillows. A couple of weeks had passed since I had last heard from Soren, and it was both a blessing and a curse. The time we spent apart had slightly changed my perspective on what happened between the two of us.

To be honest, I was surprised he was respecting my space and not trying to invade it, although every so often, I got the feeling that I was being watched but wrote it off as me being paranoid. Soren had his own business to run, as well as his dealings with the Chevaliers. How would he have the time to stalk me?

Then again, I shouldn't underestimate him at all.

The familiar chime signaling that I'd received an email

sounded, and I debated whether I wanted to pause the show I was watching to check it. I could wait, but whenever I was already on my laptop, it was super easy and quick for me to check my email. It took a couple of seconds before a small idea formed in my head. I grabbed my cell phone and checked the email from there, but I was completely confused because it didn't make sense.

There was an email from Soren, but it wasn't a regular email. It was marked with several layers of digital protection, basically a virtual lock that needed a key in order to open it.

A second email arrived before I could think of anything else. It contained the access code. Soren's brief message explained that the contents of the protected email were meant solely for me. There was no way that I couldn't open this now, so I switched to my computer, clicked on the email, and put in the code.

The email opened to reveal several attachments. The first was a couple of photographs of old, yellowed papers. It didn't take me long to realize that they were letters written by Eddison Payne, one of the founders of the Chevaliers. My eyes quickly scanned the handwritten text, and I was drawn into the historical significance of what I was reading. Payne's words painted a vivid picture of Margaret Turner, not just as a founder of the organization but as the driving force behind the Chevaliers. Her contributions. Her vision. It was all there in Payne's elegant script, which was a stark contrast to the history that had been told for more than a century.

My fingers shook as I read the words in the photographs again. I hadn't been able to find them, but at least I was able to read some of them, seeing as how I wasn't a member of the organization. I told myself I would make sure that Gran could

see this too, the next time she and I were together in a private place.

I clicked on the next attachment, a memo from Parker, to what I assumed was the Chevalier membership based on the introduction. His words slammed into me like a dump truck, even though I knew it was coming. He'd kept his word. The memo announced a groundbreaking change in the organization—for the first time in its history, the Chevaliers were allowing women to join their ranks. This monumental shift was being made in honor of Margaret Turner, recognizing her pivotal role in the Chevaliers' formation.

As I absorbed this news, I realized what this meant, not just for the Chevaliers but for me. Soren's decision to share this with me spoke volumes. It wasn't just an acknowledgment of our situationship or his attempts to make amends; it was a profound gesture of respect toward my passion for justice for Margaret.

I leaned back, feeling every emotion that I could possibly feel washing over me. Soren was obviously trying to show how serious he was about us starting anew. This act showed a deep understanding of what mattered to me, and more importantly, it showed how he was changing.

But even as I recognized the significance of what he'd done, I knew that this shift in him and in the Chevaliers didn't automatically change things. It was a beginning, perhaps, but where it would lead, I had no idea.

I closed out of the email and found the tab where I was streaming the show. I was grateful for what Soren had done, but I wasn't ready to speak to him yet. Heck, I wasn't sure if I would ever be.

In the two weeks following the revelation of Margaret

Turner's true role in the Chevaliers, my days were a blend of academics, trying to maintain a social life, and not having my thoughts drift back to Soren. I managed to succeed with two of those items.

Although I didn't see him, Soren's presence surrounded me. It was my fault that my attention outside of schoolwork returned to him often, but I couldn't shake it. There were no more emails, no unexpected encounters. His respect for my space was evident, and it gave me the breathing room that I'd wanted, even if my thoughts always came back to him.

Once January ended and shifted into February, the date of Soren's special lecture grew closer. I'd debated with myself about whether I was going to go or not, and I still hadn't come to a decision. It was dangerous for me to even consider going, given the hold he had on me, so I didn't know why I was bothering to debate this with myself.

One afternoon, I returned to my dorm room to find a bouquet of blue irises waiting for me. It was obvious they'd been personally delivered because I didn't need to go to the campus's post office to retrieve them. I walked toward them and picked them up, choosing to take in their beauty before looking to find out who the sender was. Although it wasn't hard to guess who it more than likely was.

I walked inside my room and took my time getting settled in before deciding to see if a card had been included. Once I found it, I was somewhat surprised to see that it only had one word on it.

Petal

The sight of the irises brought a mix of emotions. He was thinking about me too. I placed the bouquet near the window, its vibrant colors a stark contrast against the backdrop of my dorm room. They were stunning, and once again, I was faced with the dilemma of whether I should reach out to contact him to thank him for the lovely gift.

I pulled out my phone and debated texting him before stuffing it back into my pocket. Calling him right now wouldn't do me a bit of good because I wouldn't be able to say anything but thank you and listen to him breathing on the other end of the line. But saying thank you and ending the call wouldn't be the worst thing.

As the irises stood by the window, bathing in the soft afternoon light, which felt more like a rarity because of the time of year, their presence in my room was comforting, something I hadn't been expecting. I wasn't surprised by Soren's decision to use the word petal because it brought up memories of how he would whisper the word in my ear just before he made sure that I was coming all over his cock. Not to mention the many times he'd called me petal outside of the bedroom as well.

My phone felt heavy in my pocket as I paced back and forth. One message, one call, and I could bridge the gap between us. Yet my mind was still holding me back. Was I ready to reopen that door? To have a discussion I wasn't sure I was ready to have?

I decided to let the moment be. For now, they would just be flowers that someone sent to me. Their beauty, in my mind, would remain uncomplicated by actions and reactions.

However, I couldn't help but wonder what else Soren had up his sleeve.

43

IRIS

The irises didn't stop coming.

As I shrugged off my coat before hanging it in the closet, the fabric rustling softly as it settled among my other clothes, my gaze drifted involuntarily to the bouquet of irises placed carefully near my window. They were the latest in a series of weekly floral reminders from Soren, each as beautifully arranged as the last.

The flowers had been arriving at my door for weeks now and there wasn't any sign of them stopping. I knew I should tell him to stop, but I was enjoying having them in my room at this point. Other small gifts had also arrived, like snacks for studying and money for meals on campus suddenly appearing in my account. I knew it was him without him having to announce it.

His guest lecture on campus was just around the corner, and I still hadn't decided whether to attend. It wasn't just a matter of seeing him again for the first time in months. It was about what my presence there would signify to myself and him if he knew I was there.

Lost in thought, I absentmindedly fiddled with a loose thread on my sleeve. My gaze then drifted to the floor of the closet, settling on a peculiar detail I hadn't paid much attention to since I'd been back. The small hole in the wooden planks offered a limited view into the room below. I still had no idea what was down there, and I was dying to know.

Kneeling down for a closer look, I wondered about the figure I'd seen with the candlelight down there and what they'd been looking for. Who was it, and what was in that room that made them want to search it?

Since I'd been back on campus, I hadn't heard anything coming from the room. I was pretty satisfied with where things were, but I still wanted to know what was down there.

But that would have to wait for another day.

Rising to my feet, I looked at the flowers again before there was a knock on my door. I wasn't expecting anyone, so I was confused about the intrusion.

I debated whether I wanted to answer the door when there was another sharp knock on it. "Who is it?" I called out, approaching the door.

When no one answered, I figured whoever it was had decided to go find someone else to bother. However, I was wrong. When I opened the door, I was met with a sight I hadn't expected—Soren. He stood there, dressed in a black suit, and I could read the determination in his eyes. I swallowed hard as I took in every inch of him and how gorgeous he looked standing just outside of my door.

"Can I talk to you for a moment?" he asked. I was shocked he asked instead of demanding that I let him in.

Nodding silently, I stepped aside to let him in. Soren entered, holding a black envelope in his hand. The air between us was undeniably tense, but that was to be expected. It was something I'd been hoping to avoid, and why I hadn't reached out to him at all, but apparently the time to avoid him was now over.

"This is for you," he said as his gaze met mine.

For some reason, I'd been expecting him to apologize again, but I was happy that he hadn't. I'd moved past that already, and it wasn't something I wanted to revisit right now.

He extended the envelope toward me. He waited until I opened it and my mouth dropped open before he explained. "The Chevaliers made a decision. After acknowledging Margaret Turner's contributions, we realized we owed a debt to her descendants. As the oldest living descendant, your grandmother is entitled to it, but we also wanted to give you something for being instrumental in bringing about this change."

The amount written on this check was far more substantial than I could have imagined. It was a gesture that went beyond a simple apology. It was an acknowledgment by the Chevaliers that they messed up, and they were now trying to fix an error that should have been rectified decades ago.

Soren continued, "It's a small part of what is owed, a recognition of the legacy that was almost lost, and your role in bringing it to light. I know it doesn't change everything, but I hope it's a start."

I looked up at him and let out a shaky breath. This was more than just a personal apology. It was a step toward righting the wrongs of the past. It also added a new layer to the complexity of our relationship. I didn't know when it had shifted from being a situationship to a relationship, but it had.

"Thank you," I managed to say. The money was significant, and I wasn't sure how to wrap my head around it. I could pay off my college debt entirely and still have money left over, but I would deal with that later. At this moment, all I could think about was Soren's presence, right here, right now, in my room.

Soren's hand landed back in his pocket as he stared at me as if he hadn't seen me in a million years. "I wanted to give this to you in person," he said. "It was too important not to."

As he turned to leave, I froze. There was something in his posture, a finality in his movements, that suggested this might be more than just a delivery of a check. It struck me that this could be a farewell, and that thought frightened me enough to act.

"Wait," I found myself saying, the word escaping my lips before I could fully grasp the implications. He stopped with his hand on the doorknob. "Are you leaving?"

"What do you mean by that?" he asked.

"Will this be the last time I see you?"

Before he responded, he turned around so that he was facing me. "Is that what you want? Do you want me to leave?"

I stared at him, wondering exactly how to voice the words that I wanted to say. After several seconds of silence, my voice made my intentions known. "No, I don't want you to leave."

"You don't know how long I've been waiting for you to say something like that." Soren ate up the distance between us and pulled me into his arms. "Staying away from you and giving you the space you wanted was one of the hardest things I've ever done."

It had grown difficult for me too, once I was able to start processing everything that had happened to me. I wanted nothing more than to talk things through with him, but I was scared that I wasn't ready to have the conversation.

This time, things felt different.

"We have a lot to discuss," I said when I noticed that Soren's lips were drifting down toward mine.

"I know, but there is only one thing that matters right now."

I raised an eyebrow at his comment. "What's that?"

"That I tell you how much I'm in love with you."

His words snatched my breath away temporarily before a grin appeared on my face. "You know what?"

"What's that?"

"I love you too."

It felt so good to finally have the words out there in the world, and Soren seemed to appreciate them too. A smirk appeared on his face before he ran a finger across my jawline until it ended up underneath my chin, pushing my face up.

Before I knew it, my eyes were closed, and Soren was kissing me as if our lives depended on it. There was a lot that needed to be worked out between us, but as things stood right now, I was happier than I'd been in months, right here in his arms.

44

IRIS

I tucked a piece of my hair behind my ear as I listened to Soren speak.

I've been captivated by his lecture since the first word flew out of his mouth. It didn't hurt that his wit, charm, and good looks made him impossible to ignore or stop me from squirming in my seat.

I could sense that Professor Soren Grant was about to wrap up his lecture on media economics. I could see other students nodding along to the words he was saying as he held their attention for the last hour and a half. As he concluded, his eyes scanned the crowd, eventually locking with mine. In that brief moment, a silent understanding passed between us, as a smile drifted to my lips. He returned it and all felt right in the world.

I sat back as Soren's gaze lingered for a second longer than usual before he broke the contact. I couldn't help but wish that we were alone and that he was commanding me to get on my knees before him until I was unzipping his slacks to take his dick in his mouth.

I squeezed my thighs shut in order to dull the ache that was quickly forming. We still needed to keep our relationship quiet while I was a student here and fantasizing about him in public wasn't the way to do that.

As the audience began to applaud, signaling the end of the lecture, I found myself sucking in a deep breath as I reflected on the journey that brought us here. I was happy for the first time in what felt like forever and excited about the future versus trying to dig up the past. All aspects of my life seemed to be going the way I wanted them to and I couldn't wait to see what lay ahead.

The crowd started to disperse, and several people walked down toward the stage to talk to Soren. I remained seated for a couple of minutes, allowing the huge crowd to clear out before I decided to make a move.

That is until an idea formed in my mind.

I quickly packed my things, grabbed my coat and tossed my bookbag over my shoulder. By the looks of the people that were still standing around Soren, he would be there for a little while, so I had some time to throw my little plan into action.

I glanced around and noticed the empty halls as I slipped away, unnoticed by the students and faculty to head toward where most of the professors had their offices in the economics building. It didn't take me long to find the office labeled "Professor Soren Grant" and slip inside.

I let out a deep breath before I tossed my coat and bookbag down in one of the chairs reserved for guests. Thinking better of that this would be an extra touch, I found myself toeing off my shoes and pulling my sweater off my body. After removing my jeans, I found myself in the dark purple bra and panty set that I'd put on just before I headed over to the lecture.

I quickly walked over to find his chair behind his desk. There I found his bag, confirming what I'd thought all along. He was definitely going to have to come back here and get his things.

I sat down and adjusted my positioning and waited for him to return. A few minutes later, I jumped when my phone vibrated and I couldn't help but wonder if that was him sending me a text message because he wanted to know where I was or what I was up to.

I grinned and folded my arms over my chest. My mind drifted back to the time he and I had fucked in Professor Hamby's office. This was going to be fun.

When I heard something touch the doorknob, my heart lodged into my throat. Even though chances were that it was Soren entering the room, thoughts about how this could all go very wrong due to someone else entering his office did flash through my mind. I was taking a huge risk by doing this, but the reward could be even bigger.

I heard the knob turn and the office door open. Soren entered, his eyes widening in surprise at the sight of me. His gaze traveled up and down my body before he regained his composure and closed the door behind him. He stepped closer to me and asked, "What are you doing here?"

"I wanted to congratulate you on the amazing lecture you put together and surprise you," I replied with a smirk. "Did it work?"

His lips curled into a smile as he took another step toward me. "That it did, petal. That it did."

Soren placed the papers in his hand down on the desk

and held his hand out, pulling me up from the chair. His hands slowly moved down my body until they were around my waist just before he pulled me toward him.

The air in the room quickly shifted when he entered. Gone were the nerves that seemed to float around me and what had settled into the air was anticipation. As he looked at me, the intensity in his eyes only grew leaving me feeling exposed and vulnerable.

That is until he slowly unbuttoned his jacket, revealing his crisp white shirt undone at the collar. I could see the outline of muscles in his chest flexing beneath it as he moved to take it off. He leaned forward and I could feel his breath tickling my earlobe.

"You're so brave," he murmured, causing goose bumps to rise on my neck. I knew he wasn't just talking about what I'd done tonight. "Thank you for my present."

Soren finished unbuttoning his shirt and took both the suit jacket and the shirt off at the same time. He moved his hand and allowed it to trace my jawline gently before running it through my hair, guiding my head back as he leaned into me. Our lips met in a fiery kiss that left me wanting more.

As our kiss deepened, I could feel the ache that had started in the lecture increasing tenfold because of my desire to have him in any way I could. His tongue began to explore my mouth, tasting and teasing me. He made sure that his hands focused on every inch of my body, caressing me in ways that made me melt into him. His touch sent waves of pleasure through my body, making everything else around us seem insignificant. All I wanted was to stay in this moment with him forever because it felt like nothing could ever compare to it.

My nails dug into his shoulders as he pulled away from my lips, leaving a trail of kisses down my neck and collarbone. I couldn't help but shiver because of his touch. My body involuntarily arched into him, craving more of his touch.

With a groan, I felt his hand slide up my thigh, brushing against my lace panties. I grasped his shoulders even more, not only steadying myself, but choosing to hold onto him as if he were my lifeline.

One of Soren's hands trailed up my back, while the other found my butt, choosing to cup my ass and pull me even closer to him. I whimpered softly as his fingers traced the elastic band of my panties, once again teasing me with what was to come.

"I need this so fucking bad." The words rushed from my lips and I wasn't completely sure that I'd said them until Soren's gaze darkened even more.

"I know you do," he replied just before the hand that had been on my back shifted gear and ended up between my thighs. I gasped as his rough fingers found my pussy, choosing not to tease me anymore. He smirked and leaned in closer, his lips brushing against my ear. "Don't fight it because I know exactly what you want."

I gave him a low moan in response as my body rocked against him. His fingers shifted the panties out of his way and he hissed when he was able to slip a finger into my pussy. "You're so fucking wet for me, petal."

"Soren..." My voice was a hoarse whisper and I didn't even recognize it.

He fucked me with his fingers, testing my readiness for him. It took everything in me not to yell out. Instead, I bit my lip so hard that I swore I could taste blood.

Soren turned me around and made me lean over his desk, his roughness mirroring the hunger in his eyes. "This isn't going to be romantic," he said. "We'll have more time for that when we get back to my place. What I'm going to need for you to do is to be quiet. Do you think that you can do that?"

I nodded my head, but I wasn't sure I could keep that promise. Apparently, Soren had the same thought. Next thing I knew, he was shoving my panties down my legs.

"Turn your head toward me and open your mouth," he said. Once I had followed his directions, he stuffed my panties into my mouth just before I felt his hands grasp my hips.

Before I could take another breath, he slammed into me, claiming me in every way, shape, or form. Once the shock wore off, he began to move and I welcomed every single bit of this. While in some ways it still felt oh so wrong, this was one of the best things that ever happened to me.

We began to move together, choosing the perfect rhythm for us. Every groan, every moan, every gasp filled the quiet room and while the noises were mostly muted, I knew that if someone walked by, they would know exactly what we were doing.

Soren's hips pumped harder, faster, driving me closer to the edge. My whole world was currently nothing more than his touch, his taste, his scent. My body began to tremble as I got closer to my release.

And then it came, slamming into me like a lightning bolt. I screamed out against the panties in my mouth as my orgasm consumed all of me. My body shook as I tried to recover, but Soren continued to pound into me until he followed suit, his low groan echoing through the room.

Finally, we both collapsed against the desk, our breathing heavy and erratic. I felt a wave of love wash over me as I looked up at Soren. We were both sweaty and disheveled, but that didn't matter.

"I love you," he said as he reached forward to take my panties out of my mouth.

"And I love you too," I said as the words rushed out for fear that I would run out of breath as I was trying to calm my racing heart.

As our breathing returned to normal, we got dressed in silence, choosing to enjoy the relaxed silence between us instead of disrupting it. I stuffed my panties into my bookbag when I was done and turned to find Soren staring at me with a smirk. He leaned forward and laid a searing kiss on my lips that promised so much more later.

With that, he took my hand and intertwined his fingers with mine before laying a kiss on the back of my hand. It was as if he was savoring the private moment we shared together before we stepped out in the world that would judge our relationship.

"How about you leave first and drive over to my house? Then I'll leave a few minutes later just in case anyone is trying to figure out what we are doing," Soren said.

"That sounds like a good plan."

"Are you ready?" He asked softly.

I glanced around to make sure I had all of my belongings before nodding my head and giving him a big grin. "I'll see you at home shortly."

EPILOGUE
IRIS

The scent of freshly ground coffee beans and chatter surrounded Aria and me as we sat at a small table in Beyond The Page. I took a sip from my mug, enjoying the warmth I felt from the hot coffee making its way through my body. We'd been sitting there for about thirty minutes.

I watched as Aria's eyes sparkled with excitement. "I've recently been debating whether or not I want to try out for the Chevaliers when they open admissions for women. Are you thinking about doing the same?"

I sighed. "I haven't decided yet."

"I'll let you know if I hear anything about the change."

I assumed we would both hear about it at the same time, but I still nodded all the same. Our conversation continued, the air between us light and comforting. However, my eyes couldn't help but be drawn to a person sitting alone at a nearby table, with a baseball hat covering most of his features. What I could see was that it seemed to be a man who was reading a book but every so often he would look over this way.

"Anyway," Aria said, interrupting my train of thought. "I can't wait to see what happens...with everything."

"Me too," I replied absently, attempting to refocus on our conversation. Still, I couldn't shift my focus from the man sitting a few tables away from us.

His gaze met mine for a brief second before he shifted his stare to Aria. I couldn't help but raise an eyebrow at him.

"Is everything okay, Iris?" Aria asked.

"Uh, yeah," I stammered, forcing a smile. "I just got lost in thought for a moment." I paused, debating whether I should mention the guy who was staring at her. Deciding against it at least for now, I continued, "What were you saying?"

As Aria spoke, I tried to focus on her words, but my gaze kept drifting back to the guy a few tables over. Every so often, he would glance up from his book, his eyes locking onto Aria for a moment before returning to the pages before him. His actions made me feel uncomfortable. What did he want with Aria? Was he somehow connected to her? My mind raced with questions and I wanted the answers.

"Earth to Iris," Aria teased, nudging me gently. "You seem a million miles away."

Having enough of keeping this from her, I said, "Yes. It's because that guy at that table over there keeps staring at you and I don't know why."

Aria's eyes widened before they narrowed as she followed my gaze to the man in the baseball hat. She quickly stood up and turned to face him, her head held high. I hurried up and joined her as she walked toward his table because I didn't think she should face this alone.

My heart raced as Aria walked up to the table and the stranger looked up from his book.

"How many times do I have to tell you to stop fucking following me?"

THANK you for reading The Truth Between! While Iris and Soren's story is over, Landon and Aria's story will take place in The Whispers Below and it's available for preorder now!

DON'T WANT to let Iris and Soren go just yet? Click HERE to grab a bonus scene featuring the couple!

WANT to read Bianca and Easton's story? Keep reading to find a sneak peek of Shattered Saint!

WANT to join discussions about the Westwick University duet? Click HERE to join my Reader Group on Facebook.

PLEASE JOIN my newsletter to find out the latest about the Brentson University and my other books!

THE WHISPERS BELOW BLURB

Whispers can be deadly...

In the ancient halls of Westwick University, secrets are currency.

And my objective is to uncover them all.

My mission is to track Aria Townsend's every move.

What makes this situation odd is that she's the sister of one of the most powerful men in the world.

But not only that, her brother is the one that has given me this mission.

I need to find out exactly what she knows and how deeply involved she is in all of this.

Because above all else, I must protect the Chevaliers. No matter the cost.

Sometimes, the truth won't set you free.

The Whispers Below is a standalone dark forbidden college romance that has enemies-to-lovers themes. This book may not be suitable for all readers due to dubious situations that might be triggering. It ends in a happily ever after.

PREVIEW OF THE WHISPERS BELOW

LANDON

It was time.

I drove my black sedan with dark-tinted windows past the gates of Westwick University. I had to admit that my car fit in well here as it was an institution that not only thrived on academics, but the haunted atmosphere that was prevalent here.

It made me think that what I was being sent here to do would be even easier for me to do. There were so many dark corners that I could hide behind and the shadows that surrounded this place would become my best friends.

The assignment I accepted flashed through my mind: Follow Aria, a student at Westwick University who was seen getting close to Iris Bennington. Uncover the truth.

I forced my sedan to a stop in a deserted parking lot. The hum of the engine came to an end as I turned off the engine with the click of a button. Silence surrounded me in this space, and it was heavy and expectant for what lay ahead.

It was time.

I slid out and the blistering cold greeted me as I scanned

the courtyard. A flurry of movement caught my eye, leading my gaze right to her. A girl with long, curly brown hair wearing a blue hoodie with a navy backpack slung casually over one shoulder.

Aria.

I inhaled quickly as she came into view, clearer and clearer with each step. Aria Townsend, Parker Townsend's beloved sister, was the person I was supposed to watch under the guise of me being the newest transfer student to Westwick University.

Our gazes locked across the distance, hazel eyes meeting blue. A jolt shuddered through me as she gave me a friendly smile.

She didn't fucking know what she was getting herself into.

I gave her a smile in return, but I didn't approach. That would happen in due time.

She wanted to play with fire and force her brother to call me in? Fine.

Let the games begin.

∾

The Whispers Below is available for preorder now. It will be released in 2024.

SHATTERED SAINT BLURB

This never should have happened...

He was supposed to be off limits.
The one I couldn't have.
There were lines that should never be crossed.
At least until one fateful night
That changed everything forever.
Now we hated each other
And nothing was going to change that.
Ever.
Or so I thought...

Shattered Saint is the first book in a dark college romance trilogy that has enemies-to-lovers themes. This book may not be suitable for all readers due to dubious situations that might be triggering. It ends in a cliffhanger and the next book in the series will be Shattered Sinner.

PREVIEW OF SHATTERED SAINT
BIANCA

I wished I could make it stop.

The panic. The busyness that surrounded me.

All of it. I just wanted to make it all stop.

I took a swig from the glass of wine that I had in front of me and stared off into the nothingness that was my apartment. Sure, I'd had all I needed here and could do anything I wanted, but staring into the abyss seemed much more attractive to me.

On the surface, I had it all. I was the mayor's daughter who never wanted for anything monetarily. Sorority sisters who loved me. A mother and brother who cared for me. I would love to say that my father did too, but that was a story for a different day.

I took another big gulp of the wine in front of me. It was my third glass of the night. While I knew I should stop, I didn't want to. The alcohol was helping to numb the pain that I felt and I was alright with that for now.

Tomorrow I would deal with the consequences. After all

this was means for a celebration, even though it looked as if right now I was doing anything, but.

I'd kept my cool over the last couple of days and I was proud. I didn't have a sip of alcohol throughout my whole time in the city including at a gala I was forced to attend tonight. The urge to wash away my feelings about having to be somewhere I didn't want to be was strong, but I resisted.

But that ended as soon as I got back to my apartment. Once I was in the comfort of my own space, I took it as an opportunity to unwind, although by the looks of it, I probably should have stopped drinking a while ago.

I stared at the wine glass in front of me, debating with myself whether it made sense to drain the rest of the wine

I had to spend most of the night with my brother's best friend. The man I might have hated even more than my father.

Easton knew why I couldn't stand him ever since he did what he did to me. Yet, he did everything in his power to insert himself into my life just to piss me off. Although I would miss Nash, the sooner they both graduated from Brentson, the fucking better.

When my phone vibrated on the table, I was jolted out of the memories that I tried so hard to push away.

> Unknown Number: B, the fun has just begun.

My mouth dropped open as I reread the text.

Who the hell was this?

Shattered Saint is available now!

ABOUT THE AUTHOR

Bri loves a good romance, especially ones that involve a hot anti-hero. That is why she likes to turn the dial up a notch with her own writing. Her Broken Cross series is her debut dark romance series.

She spends most of her time hanging out with her family, plotting her next novel, or reading books by other romance authors.

briblackwood.com

ALSO BY BRI BLACKWOOD

Broken Cross Series

Sinners Empire (Prequel)

Savage Empire

Scarred Empire

Steel Empire

Shadow Empire

Secret Empire

Stolen Empire

The Broken Cross Series Box Set: Books 1-3

The Broken Cross Series Box Set: Books 4-6

The Ruthless Billionaire Trilogy

The Billionaire's Auction

The Billionaire's Possession

The Billionaire's Vengeance

Brentson University Series

Devious Game

Devious Secret

Devious Heir

The Westwick University Series

The Lies Beneath

The Truth Between

The Whispers Below

The Shattered Trilogy

Shattered Saint

Shattered Sinner

Shattered Reign

The Devilish Billionaire Series

The Devilish Billionaire: Season 1

The Devilish Billionaire: Season 2

9 781956 284881